Everything Breathed

Everything Breathed

Struan Sinclair

Granta Books
London

Granta Publications, 2/3 Hanover Yard, London N1 8BE

First published in Great Britain by Granta Books 1999

A CIP catalogue record for this book is available from the British Library.

1 3 5 7 9 10 8 6 4 2

Typeset in Goudy by M Rules
Printed and bound in Great Britain by Mackays of Chatham plc

For Cedar

Acknowledgements

For their many contributions to the many stages of this protean manuscript, I am indebted to Stephen Heighton, Isabel Huggan, Greg Hollingshead, Caroline Lonsdale and Michael Redhill. Thanks also to Edna Alford and Rachel Wyatt at the Banff Centre for the Arts Writing Studio, to Anne McDermid, and to Frances Coady and Shona Sutherland of Granta for their insight and understanding through the home stretch. Finally, I wish to acknowledge the continuing patience and kind support of the Sinclairs, Sarah Wang, Chris Buxton, Stefhan Caddick, 4dt, Warwick's of Hammersmith, Hatch & Lawrie and the denizens of 4 East Grove.

Several of these stories use found, non-copyright text. 'Building Marrakesh' samples from *Marrakesh: City of Fascination*, a brochure produced by the Morocco Tourism Board. 'Terminal Wheel' draws on the 1773 *Newgate Calendar; or, Malefactor's Bloody Register*, as well as a Salvation Army pamphlet entitled *First Things*, distributed locally around Cardiff. Finally, my research for 'Attempting Archaeology' involved prolonged tasting sessions with a wide range of Thornton's and Marks & Spencer's superb confectionery.

Contents

Triage

Sara wrote me twice in a month. She wrote: *I know I missed your birthday and I'm sorry. We were away for a change. It was very nice . . . Jessie is reading now, overnight she has become a little bookworm . . . Mom came for a week's visit and the kids thought she was neat. She brought them each a souvenir bark canoe (oh boy!). She spent a lot of money on them . . . We're thinking of coming up north.* She wrote: *You and me and Mom and Tim – I can't remember the last time we were all together. I must have blocked it out in the way we do, the good with the bad. You know?*

June 22 was the day Tim died. It was a dull hazy morning, just like the one before it, the sun and moon both out, barometer rising drowsy. I was at the sink, washing up strawberries for pie, looking out through the screen door our hockey sticks tore, trying to shape my eyes to fit the holes. I could hear Mom coming downstairs, tap-tapping in her wooden shoes, and Sara outside, flailing at the eaves with a bristle-brush tied to a long paint-roller handle, bendy and hard to manage.

Mom walked past me in her old plaid shirt and jeans shot-gunned with bleach stains, submarined a strawberry I was reaching for, leaned in for the pastry pin. Outside Sara stormed, broom bouncing into the side of the house, *bam, bam, bam!* The broom stuttered, then paused for a moment, and Sara wailed, *Mom . . .*

Then Mrs Shorter was in the kitchen. She must have run like sixty – no coat, cardigan undone three rows down, wig-line pearled with sweat and the rosewater she freshened up with, twice daily. Mrs Shorter had never been inside our house before. Probably she thought it was distasteful, barefoot kids begging for money. Dangerous, bat guano bundled in the ceilings, poised to drop into her lungs.

I came right away. May the Lord help us, Mrs Purves, your son—

Right then the phone, which never rang, rang and none of us was up for answering it: me, hands soaking, doing little girls' work; Mom, caught in clothes she mustn't be seen in; Sara, wisped with spiders' mansions, still toting that broom. The phone rang, a brisk trilled rattle, and none of us moved.

Your son . . . Mrs Shorter began. She knew what she was going to say, maybe had run through it once or twice in her head, and then that darn phone ringing, and messing her up. I watched her hard rouged mouth prod the air and thought of chickens pecking for pellets in the frozen ground, so single-minded.

I am sorry to have to tell you this, Mrs Purves. Your son . . .

Even then she couldn't bring herself to call Tim by his name, as if saying it could contaminate her, as if he were the common cold.

Sara's broom stuttered along the floor. Mom began to cry. I watched my hands underwater, wrinkles scribbling down my thumbs like ski trails in the snow. The strawberries floated in ever-widening circles, lonely planets knocked from orbit, their crowns poking up between my fingers where the skin was tender.

Mrs Purves . . .

Answer the phone please will you please!

None of us moved. Then Mrs Shorter looked at Mom, who nodded at her, defeated, and Mrs Shorter picked up the phone, and spoke into it.

Hello, she said, and listened. No, she said, he isn't in. And he won't be in. Because your friend is dead!

She hoisted that phone like it was the staff of Moses, brandished it at Mom.

I can't be blamed. I've been trying to tell you, Mrs Purves. Your son is dead. The police will be here shortly. But I thought, since we're neighbours . . .

In that moment of breath held, the voice on the phone squawked like sirens, rude in the quiet of the room. Ronnie Tumbler's voice. Ronnie was Tim's best friend. Or had been. Tim was dead.

Tim was the oldest. Sara and me, our whole life was hand-me-down. Whatever we wore or read or played with had once been his: Tim's sweatshirt with a football patched right over the heart; Tim's busted ukulele; Tim's old bike, red with black fenders, that I had to push all the way to school with him riding broncobuster, until a teacher noticed the blisterclusters on my palms that didn't quite heal. Tim's Remington Sure-Shot that he used for squirrels he never killed but only wounded with off-kilter shots that left a dazed odd wetness in their fur. That was Tim's way. He couldn't find the end of anything.

He lost that gun after pulling it on Mr Ellis who ran the Solo store. The store was a business, not a lending library, and Mr Ellis kept a paddle behind the counter to make sure it didn't become one. Tim strode in there one day and picked out a dozen comics; took a whack on the rear and another before he raised his gun and held it to Mr Ellis's sprouty red ear. Then he propped the gun beside him and read at his leisure: *Creepy and Strange Tales* and *Captain America*. People said it was that day Mr Ellis got his heart difficulties. Tim said he was so loggered he couldn't have fired that gun anyway. Tim was getting regularly drunk by the time he was eleven, cached behind the LCBO with old Gordie Cummings, knocking back Still Cold Duck. No one knew how he paid for it. He wouldn't say.

When he was younger, and sober, Tim stuck around. He made up games by the dozen. Tough running games, hiding games where he was the leader and got the best weapons and titles. I dragged around as second-in-command, and Sara got to stay with the fort, the spacecraft, the castle. Where we lived was shady spruce forest, sewn right into the rock and our town was a stitch on its seam. Heads low, careening through the deep bush, we could divine a path to anywhere. Tim always went where he wanted, and as he got older he wanted out.

I got engines in me, he said. When they tick over, I gotta go.

Sometimes he'd go for days, and we relaxed a little, and ate our fair share. It was just like a holiday, except Tim was guaranteed home on holidays. We'd ask when Tim was due, anxious that it would be soon, and Mom would be anxious too, though for the opposite reason. When he got in, he'd bang around no matter what the hour, bolt whatever was left over with the biggest spoon he could find, leave the radio at full volume for me to get up and go down and turn off.

Tim always bailed when company came by. Company chafed him. He left, and we got the mops out. Relatives and friends got use of the front door and a clean house, and maybe the door was freshly trimmed with the paint dregs Mom got for the asking from Beaver Lumber, and maybe the house was spruce with new curtains made from the off-cuts of the dresses she sewed for weddings, graduations, sweet sixteens – one alteration included in the asking price. It was a mantra with Mom that the house was just about finished, and it might always be just about finished, and this was at once a shameful trial and a strange comfort.

The Rentons came and I got the door and Mom made an entrance and Sara served and cleared. Mrs Renton said, Where's my big boy? and I said, I'm your big boy, dutifully, and she said, No, I mean my biggest boy, shooting Mom The Look, and Mom hung a fragile smile like a glass bell off her steepled hands and said she thought Tim was out looking for useful work. She might have said he was perched in a treetop charting the planets for all they believed her. Mrs Renton said she guessed me and Sara were good enough and I smiled and blushed on cue and I was Mrs Renton's sweetie, and Sara was really just the picture of a lady, and we were Tim's diversion and also his mirror and wasn't that fine.

After some chat Mr Renton asked us to bring in the baking from the trunk, and at the very same second Mrs Renton asked if we could maybe find a little iced tea, oh, and in frosted glasses, wouldn't that be nice? And we asked well, which? And the

Rentons exchanged glances, and Mr Renton said the baking would spoil but the iced tea would keep, and Mrs Renton added that we could lay the sugar-tarts out on a tray with the glasses. Sara yelped, Sugar-tarts! and hooked on outside. Mr Renton leaned forward, his voice got low and tight, and I knew he'd lit into Tim.

When we returned we brought iced tea and twelve sugar-tarts less two. Mom's face was wet, and shiny-bright. For a few minutes the whole room crackled, then Mr Renton sighed and looked at his wife, sighed and looked at Mom, sighed and rubbed his knuckles, pink and smooth and bald like babies' heads. Well, we'd best move along, he said, and Mom said automatically, So soon? And yes, it was so soon, and yes, they had enjoyed themselves, and yes, they'd be sure to drop by once our here-and-there house – now just about finished – was truly fit for guests.

Sara gave a little curtsy and I shook hands hard as I could manage, with a little twist Tim had taught me. You better be careful with that handshake there, fella, you could hurt an old man like me! said Mr Renton, and I said, Sir, I'm sorry. Tim teach you that? Sure he did, I told him, it's got a name: The Disabler. He gave Mom a pretty good squeeze, though not a Disabler, and told her, Remember what I said. People are talking, and it is bound to get worse. The boy needs help and he had better get it.

Goodbye Mary, Mrs Renton said, and Mom fluttered bye-bye.

The Rentons drove off, and Mom hugged us so hard and long that Sara got the hiccups from being squished. Then we wiped and stowed the nesting tables, and Mom herself put away the good china and sleeved the plastic covering on to the good sofa and chairs. Tim walked in cool as morning clover and tugged Sara's barrettes and threw me a suckerpunch that spread a cold queasy stain in my belly, and sloppy-kissed Mom, and crooned, Hey gorgeous! Where's dinner? I'm freakin' starving!

There were hunting camps in our woods, clusters of tiny bowed cabins with a chair and a cot that lay empty most of the year – perfect for playing War Party and Survival and Capture the Flag. Older kids used the cabins for drinking and fooling around, and it was the custom to plant your peg out front, like signing in. Tim tagged his pegs Tim the Great, and the other kids used to mess with them, substituting Tim the Full of Shit and Tim the Brain-Dead and such. He let it ride. But when he was up there everyone else stayed away, because it was understood he'd have a bottle or three and be well on his way to a force-ten bender.

The path to the biggest camp traversed a pipsqueak river, bridged by two logs flattened and lashed together with metal plumber's bands. The river boasted yellow perch and a couple of old whiskerfish not worth the worm, and scads of frogs. At night those frogs belted away like a veterans choir and made a kind of music, meaty and wild. They thundered the last night Tim was there, sang themselves dry, and the cops figured that anyone who caught the racket from the cabin, the swearing or the screaming or the short dull thuds like an axe through wet wood, must have had supersonic hearing, so ripe and rowdy was the frogsong.

Some days after they'd picked up the body, the police told us that Tim had left a will. It was rolled up inside his pool cue that stayed at the social club for safekeeping. Mr Rollins who ran the club drove it over, and inside was this paper, and it was a will. I guess everyone was pretty shocked, and of course everyone found out about it. Everyone always knew everything about Tim, and the will fit nicely with what they always knew. Typical! people said. That bad apple! Going around drawing up wills, thumbing his nose at those he'd hurt most, wasn't that always his way?

The will was recent, early March. The witnesses were Ronnie Tumbler, which wasn't surprising, and Ronnie's mother Pearl, which was. No one knew she could write her name, but there it was, in crinkly broken letters that might as well have been grated on to the paper. We showed the will to Mr Steely, a lawyer in Moraine, who told us it was legal and, more than that, showed real competence. He was very, very sorry for the tragedy, and to happen to such a bright young mind.

When we left, Sara asked what did Mr Steely mean about Tim and his bright young mind, and Mom said forget it, it was a good thing we hadn't gone to lawyers in our town, a town like that, where no one could keep their mouth shut. She was crying, and I had just under a buck, and Sara had fourteen cents, so we pooled and bought Mom a Horn of Plenty, a triple-scoop of blue-liquorice on a curvy sugar cone.

Let's go somewhere, Mom said. Oh, let's get away!

Tim would have liked where we went that day, to Blind River gorge, a huge gash in the land, rooked with high crooked cliffs he'd have been the first to scale, calling us cowards; the first to jump off, hooting like a birthing cow, browned swizzle-stick legs breaking into a jack-knife, arms waving in wild circles.

Mom sat on the edge beneath a blue–grey stone overhang, her old clothes much baggier now than a month ago. Sara and I played a rough game of tag, leaping like antelopes through the tails of surf. I dived out too deep for her, she stayed to skim stones, and I didn't twig then and neither did Mom that Sara was screaming, and the stones were thrown too fast, too hard.

I went for her legs, brought her underwater, her screams

became bubbles that scudded and burst right before us, and told our future, and changed our vision. We were shingled in the knot of sun and current; we grew longer, sleeker, sturdier. Sara laughed at my crummy handstands, my white, wiggling toes. Suddenly I was funny to her. I was funny. Tim was dead.

The reading of the will took place in Mr Steely's office and was for next-of-kin only. In the will, Tim left Sara his bike with no chain-guard and one bent rim. Before she could take possession, she had to agree to turn it over to Mr Steely in the event that she got a new one, and she had to sign her name in that full knowledge. Did she accept these conditions? Sure she did. She signed, careful not to lefty-smudge. Sara also got his records and a hockey-card collection we didn't know he had, and the pennies in the ukulele case we'd been sneaking for maybe three years already. Mom got his pocket watch that she'd given him anyway, his savings account that held eighty dollars, and his baby bonds that she had rolled over, year after year, for the university he would never have gotten into with his low, sullen grades. I was to keep what we took away from George's. That's all. *What we took away from George's.* Mom and Sara and Mr Steely were baffled. I said I'd have a think about it. Mr Steely said wills were funny things.

I read the plaques on the wall that attested to Mr Roland Steely. I liked the way the name felt in my mouth, the mix of long and sharp, warm and cool. I thought it might be nice to spend more time here, but we were limited by that hour. Even so, Mr Steely didn't rush us. He asked if everything was sufficiently clear and patted our heads when we got set to leave, and I thought of the billboard outside the United Church: 'Charity is kindness without levity.'

Mom rose first and took out her purse, fiddling with the clasp, businesslike, asking him, And what do we owe you for your time, Mr Steely? He nodded politely and asked her to recall what they'd agreed, that he would handle it pro bono. She said of course she recalled what he recalled, but he needn't imagine she'd cut out on paying the fee. One moment, he said, and glided over like a waterpark swan, threaded Sara and me through the high noiseless doors.

While we waited, we explored the corridors, plush-carpeted; the washrooms with marble basins, brass taps, clove-sweet soap dispensed in flat waxy wafers. Sara wrapped up a stack to use for company, to flake on her wrists as a kind of perfume, and as many paper sipping cones as she could pocket. Mom strode out, fast, flushed, head high, told us that Mr Steely had been very kind. Later she found Sara's soap and was angry, and asked her, Did I bring you up to steal? It is wrong, don't you know? Have you learned nothing by example? Sara cried no; she knew; she had; she was sorry. But she kept the paper cones.

Sara was friendly with the wind. She stood outside on breezy days to let the wind push her downhill. She followed the wind gust by gust, watched it drag the tops of creeks, chasing it, jumping, shouting. She liked to stand in the wind in the chewgrass in the bottle-strewn vacant lots out back of the house. More than once I watched her and wondered. I saw her aeroplaning, her hair whipped round her face like halyards on a mast. She had lost us all and was victorious. I saw her standing still, her hair a silted river in the wind, running down her shoulders, over her narrow arms stretched out from her sides. She was alone in front of the house, door open. The same wind blowing Sara had blown someone's laundry on to the hump of our roof and a bed sheet draped the attic like a funeral veil. Sara looked up, dipped over, came reaching with her long broom, trying to unhook it, then she was underneath it, both of her arms poking out. She didn't move, didn't drop the broom, just stood there, hollering, in surprise not rage.

Sara shrank after Tim died. Always limber, tall like a poplar, she seemed to compress herself, her size and voice, her presence. She tied her hair with raw elastic bands that caught and tangled, left them there until I went after them with the safety scissors. Why won't you talk to me, I asked her, I'm his brother too, remember? I was worn out by her and it wasn't fair. Everything was harder now, all of the looks we got, the people we had to step around.

Mom took Sara on a trip to clear her head. They went to Sudbury for a visit and some shopping and came back with a new pair of shoes each, some stuff for the house and a sweatshirt for me with this huge nickel on it.

It's a famous attraction, Mom said. The Big Nickel. People come from all over. You wouldn't believe it.

I believed it. I believed that people lined up to gawk at an overgrown coin. But the fact that they did – well, that was the trouble with everything.

The trip to Sudbury didn't do the trick for Sara. Nothing seemed to. What have you lost anyway? I wanted to know. As far as I knew, Tim had never bothered much with Sara, except to put her down, calling her The Yapper and The Little Witch. She thought he called her that because of her witch's black hair, so she poured Clorox into a swim cap and wore it for an hour to make her head shine white. I was the one who flushed her down and bathed her. Tim was weirded out.

But Sara couldn't forget. She talked about Tim all the time. About how strong he was, how fast with his elbows in a fight. How brave and dangerous, chest puffed out, shinning up our chimney while Mom called for him to get down, pretending to fall, then catching himself while our stomachs tripped and thundered. How kind, walking her to the clinic when her wrist snapped playing murderball, treating her to a pack of peppermint gum. I didn't know if Sara remembered these things or whether she'd gathered them from the books she gulped up like oxygen. Books about young detectives who drank bottled lemonade and travelled in caravans. Books about the pioneers. The unexplained. The fish of the sea.

For almost two weeks there was a trial to determine how Tim had died and who should suffer for it. It was held in Woborne, which boasted a real courthouse and a television station and was far enough removed from our town to be neutral ground. Sara and Mom went every day. I didn't feel like going, I didn't want to know.

Instead, I went to the attic, where the spiders crept and the moths jiggered their sleek cocoons. There it was warm and dark, and I had space for my thoughts. I imagined the insect looms winding out their warm-glass thread. I listened for whisky-jacks and the trucks turning out of town, bound for other places.

On the last day of the trial, I didn't go to the attic. Instead, I sat in Tim's room and tried to feel something of him there. The room was pretty much as Tim left it – close, untidy, full of his bent and broken things. The sun painted shapes on the floor that reminded me of Tim's kite. He got it for his birthday, tried to build it without the diagrams. It's a kite, he said. Why do you gotta have instructions to build a fuckin' kite? He built that kite by will and intuition; and of course he made a mess of it; and of course it was my fault because I must have misplaced a crucial peg or tie. Well, it looks okay, he mused. I agreed. It did look okay.

So he ran with it through the fields cushioning the highway. Finally aloft, it peaked and dived for a few seconds before the frame snapped and the kite went limp, hung, plummeted, a red billowy bird that had forgotten how to fly. Tim didn't move to correct it, just stood there, wreathed in gently collapsing string, and I knew it was because he'd worked so hard on it that he'd believed it would fly.

I sat on sore haunches in that field, watching the sky and then the ground, imagining myself as a kite, long runs of cornsilk connected to my body, doubled-up around my hips and head where I was heaviest. My bones were my balsa wood, and my chest unzipped like a pillowslip to catch the wind. Lifted in jerks and jolts, a kick in the stomach that I shrugged off, a buffeting about my weary knees. Spread to the wind, spinnakered, I leaned down and cut my anchors, leaving Tim behind. His mouth was open, it was a pit I had climbed out of.

The trial ended. Sara locked herself in her room with thoughts that were to Mom and me a strange language. Just leave me alone will you? I am busy can't you see! Sometimes I found her in my place in the attic among the moths spooning drunkenly, jumbling up against the window, fighting for the place through the gap between glass and frame. She didn't seem to mind, like I was starting to, that the moths were mostly dead. She spent more and more time up there. Mrs Giddes called.

Sara is a good student, she explained to Mom. But she is struggling. Understandably, of course. We think she ought to—

No thank you, Mom replied, as though Mrs Giddes was at her door, peddling goods she would rather not purchase. It's just overreacting to her other troubles. Don't you mind her. I'll see she gets back on track.

I was doing better in school and elsewhere. I was losing weight, firming up. Starting to grow muscles in my arms like the other kids, and a band of iron-red sandpaper along my upper lip, a few long hairs in my cheeks. People said that in my colouring, the way I smiled, I reminded them of Tim. I am not like him! I wanted to shout. Go on – ask me anything – you'll see! I floated stories to explain our deep and lasting differences. I hinted mysteriously at different dads, babies in baskets, strange doorbells rung in the anthracite night.

Sara never really got near the house, though she came close enough to torching herself, stinking of gasoline when she finally came home that night. I'd gone by at the nick of eight to pick her up from Girl Guides, and she wasn't there, but they'd quit early because Jodi had barfed during a game of spinners, another waiting girl told me. Barf is not a word, something called a Grey Owl said sternly. I nodded, headed home. By nine Mom was dialling.

Hello, is that Mrs Boult? It's Mrs Purves. Sara's mother . . . We can't seem to . . . I wonder if . . . Oh, I see . . . Hello? Sorry to trouble you, Mrs Reid. It's Mrs Purves. Sara's mother . . . We can't seem to . . .

No one had given Sara a lift. No one saw her arrive or leave. Mom began to pace. I said, Hey, don't worry, you've still got me. She gave me a strange look, like she'd heard something I hadn't said. She put her head on my shoulder. Her body was damp. She was trembling. I didn't really like to touch her.

Sara came in much later. Some of her hair was burnt and the back of her coat from the hem to her shoulders. She didn't speak, just fell, and Mom gathered her up. I left the room while she stripped Sara down, folded her into a cotton comforter. I touched base from the kitchen, washing up under a trickle so I didn't miss anything.

What's wrong with her? Does she need anything special?

The knock on the front door was loud, percussive. Constable Art Durkheim, Ontario Provincial Police. He asked for Sara. If Sara J. Purves lived at this address. People had seen Sara near the Freed place, carrying a pair of half-gallon cans. The police guessed she'd fashioned wicks from loose-rolled newspaper and that's when her coat caught fire, and she ran, keeping hold of the cans because they still held eight bucks' worth of gas. All around her, moths were raised by the light. Moths with tracing-paper wings, shielding her like a mobile cloak, their crisp bodies tinder to the fire, tarnished and popping like husked dried corn. Sara was burning when Joe Oliver got to her, prised the cans from her fingers, rolled her in an army blanket. Moths covered her, nestled even in the edges of her eyes and the hollows of her ears. They might have saved her then.

The summer before Tim died, we spent three weeks together. Our grandfather George was alive then, six feet tall, with brown eyes that shone like the boat deck he polished once a week. One thumb missing from an accident that happened when he was a boy, when fingers, like lives, were more easily lost. George hired us as casuals at his cottage, providing room and board in exchange for our labour.

Boys, he boomed, you're nearly men and here you can work

like men and I'll treat you like men, and you'll call me George, like equals.

Mostly true to his word, George treated us like men by working us like dogs, and when Tim figured that men like us ought to get a nip of the beer our grandfather took with supper or the Scotch he took before and after, he laughed, poured a shot and said, You can wet your whistle but you sure as shootin' won't soak it! Later he phoned Mom and claimed he didn't know whether to shit or wind his watch when Tim hit him up for hooch, and what was she raising, anyway, a couple of winos?

At George's we had our own cabin maybe sixty yards from the main house. It had two rows of bunks and a screened verandah with a small deck. I slept in the top bunk and Tim the lower, so that he could get in and out easily and thump me from below if I snored or got farty. The windows were opened to draw a breeze. We fell asleep to the crackling passage of wood mice and garter snakes and the buzzing from the domed iron pathlight, hot locus of an insect cavalcade, a deafening revolving nimbus. When we got up in the night we were careful to shut the door against the bugs that broke ranks, dizzy from the brightness.

In the mornings it was cold and the grass was wet and prickly. We got up at six or thereabouts because we had to get cracking and we had to pray. George's prayer was always slow and salty and full of thanks. He'd been saved in the War when he should rightly have died, been saved by God himself, he told us, plucked up by God's big warm hand and born again. I said, from the way Mom carried on, being born even once was asking a lot. George didn't laugh. I said it was lucky he hadn't been crushed by God's big warm hand. He didn't laugh. Tim didn't laugh.

George broke us in by having us scale the hard black lacquer from the log siding. Then we tilled and seeded the septic-tank garden, polished the outdoor lamps, painted trims, sanded the ladders and diving board, pulled watergrass and nettles. My back hurt and my hands split, then hardened, and the nettle and tansy puffed my eyes. Tim surprised me by doing his share; together we swam to get clean and slept to lose the feeling in our limbs.

At the end of each week there was this big deal where we ticked off the jobs we'd finished on a big assignment chart in George's kitchen, and reported for pay. Once we got six-tool Swiss army knives; mostly it was a few bucks to spend in the dinky town half the size of our own. I bought candy and comics. Tim ate my candy and read my comics and blew his money on mickeys of rye. At night he pulled at the bottles, not getting much drunker but only quieter. When he slept he was silent, and his silence broke my sleep.

After maybe a week I was angling to get back home. I asked him, Hey Tim, you like it here? Sure I do, he said, I like the work. I don't feel itchy. I said I wondered why Mom never told us George was a Jesus-freak. He's not, Tim said. He sounded angry. He's a religious man. There's a difference. I thought, Oh holy smokes, Tim a convert? But I didn't push it.

Stacking cedar roofing shingles under the house, I found some envelopes, caramel-coloured manila, slowly blending in with the topsoil. Each was packed with bundles of photographs tied with elastics – snapshots and portraits of men in hats and long shorts and women looking straight into the lens, not smiling. Some of the men were in uniform, lean and hard, steady and drawn straight up, very different from the men I knew, from Tim. I called him to come have a look at this, whatta goldmine! We flipped through the photographs, scanning for names, dates. One showed a very young man half lying on a kind of cot. The caption read: Captain George Barnes in Triage, 1917.

That night I asked George what the word meant and his eyes narrowed. Triage was a system they had in the War, he said, for treating men who went down in battle. Yeah, but what's it mean? I wanted to know. It means the sickest ones are the first to be attended to, he said, but sometimes it means something else, and then they're the first to die. How can it mean something else if it means something in the first place? I asked him. Everything means something else, he told me. Everything. Your paint brushes'll harden for sure, left out in the sun to bake like that.

After that Tim was different with George, quiet and solid and never swearing. I did my best to pick up the slack, swore like an oil-rigger, beefed him like crazy, and he just said, Keep it up and I'll give it right back to you, plus, and I did, and he did, but not in front of George, oh no never. I said, Hey, I like George fine but so what, and he said George was a hero, which was more than I could expect. Sure, I said, to humour him. Sure. You're right. Whatever.

In no time at all Tim became George's smaller shadow. When he'd finished his work Tim would head up to the main house, sit with George, tuck into soda-water and lime, and shoot the shit about God, the War, history, politics and what was wrong with everything.

So what's wrong with everything? I asked Tim.

Everything, he said.

Great. What do you really do up there?

Talk, he said. You know, *conversation*. Little a this, little a that.

Little a what? Bullshit, maybe. All *you* ever gab about is booze and guns and pussy. What's George care for that?

He slapped me hard. You got a nasty mouth, squirt.

Oh shove it, Tim. What, you're some preacher now?

None of your business.

And what'll you tell them back home? Think Ronnie and them'll be pleased you suddenly got religion?

Don't think I won't bust that mouth, 'cause I will, religion or no. And he walked away, right back up to George's.

Painting the trim on the sunroom windows, I smelled George's smoke and heard his level voice. You got to make room for what's coming, Timmy, he said. Make room right here and right now, in this life. I wanted to hear the rest, but my painty feet were sticking to the rungs of the ladder, and I hated that feeling more than I wanted to hear the rest. So I squelched off, went for the turpentine and swooped it on to my green-gilded feet till they stung and the gathering fumes drove me down for a swim.

The kayak floated off in the night and George never noticed but I sure did, the next afternoon. George was resting, and wasn't to be disturbed. I saw the hashed, frayed lines flapping from the dock cleats, and called for Tim. I asked, Do we wake him? Well, we're here, right? Tim said, hot and pissed off. So I knocked and walked into George's room. Sure enough he was sleeping, mouth snored open, glotted shut. I knew I wouldn't budge him. Tim was outside, buzzing, fists on hips, and I knew he'd call me sissy when I told him I didn't wake George.

Well? he demanded and I said nothing and he said, Fuckin' wussy! What, too chicken to get the old man up? and I said, You do it, you're such good pals, and he laughed, short and disgusted and said, I figured, and I don't know, I snapped, and gave him a clout, and he looked so shocked and gave me one back, and soon we were going at it, him saying, Shitpants, shitpants, and me screaming and crying, not nearly as strong as Tim nor as crazy, and finally I said, to save myself, to escape being a sissy, because I was angry – I don't know why – You idiot you fucking idiot I didn't wake him 'cause he wasn't even asleep just jerking!

Tim backed away. What's that?

What's what? I said, screaming in earnest now, caught up and no way back. Maybe you wanna go give him a hand?

Tim's face went strange and rigid, and his voice went dim.

You don't know anything, he said.

But his face and voice told me I did. I knew what Mr Renton said about people talking and Tim needing help. I knew about Tim and Gordie Cummings drinking together, all those years. I knew about sly old Gordie. And I knew how Tim paid for all those bottles.

O holy Jesus, Tim, I said. Is that what you do with George?

He roped an arm around my head and yanked so fast my neck stung hot. Pulled me from the house. Then walked away and left me there.

Sometime later George came and asked, What was all the ker-fuffle about? I said Tim and me had a scrap, you know, it was my fault, and he smiled and ruffled my hair with his big right hand no thumb.

That night Tim skipped dinner and when I asked him did he want a plate brought down, he just looked right past me, like I was a flicker in his vision.

I'm sorry, okay? I told him, and I was.

You don't know anything, he said. And for the first time in my life, I thought Tim was dead right.

On our last night, George cooked up a storm: flank steak, grilled corn, Saskatoon crumble, two bottles each of cream lager. Afterwards, Tim and me lay beached in our bunks in the dark, draining a thirty-sixer together, getting nicely and quietly plastered. We had the radio on low. It might have been Supertramp.

They rule, Tim said. They royally rule. But he turned the radio off and the only sound was our breathing. It was that way for a long time. Then Tim said, What would you say if I asked you for help?

You wouldn't, I told him. You would never ask for that. Not you.

When he spoke again his voice was calm and large.

That's right, he said. I wouldn't ask. Not me. Not Tim the Great. Then he laughed – a blade whirring at the bottom of a blender.

Damn straight, he said.

Soon we were sleeping in that throbbing, soggy way you do when you're drunk. I had to take about a thousand leaks, and during one of them the door was open and let in a triangle of light, and a moth that went to ground. I hated the idea of it in the room, crawling down into my windpipe, up the tunnel of my ear. I flicked on the lamp by my bed, to attract it. For long minutes, I lay in wait. Finally I heard then felt a flutter, flapped my hands, batting, snaring. The moth beat its dusty oaky wings, went low, landed on Tim's face. He grunted, swept it away with a wrist, smearing its shape.

A major coronary robbed George of his time that wasn't near up. At the funeral, Tim and me were pall-bearers, a gesture to the man who'd given us a life experience. The coffin was rubbed oak, and in direct sun I saw my face in its panels, wider than normal, and my smile met Tim's smile and overpowered it. At the wake Mom got very drunk and cut her finger on a glass, hugging Tim and bleeding over his new-pressed shirt. The next day was the reading of the will. Tim took notes all the way through.

Mom asked Tim how he remembered George and he said George was fine. She asked me and I said I thought he was a slave-driver, but maybe the best man I'd known. I said I credited George with teaching Tim and me the qualities of sin and prayer. I said I recalled George seeing us off on the day we left the cottage. He'd brought his clippers for something to do in case the bus was late, and it was, and he went to work right there on the hedge at the end of his lane.

When it finally came, I sat facing backwards, watching George waving his clippers under a cloud-curled sky, the leaves helicoptering down from the big oak trees. The bus speeded up going around a turn and George escaped my view save for one tough, gnarled arm, waving and tilting, like a tree when the soil around its roots grew loose.

Mom was crying. That is how George ought to be remembered, she said. Like that. *Doing* something.

That was George all over, I said. Tim looked at me, his stare hard and then thoughtful. And as we were getting out of the car, he held me back. Very soft, weird-soft, he asked me, Why do you hate me, squirt? Why?

I said, I don't hate you Tim. I said, Jesus, why do you *think*?

He let me go. Climbed out. Walked away, goofy grin right back on his face. And he never spoke to me again before he died. Not once.

Sara and I don't see much of each other, but we write back and forth. She is a teacher now, married to a doctor. She has two young kids I met a few years back when she brought them up north for a flying visit. Two good kids – nice, smart.

In her letter, Sara reminds me that it's twenty years since Tim died. Do I want to do anything to remember the occasion? She intends to have Mom over for dinner, and then maybe they will go to church, though not to a service, just for some silence with his memory. Of course, it's our memories she means. Our very different memories.

At the trial in Woborne, Jonathan Collins Freed claimed innocence. Tim and he were drunk, he told them, drunk as skunks, rocking out and popping shots. Tim was the one wanted to play Mercy, wanted to use the pipes they'd found under the shack, wanted to keep playing long after it was obvious he was hurt. It was Tim who just refused to quit, screaming, *Hit me! Hit me for real you stupid shit you stupid fuck!*

It was Tim who wouldn't say mercy, never once said mercy, just stood there in the din of frogs and bones, under deadly pressure, egging Freed on like he had all of us, one way or another, his whole life through. *He got so under my skin,* Freed testified, weeping openly. *Right under my skin! He did it on purpose I'm telling you! I was wasted, he was wasted, slapping me, screaming at me – the whole fucking thing was his idea,* his *idea it was* his . . .

I wasn't there, of course. I had already done my part. I was in Tim's room, dreaming of kites. Only the kite wasn't me at all. It was Tim. I was flying Tim, threading him through the turrets of a walnut tree, combing him along the teeth of a widow's walk, paying out line as he shouted, Bring me in, bring me in, I can't get any air up here! I was flying Tim by moonlight and all was quiet on the Northern Front. We were in triage, and I had to make a decision, a routine weighing of scales. I had to signal who to save. I pointed. Mom would be saved. Sara would be saved. And me. Tim was still rising, very high now, bicycling his legs, trying to gain a purchase. He had to be told. Cut yourself loose, I suggested. The grass is plenty thick enough. You'll land gentle.

I write to Sara. I send her some snaps of my husky team in harness that I know will thrill her kids. I write: *I think your idea is wonderful – would you believe I'm out of town that week . . . The snow here is six-feet deep. I can ski off the top of my truck . . . Gerri (yes, we're still talking) would love to see you if you're passing through Thunder Bay . . . I'm sending you something. Show it to Mom. Then do what you like. This was what Tim meant in his will*, I add. It was Tim's will.

Carefully, I wrap the print of Captain George Barnes that Tim smuggled out. On top, I lay a snapshot I took with George's camera. He sent Tim and me copies in a letter I don't remember, but was probably brief and awkward and godly/profane.

In the photograph, Tim and George are standing on a dock. Tim wears his underpants, George his regulation bathing trunks with a go-fast stripe down the sides. Tim is very tall and dark; even on the black-and-white film you can see his tan, a farmer's tan, his chest milk-white. Behind them is a raft they've been fixing, plywood lashed to old gasoline barrels nearly five-feet tall and four-feet wide. Tim is in front of a barrel whose shadow takes a queer turn. It must have been evening, the sun lowering, crossing Tim at the knees, and he is floating, untethered, with his famous old open grin. I got all of George, bright blue-jay eyes, gappy smile. I planned on being in this picture, but the camera's timer never once worked.

There is another picture, which I never took. Though I might have, so square and sharp is it in my mind.

It was the night the moth got in. I lay woozy, throat burning from the whisky, feeling the drink siphoning into my bladder;

restless, knowing the moth was in the room. I waited there in the half-light, staring over the edge of my bunk, watching Tim shift in his blankets, watching for the moth.

I was startled by its wingtip. I windmilled my groggy hands, saw it cartwheel down on to Tim's cheek, crouch and settle its wings. Tim never moved. His eyes were shut. Then his hand whipped out quick as a frog's tongue and as dangerous, swatting then polishing something on his cheek.

He might have been dreaming still, in the patchy burn of the pathlights. He might have been acting on reflex. It was only later, with the clarity that comes just before sleep, that I realized his eyes had been wide open, intent and frightened, looking up with complete conviction.

Maybe he was pleading with me.

Maybe he knew.

But truly at the time I believed him to be sleeping.

Attempting Archaeology

'So I'm right into your old lady,' Murray says. He palms his phone, flicks his fingers over its illuminated keypad. 'It was an accident waiting to happen.' He laughs at this; his freckles knit along his brow and form pinched reddish galaxies. The boy doesn't say anything. Just watches Murray's phone. The phone beeps like crickets and Murray talks. When Murray isn't on his phone, he talks like he's on it. Murray is always buying something, or selling something, or buying something to sell on, or selling something to buy something better. The boy watches Murray's phone and forms a dull hope that it will ring, right now, and release him. Murray sighs and hitches up his shoulders like he can't believe his luck or something, tousles the boy's stiff buzzed head. 'Hey *hey*,' Murray says. 'Right?'

*

The boy leaves his apartment at ten past noon. At the door, he turns to his mother. 'Gotta shoot,' he says, like Murray does. He waits for her to notice this. 'Be good,' she says, simmering up from her TV chair. 'Cable's gone buggy,' she complains, lobbing a Molson coaster at the set-top box and in the very same motion pressing the favourite button on the one-for-all remote. The onscreen volume bars rise like temperature as he pulls shut the door and stands in the hallway. From behind other doors, he hears plates being stacked and scraped and, settling like sump oil around these noises, the same dark television din.

The boy does not go to school as he is supposed to. Instead, he ducks into the alley behind a for-lease Mr Transmission and changes some items of his clothing, climbing into the grey flannel shirt and red-and-green kerchief he's kept from two years ago, when he was a Boy Scout. In his shoulder bag, the boy carries fourteen large chocolate bars, each containing over eighty grams of high-quality milk chocolate. Also in the bag is a clipboard with a pen and several sheets of paper, some with bold-face headings, one with a list of names. He empties his pockets of change except for a few nickels and pennies. Under the rim of his beret he tucks a compact aerosol screamer. Young kid in uniform – you never know.

The boy walks quickly but carefully down his own street for several minutes, crossing a busy intersection, nodding to the palsied man who collects for the Sally Ann. He continues fourteen blocks west to a street where the houses are nicer, bigger lots and bigger buildings with periscoping sprinkler systems. As the boy walks, he is alert. He watches for cars. He avoids stepping on the worms which wetwool the coarse pavement. Stepping on worms will shrink your willie.

The boy hits a good patch right away. He sells two chocolate bars to a young woman with a baby on her hip. She is a nanny and she loves chocolate. She grins while the boy goes through his routine: Good afternoon. May I interest you in a chocolate bar, a delicious way to build a better world. By purchasing this quality confectionery, you will assist in many important projects. You will help send an inner-city kid to camp; you will subsidize jobs for kids who really need them.

'Four dollars per,' he tells her. 'Half goes to charity.'

The nanny laughs, and says, 'All this delicious chocolate – and me just putting on my winter fat!' She tells the boy he is temptation in trousers and never mind the change – last thing she needs is a pocketful of pennies.

The boy doesn't sell anything at his next house, but the woman there asks when they will be calling round with the apples. Raw apples have never agreed with her, but thankfully this is not the case in pies. The boy says he'll be sure to call round again, with the apples, and he carefully takes down her name and address. Beside it he writes, in his neat square hand: *Apples?* He is thinking ahead.

The boy rings at three houses where no one answers the door. He notes the street numbers, adds: *Try evenings*. He thinks of the palsied man, his coins ching-chinging in time with his weird inside rhythms. He wonders where the palsied man got himself that bucket.

The boy has a little trouble with a man on a construction site who tries to bargain him down while waving a high-torque drill. No sale. Then he has a string of luck and he sells six chocolate bars, all of them to nannies who are not white. He also sells one to a big, oily-bellied man who complains about nannies who are not white and tells the boy he hasn't moved house and home all the way from North Bay just to end up in the Philippines. The boy has no opinion. Opinions are bad for business.

The boy takes a moment to transfer his earnings to a zippered pouch under his shirt. Then he thinks about where to go next. He can't decide between two houses across from each other that both look good. The first is a red brick with coach lanterns on each side of the door. The second has a real-estate sign on the front lawn: *For Sale*. The boy thinks someone who is selling might also be in the mood for buying. But the red brick house has tended window-boxes, and in the boy's experience this means that an old person lives there. He checks his watch. Game shows and soaps – prime time for old people. He tugs his beret further back to emphasize his youth, reaches delicately down and fingerballs a little dirt on his cheek. An old person will spot the dirt and offer him a tissue and buy some chocolate as a kindness. The boy looks at the house with the real-estate sign. A man gets out of a car in the driveway and stands by the door. He turns around as if to leave, then turns again and walks into the house. The boy sees that there are no blinds on the front windows. Through a bare window, he watches the man walk slowly around a big bare room. He glances back at the red brick house, at the Neighbourhood Watch decals, at the neat, very green lawn.

Inside the red brick house, an old man is watching but not watching *Wheel of Fortune*. Three people behind three podiums jump wildly up and down while the massive wheel ticks round and round. On the wheel are numbers and dollar signs and exclamation points. There is a loud *ding!* and the old man thinks, It is all over. There is a loud *ding!* but the wheel has already stopped.

There is a loud *ding!* and the old man uses the arms of his chair to haul himself upright, waits a moment for the blood to swab back down into his feet, shuffles to the door, steadies his hand long enough to tuck back one of the lace curtains dressing the windows, peers out at the boy peering in.

In the house with the real-estate sign on its lawn, the man takes his time closing the front door, double-locks and dead-bolts it for no reason, kicks the sheaf of mail out of the way, not bothering to look for his name on any of it. The place smells fusty, part maybe bacon grease and part maybe cold cream. The smell gets stuck into his nose and between his teeth, like cut grass. He unlatches a window, taps on the screen to shake loose the dead flies gathered, and the cool air spills in and soothes him.

He doesn't need his glasses to see that the place is basically cleaned out. Wall to wall. He tries to remember the way things looked before to compare with the way they look now. The lighting fixture is gone. The chairs are gone, and the sofa that turned itself into a bed with the flip of a switch. The television and the VCR are gone. And the two clocks; one fast, the other slow, whose median gave the correct time. What's left is a floor lamp complete with dimmer. Matching brass-effect magazine stands. An embossed fireplace set. The thermostat, set to frostguard.

A rectangular outline on the wall marks where a painting once hung – a watercolour of a wasp burrowing into a cantaloupe, that Sharon bought from a local artist with leukaemia who sold door to door to help pay for the chemo and the hash he smoked to gentle it. The wasp in the painting had a hunger, its silkscreen wings beat and buzzed, it drove its mandibles through the melon's stiff skin and sucked forcefully. That was the painting. Now the painting is gone.

Jenna, their realtor, will be by at three with the buyers. It's one, now. He had better get a move on. He deepdives his pockets, hunting for his agenda. Pulls it out, flourishes it open, makes a heading: MY STUFF. Then crosses it out, tries another: THINGS I HAVE LEFT.

He looks down and sees that the floor is under dust. It has been settled by dust, colonized. The dust is fine like dry mustard and then it is felty like shed fur. He takes a step, watches the dust cumulus through the room, leaving behind a bare blurry sickle of floor. His breathing bounces around a cavity in his head, and bumps some things loose, and brushes away some scale.

Under THINGS I HAVE LEFT he writes: *Dust.*

He gets up, walks, heading for the space where they ate their suppers, the open pentagon Jenna insists on calling the 'dinette'. He sees that the sideboard has been left for him, as promised. It's a good piece, well built, veneered in bird's-eye maple, with glass swing doors. Once it housed a dozen place-settings of sterling, a wedding gift, and a few bottles he drained and topped up with water so many times that every drink but the first one was a mixed drink, and at least once he must have been wasted on just water.

To his list he adds: *Sideboard.*

From outside he hears clear high kids' voices, pleading, scornful.

He continues into the kitchen. The cupboard doors are flipped askew like the wings from the flies that stick to window-screens. There is an odour of ammonia. An old calendar is fixed with magnets to the refrigerator door – twelve exotic cars, a promo for Raymond's Automobiles. The month displayed is December. Two Lancias – one red, one white – rest side by side, friendly, sleighbells draped across their hoods. The caption assures that Santa does not drive 55. The date is 1987. A good year? Maybe it had been. The magnets, red ladybugs, goggle at him. He opens the refrigerator door and it hums impressively, but the light is off. He closes each cupboard door carefully, considers, and opens them again. Then he goes back to the living room and sits in the lone chair and thinks. He headsinks into his hands, finds he can't exhale properly in this position. He rises, dips his toe in the dust and draws the lazy lower lip of a circle.

Then he expands his list: *Calendar (1987)*. *Ladybugs*.

The kids outside are insistent. 'Why don't you take a flying fuck?' one of them suggests, and another hoots, 'Why don't you?'

He finds the twins' bedroom, sees that the walls have been rollered over with a light beige. Years ago he had the itch to be handy, spent weeks checking out swatch pads and paint chips, isolating that single shade of lemon that would suit the twins, working overnight in coveralls and goggles with poor ventilation while they slept at their auntie's so the fumes wouldn't spoil their innocent insides. He has to admit, the beige looks better.

Back in the living room, he stands a while before his shape in the dust. It reminds him of the traces of sticks in sand, shallow channels blown slowly over, tenderly, relentlessly. Like on a programme he has seen about a nomadic tribe whose art is of the sand – temporary etchings, subtle networks scooped by damp hardwood spears blessed by their rarity. These people believe that the motion of sand belongs to a cycle of absorption extending deep into the earth, where water is cool and sweet and plentiful. What they draw in the sand is recycled as water, transformed to become life, become piss, become sand.

He looks out the window and sees a boy in a hat in the middle of the street. In the wind, the boy's hat is disfigured, it slinks across the landscape like a soft watch. The boy in the hat in the street looks one way and the other, shrugs, and maybe makes up his mind, because the man can't see him any more.

The boy stands outside the door of the red brick house and rings the doorbell and waits for the door to open. He sees the corner of a curtain lifted at one of the kidney windows that flank the door, smiles, waves his sample chocolate bar. There is a period of no movement. Then the door opens and an old man in Chinese slippers backs into gloom and the wavy blue light from a tele-vision.

'Come in, come in,' the old man says, and the boy does so. He is careful not to look too closely at anything. Being nosy is bad for business.

'What can I do you for?' the old man asks, and laughs. He laughs and coughs and wipes his hands on his trousers. Watching the old man wipe his hands, the boy thinks he might come back with a chamois or two, best price in town.

The boy introduces himself. He scans the list of names on his clipboard, picks one, and carefully crosses it through. He says, 'My name is Johnny Rombouts and I am a Boy Scout and I am not from this neighbourhood.' He says, 'I am selling chocolate bars for charity. Four bucks buys a chocolate bar.' The old man nods affably, his hands spinning into one another like waxed furies. The boy finishes. He smiles, but the old man does not meet the smile. The boy thinks he should have watched his mouth, a little more 'please' and 'thank-you', 'dollars' instead of 'bucks'. He smiles and shifts his head so the old man can see the dirt on his cheek, the result of his honest labour in the fields, picking chocolate bars. He displays his sample so the old man can appreciate its large size.

The old man asks, 'So where does the money go?'

The boy reaches up and fiddles with the dirt on his cheek but the old man doesn't notice. He returns to his routine. 'A kid will go to a summer camp,' he says. 'This kid maybe has never seen a pine tree or dunked his head in a freshwater stream. Another kid will get hired somewhere. It will be a position of trust. These are *opportunities*,' he explains to the old man.

'Where is this camp?' the old man wants to know. 'Up north?'

The boy isn't sure, it might be. What the boy knows of the north is that it teems with black flies that lay eggs in the ears and throats of those dumb enough to sleep on their sides, or snore. Then the eggs hatch and maggot flies harvest the brains – this happens all the time. On a camping trip he and the other Scouts sang 'There ain't no flies on us', and a sloppy turtlenecked man with a smoker's voice, someone's father, explained about black flies as they ate coloured marshmallows. This is what the boy knows of the north. But he doesn't pass this on to the old man.

The boy tells the old man that some of the money goes elsewhere.

'To a good cause?' the old man asks.

The boy guesses so. He guesses it's earmarked for medical research. No one has ever asked this before, so the boy is not prepared. He smiles at the old man and jots in his pad: *Where does $ go?*

The old man shakes his head. 'I can't help you,' he says.

The boy points out that they're four dollars, and you get a lot of chocolate – eighty metric grams. He offers the old man the bar to heft. He lets slip that he has tried one or two himself – eating into his own profits, ha ha – and they are delicious.

'Well, see, the way it is, I don't keep the purse strings,' the old man says. 'Cissy keeps the purse strings.' He wiggles his hands, to signify purse strings. Then tips his head to indicate upstairs, and pulls a comical face that shows his denture plate working in his mouth. In the old man's mouth, the boy pictures one of his chocolate bars, a bargain at four dollars.

The boy steps up the heat a little. He explains that there are no peanuts in the chocolate, if the old man is worried about allergies and such. No peanuts, no peanut oil. Only the very best one hundred percent natural milk chocolate. The boy becomes inventive. He tells the old man that the manufacturers of this chocolate are an old family firm, crazy for hygiene. No peanuts are permitted anywhere near this family's workshop. 'This chocolate is handmade by trained craftsmen,' the boy says. 'Strictly following an old-fashioned recipe. And in line with Bavarian purity laws,' he says, thinking of his mother and Molson coasters. 'Dating from 1613.'

The old man listens along. 'It sure sounds like good stuff,' he says.

The boy narrows his eyes until the room is flicker-blurry and only the old man is stable. Selling is all about focus. Easier to bring in the fish on the line than to hook a new one. The old man is a weighted wriggle on the boy's stretched-out line. He will be collected, creeled. He will buy a chocolate bar, and that will be that. The boy takes a long, slow breath, flashes the old man his best sheer grin.

'This chocolate is rich in soya lecithin,' he says. The old man can see for himself – it's right there, on the label, in plain view. He won't hide anything from his friend, the old man.

'I believe you,' the old man says.

The boy continues to quote from the label. The chocolate contains real eggs, and is chock-full of emulsifier. It has a minimum of fifteen percent milk solids. The boy marvels. 'Fifteen percent!' He shakes his head. How can they do it, and make a profit? His expression darkens. 'Competing brands have maybe five or six percent,' he scoffs. And who suffers? The customer – the old man! Because the extra milk solids have healthful effects. Some folks see improvements after only a chocolate bar or two. It's like a miracle. 'Their cholesterol goes down, and their heartrate,' he says. 'Look at me,' he says.

'You're certainly a fine, tall boy,' the old man agrees.

'Thank you,' says the boy, graciously. 'For you,' he adds, 'I have a deal. No, don't argue, just listen. I'll give you two-for-one,' says the boy. 'Two for five dollars.'

'I thought they were four dollars,' the old man protests.

'Not in a two-for-one!' snaps the boy, flushed now, heated.

The old man scratches absently at a scar above his lip. From the television sifts an applausy noise that the boy feels might be mocking. A slidewhistle becomes a sine wave and the boy's stomach jumps.

'I can't hear myself think,' says the boy. He pushes by the old man and switches off the television. He turns away, then reaches back, and unplugs it. 'That's better,' he tells the old man. He points at the television. 'That is what they call an idiot box,' he tells him, wanting to imply something. The old man shrugs, brisks his fingers. The boy thinks he'll pack it in, what the hell, try across the road. Then he thinks of Murray.

Murray used to come by on weekends to have French sex with the boy's mother and do a guest spot as the boy's dad. The rest of the time, Murray sold electronics and went home to another family he had a stake in. When he played the boy's dad, Murray had certain rights: territorial rights, buddy rights, walloping rights. Now these rights have been extended. Now Murray's stake includes the boy's mother and, through her, the boy. Now the boy's home will be Murray's home, and the boy will be Murray's boy.

The old man takes a few dysplastic steps and halts, looking up the stairs. Picking at his lip and looking up the stairs.

The boy sees an opportunity. 'That's some ding-dong on your face,' he says, jovially, to the old man. 'What you could do, you could make a poultice, melt down one of these bars.' He makes believe that he is stirring something, then rubbing it on his face. 'That'd do the business,' he tells the old man.

'I hadn't thought of that,' the old man admits.

'Why not enter our sweepstake?' the boy asks. 'One proof of purchase, and an SAE. Win a cash prize. With *that* . . .' The boy shrugs to suggest possibility.

'You've got great patter,' the old man says, eyes on the stairs.

'This is not about me!' replies the boy angrily. 'It is about quality chocolate. It is about kids falling through cracks. It is about summer camps and medical research, life and death!'

The old man looks up the stairs. 'Well, Cissy will say aye or nay,' he says. 'She'll give the go-ahead. She ought to be down directly,' he says. 'But she might be in the bath and then you'd have a wait on your hands – Cissy is some tadpole!' The old man rolls his eyes humorously. 'You can come back later, if you like.'

The boy walks to the door. Sun winces along the curvy glass and he sees the old man behind him, quivering, and briefly he sees himself on the steps, looking in; he jiggles his eyelids to clear this. He glances across the street, spots the figure pacing against unblinded windows. He turns around and studies the old man, his eyes still on the stairs, picked-over lip churning in his fingers.

'I'll wait,' says the boy.

*

In the house with the real-estate sign on its lawn, the man checks his watch.

'Just, you know, spiff it up a little,' Jenna told him over the phone. 'Folks want to see a house they can fix up if they want to, not a house they need to fix up.'

The man wonders just what Jenna means by 'spiff up' and 'fix'. Maybe he ought to take a mop to the living-room floor, all that dust. And turn on a few lights.

He thinks he'll have a little fun first, while no one's around. He steps out of his shoes, flexes his feet to relax them, awkwardly toe-traces a word in the dust. It isn't easy. The characters smudge, their contours dither and dip like runes.

Eventually he manages to spell out his name. Then the word *welcome*. Then a rude word, which he scratches out self-consciously. Every so often he stops to listen for the clickety sound of keys in the door which he has locked and bolted, but he doesn't hear a thing.

Soon he runs out of dust to draw in. He hips up against a doorway, crooks his right foot over the left knee to see where the dust has mingled with the combed wool of his sock, and matted it possum-grey.

Under *THINGS I HAVE LEFT*, he inscribes: *More dust (much of it on my socks)*. Then he claps the agenda closed. Two more rooms. He is making a dent.

In the bathroom, he flushes the toilet in order to hear some noise. Blue dye tendrils sluggishly through the bowl, turning the water the universal colour of clean. On television, men sweat blue and women bleed blue and babies wet blue. Blue is the great euphemism. He hand-dips into the tank, smells the chlorine and the blue, that acrid, needling smell of blue. Closefists around the blue perforated cube. Hand-dips again for the bloated copper ball and bends it back and up, and the toilet flushes and flushes, and the water is finally clear.

A tail of breeze flutters the shower curtain – a translucent two-ply stamped with anthropomorphic fruits, each with a musical instrument trailing quarter-notes like jet stream. He tries to imagine the tune and can't. When he pops the curtain from its acrylic hinges, it makes a styrene ripping sound like the plastic under-sheet that one twin never wet though the other did, and in that percussive collapse he feels the void of modern composition. Crackled around him cloak-fashion, it fits his body like the closest harmony, and makes him waterproof, so that even the shower dialled full on doesn't touch him, though he stands, eyes ratcheted open, just inches from the bulleting spray.

The water – still flushing – soon thins the shower pressure to a hot, bending drizzle. On the mirror, steam has laid loops, by turns opaque and translucent in a kind of batik. From his right pectoral a hyphen-browed apple blows a plangent tenor sax, which reminds him of short whiskies, which reminds him of sideboards, which reminds him of his list. The toilet that won't stop flushing and the too-hot, too-cold shower are, he decides, 'fixed appliances', belonging to the house.

He squelches back to the living room, where already dust is beginning to veil his handiwork. Patiently, he retraces. The dust cashmeres his wet bare feet, the shapes he leaves behind him are sags in a flexible cord.

Outside, the kids fight over a turn.

He circuits the living room and tries to do what he came here for. The list. The list. To the list he adds: *Shower curtain (fruited). Refrigerator. Lamps no bulbs. Magazine racks x 2. Dust (in places, deep).*

By now the agenda is soaked with blue, causing the ink to

run – more blue. He drops it. He'll have to rely on his noggin. The sideboard and the lamps and the magazine holders and the ladybugs and the shower curtain come to a certain value. He'll get something for the refrigerator, though he isn't sure it's his. He'll try and sell the sideboard and the refrigerator, if it is his, and give the rest away.

He checks his watch. Nearly two. He had better get cracking.

He should have come by months ago. In March, Sharon phoned and they talked a spell. She asked how he was, and he asked how she was. Turned out they were both fine. The kids were doing well in their new school, a small-town school with its own library, good new facilities and x number of teachers per head. The town was spoilt for parks. Its recycling programmes were a beacon for other, lesser towns. The curling rink was taking on new members, all joining fees waived.

Sharon phoned and they chatted, keeping the tone limber.

He said, 'Is that right?' to nearly everything. And also, 'I'm glad. I'm real glad.'

They both thought it might be nice to get together when he swung by for his visit with the twins. They would go out for coffee, and she'd catch him up on Danielle's problem acne and Katie's below-par math, and the wisdom of sticking with piano lessons which, okay, provided an artistic outlet and honed motor skills, but at twenty-two bucks per hour per twin.

As he listened on the phone he tried to hold on to some-thing – a shared memory, scene or conversation – that might be navigated to advantage. He thought Sharon sounded very near, perhaps was near, and the phone just a prop. He told her so.

'Don't,' she said. 'Oh shit – don't start.'

He said he wasn't starting anything, he was just observing. 'It was just an observation,' he said, though knowing by now that the words, like the moment, were aspic. *It was just an observation.* But maybe the observing held some hoping.

'You left a lot of stuff there,' she said. 'I'd hate to just throw it out. What do you want me to do with it, if anything?'

'No, that's fine. Go ahead and throw it out. That's fine.'

'I'd give it away before I did that. Someone could use it. All that stuff.'

He thought that would be fine too, giving it away. Someone could use it – wasn't that funny. Better than he had. In a better way.

Over the phone there was a surge like lightning and he thought he'd lost Sharon. Waiting for her, he closed his eyes and sang. But she was still on the line, still there, only quiet. So he stopped his song. He said, 'I'm sorry.'

'Just please don't get fancy with the house when you clear it out,' she said. 'We've got buyers. It's the twins you'll be hurting,' she said. 'Please, okay?'

On the wall where the wasp once hung there is a substrate of buzzing that draws him as though by common cause. He goes to it, breathes in his own breath, reflected off the wall like a wax transfer, and thinks that Jenna and whoever will be here soon, and he had better spiff something up, and he had better get presentable.

As he rises, a nerve in his back touches another across terminals, shooting painful sparks in a griddle pattern across his vertebrae, up along his spinal column, into his brain. He remembers. He remembers that once, when the twins were finally sleeping through the night, he had awoken early, slipped his hands thin as playing-cards under Sharon's legs, lifting, and knelt in the hard ringing sun like polished copper, and gone down on her with the tip and then the roughness of his tongue.

'Mmm,' she said, drowsy, lissome. 'Why don't we do this every morning?'

It had seemed to him then that this was love as a kind of gust, localized, potent. 'Maybe we will,' he replied, as if in a pact, but as far as he could remember that had been the only time. *Maybe we will.* But it had not been like that. Not once did they guzzle champagne from plastic cups, or meet like tigers in corners. The twins bear the names of dead relatives.

He starts back to the bathroom to check on the shower. Then stops. Well, it's now or never, he tells himself. Come on! He walks to the master bedroom, main selling point of the house, with its garden view, its sheafing morning sun. Finds the brass knob which twists soundlessly as though it has recently been oiled. The room is empty except for the four-poster bed. The awesome, king-sized bed.

He remembers that the bed was the first thing they bought for this house. It was too big and too expensive, but they bought it anyway. When they got it home, finally, and into the room, finally, he and Sharon jumped right on to it, bodies loose-tangled like macramé, everywhere overlapping; her hair was their shield, and where it caught in his mouth it tasted of promise.

Now the bed is huge, massive, a football field. It has grown on its silent diet, fed on the dust and quiet until now. Its sides touch each of the four walls. Stripped of sheets, the mattress is a matrix of coil springs individually adjusting to the pressure of his gaze, each cushion scientifically designed to provide lumbar support, to prevent bumps and lumps and valleys, to preserve correctness in sleep, to legislate decent rest.

He touches his face. It is wet. He is getting wet around the gills. The steam. There are still blinds on these windows, they clatter up the pane as he tugs the string. Better spiff the place up.

Air it out. The window floats up, letting new air in, the sill is stained blue where he grasps it.

He remembers that gradually the bed aged and worsened, learned creaks like a second language. And in that bed they grew mindful of disruption.

Under the shower curtain, he sloughs his pants, socks, shirt and undershirt. His boxer shorts are worn through in places. Once, a word on the shorts glowed in the dark: *No* in daylight and *Yes* in the dark. It was a tourist's joke. Now, on the floor, his clothes seek dust. On his cool body, the shower curtain sings up a storm – a warm, slick shuffle-beat. He climbs on to the bed, begins to bounce, hesitantly, finding a rhythm.

The boy is tired of waiting. He still has five chocolate bars left of the twenty he stole from the grocer's down the street at a buck forty-nine, retail. He doesn't want them mucking up his bag. He wants this old man to buy one so he can leave. He asks the old man, 'Why don't you just go get the cash? Two-for-one,' he adds.

The old man doesn't look so well. 'Cissy's got her things to do,' he says. 'It's not right to disturb her.'

The boy shrugs. He concentrates his eyes on the old man. He is tired of waiting, but he keeps his eyes fixed right on that old man.

'Cissy don't have the best of sight,' the old man says. 'Can't see distances worth a damn. Fact is, she's had trouble doing anything, lately,' he says. 'Couldn't get into her walker, couldn't take a bath, too painful.'

The boy watches the old man. He thinks the old man maybe is weakening.

The old man's hands whiz like gypsy cymbals, releasing a thickening stink of glue.

'My hands,' the old man says, sadly. He thrusts his hands towards the boy. 'All beat up – see? Used to run a hobby-shop, "Hobby-Heaven". Trains, puzzles. Nothing video. No time for nothing video.' He shakes his head. 'Sonuvabitch, keeping it going. Couldn't compete with the strip-mall biggies. So I offered extras. Value-added, they call it. One of the extras was, I would finish any project a customer couldn't manage. No charge,' the old man says. He follows the boy's glance upstairs. 'A watched pot never boils,' he says, and wags his finger.

The boy crunches some numbers. 'Three-for-one,' he tells the old man. 'Last offer. Your vision will improve,' he says. 'Not to mention your old lady's. You'll run like a deer – both of you. You'll be hell in the sack.'

The old man nods, picks at his lip. Flakes of something sift to the ground.

'Just buy one,' pleads the boy. He turns up the heat. 'Kids in the city are dreaming of summer camp. They are dreaming of opportunities. Here I am offering you a delicious way to build a better world, to make a needy kid's dream come true!' He hears himself become shrill. 'All over, kids are dropping dead from cancer—'

The old man interrupts him. 'When I came home I had to wash and wash my hands to not get stickum on the furniture. I had to zip it all off my fingers post-haste, or Cissy called me rubberfingers—'

There is a knocking at the door like snareshots that makes the boy jump. Then there is some outside talking between a man and a woman.

The woman says, 'I don't think that's right.'

'Well, who was supposed to arrange this?' the man wants to know.

'Fourth house from the corner,' the woman says. 'Fourth house.'

Knock, knock at the door. The sound of ringed fingers pressing the mail slot.

'I don't know,' says the woman. 'There's no light I can see.'

The man sounds disgusted. 'Will you look at that,' he says.

'What?' the woman asks, from low down.

'Over there,' he says. 'There – the house with the sign.'

The woman counts: One, two, three, four. 'Oops,' the woman says.

The man and the woman leave behind their echoes. The boy walks around the back of the television, plugs it in, turns it on and off rapidly, turns up the sound.

'Zip zip off my fingers,' the old man says. 'Gave me an idea.'

The old man shoots the cuffs of his shirt. Glue lies like salt flats along the serpentine of his arms. Like a scene from the on-again off-again television, the boy watches the old man rub himself down with the stiff white glue, spoon into the bed, sculpt himself noisily to another body, wait patiently for the bond to set.

'It took a lot of glue,' the old man says. He picks at his lip – scarred with glue, the boy sees now. 'I had to be sticky enough to catch her, when she slid under . . .'

The boy feels his legs go snakebendy. He starts to walk past the old man, but the old man blocks him.

'Cissy didn't want my rubberfingers,' the old man says. 'She was all done with things. But she couldn't finish on her own. I helped her. It was a service I offered,' the old man says. 'No charge,' he says.

The boy and the man don't look upstairs. The old man takes a sun-shaped pillow from the couch. He holds it high, passes it through the air in a broad arc, swivels it gently down.

'This is how I held it,' he tells the boy.
The boy doesn't move.
'I'm not a killer,' says the old man.
'I'm not a Boy Scout,' says the boy.
And that is how they leave it.

In the house with the real-estate sign on its lawn, the man is getting a good workout. He is bouncing quickly. He is surprised to note that the bed doesn't creak very much after all, that it's actually pretty quiet. As shower steam weaves into the room, he scoops it against his skin, his face, his chest; his blue face, his blue chest. His head is nice and loose from the bouncing. He understands a few things. He understands the courage of the wasp in the painting; that though it seemed to be mired in rot, it was a wingbeat away from transcending it. He understands that blue is not a colour but a layer. He understands that names are incantations. He understands that what Sharon has left for him is dust – that everything is of the dust, belongs to the extended cycle of dust, is absorbed and transformed and preserved by it. And he understands that his task in this house is a kind of archaeology, an unearthing of who knows what, that in time may prove a surer trail.

The boy leaves the red brick house. He feels queasy. He wants to go home, but he has these chocolate bars. He trips on the steps and his head goes bang! and then is warm and sticky, but he has these chocolate bars. He stands upright, forces himself to look at the house across the road with the real-estate sign on the lawn. How can he get there? He lurches for ages, looks down and realizes he hasn't really moved. No one will help him. They are snug inside, feasting on his bargain-priced chocolate. With his mind he fashions a kind of harpoon and aims it at the door of the house with the real-estate sign. Once it is anchored he reels himself slowly across the road, and, on the same principle, makes his hand touch the button of the bell.

Inside the man hears the doorbell and ignores it. He feels badly that Jenna is locked out, but there will be other days. He jumps higher and higher. A coil pops beneath his feet, then another, bursting through the fabric like worm-driven shoots.

The boy works his way around the house with his hands on the bricks. He finds a window, bangs on it. He worries about the chocolate in his hand; the wrapping has gone wet and dark. Sticky hands and head are bad for business. Falling down is bad for business. He finds another window, partly open, manages to sling a chocolate bar through. He is having trouble speaking, so he briskly rubs his stomach to convey the chocolate's superior ingredients and flavour. He hopes he is smiling. Then he forces up four fingers. *Good deal*, he tries to say.

It takes the man a moment to realize that something has landed on the bed. He scoops and mouths it, biting through the paper and the silver foil into a rich pulped mass that tastes of chocolate tinged blue like his mouth, his blue mouth. His body too is streaked – no matter. He jumps higher, falls harder, each landed leap a skilful shovel-thrust, an act of excavation springing treasures from the dust.

He is mildly surprised to see that a boy has materialized before him.

'GoodafternoonI'mMurrayI'mnotfromthisneighbourhood,'

gabbles the boy, and the man sees that he is bleeding and that his hand is out.

The man slows, flaps his curtain welcomingly. He is pleased with his progress. Already he has unearthed this boy.

'Murray,' the boy manages.

'Dust,' says the man.

And that is how they leave it.

Building Marrakesh

Laura is still a young woman when she arrives in Marrakesh, well into the evening, in the longest light of spring. Just beyond the town limits she leaves the road for the shoulder, grinds the stiff gear into park. Stretching, yawning, she takes inventory: gasoline receipts; the shoes on her feet, unlaced; clothes and some books and a pocket knife still in its box. These are her possessions now.

Seven kilometres from Marrakesh, on the road to Taroudannt.

Down the road, headlights flare then disappear, and for an instant, from all directions, hers is the only car on this freshly paved road, a flawless black cord uncoiling into the middle distance. She lifts the latch, eases the door open, checks her watch: eight-fifteen. The luminous second-hand performs a full revolution as she steps from the car and pauses, her body, her breath suspended in the levelling light.

The sky is ablaze as the sun sets, browed by the Atlas Mountains.

She stands there for a long while, as insects, metal-blue and gauzy, melt into the dusk, and here or there the sky reaches back for a misplaced shard of light. She watches, listens, feeling for the pulse of this place. To the east, the crowded rivers; to the west, the scalloped hills. Above her, a wide copper sky, exhausted in recent days by hard heavy rain. Everywhere the cormorants, smooth-diving black chevrons. She can smell the sumac, hear the offbeat clatter of mountain goats, feel the sedimented soils beneath her feet, steeped in spice and ancient bodies, and maps long ago torn up.

Behind her in the shadows, along a path in the slumping grasses, someone's radio begins to play hot music, headlines, traffic bulletins, still-warm images of home. A newswoman breathlessly announces a tumbling Dow index; a weatherman forecasts night upon night of sea-borne storms.

Outside the ochre ramparts, the rhythm is broken, the colours change.

'Where will I take you?' Peter Michael asked her once. He smiled rivetingly, and offered the words with that look and that tone that meant, I will take you anywhere.

Marrakesh, Laura thought then. Marrakesh! But she told him that he needn't do that for her. And later she grew to understand that his offer, like her demurral, had its terms.

'Well, I'm free now,' she says aloud. 'Out of reach. I'm out of reach!'

The city slips its slumber just as it has done for more than 800 years. The morning call of the muezzin from the seventy-metre high Koutoubia, the spiritual beacon of Marrakesh.

The night ripens, heavy and hanging and almost too rich –
the air seems to thicken and bend. She leans back against the
hood of the car, hands along the fender, blending its warmth
with the heat of emergence, impatient for the new sun; no need
for sleep's unravellings, waiting on daybreak, in Marrakesh.

They do not try to follow when they discover she has gone. They
have things to do and mouths to feed and lives to moisten, and
they like it here, where they are. But when her first communi-
cation arrives, in the short hot spring of 1971, the whole family
assembles. Thirty-odd people, from barely born to ninety years of
age, sit restless in Aunt Cath's living room, munching and sucking on biscuits, drinking hand-squeezed lemonade.

Aunt Cath herself stands immobile in the centre of the room,
tall and composed, in a close-fitting camel skirt and jacket. She
carries a postcard from this morning's mail, a photograph of a
shell-white city surrounded by receding dunes. The buildings are
squat and crumbly like blocks of shortbread, with round holes cut
for doorways – they don't look anything like real homes. In the
distance stands a cluster of humped shapes that Bea is sure are
camels and Aunt Patti just knows are sand-doused rocks. At the
bottom right of the card, an exotic look-at-me script announces
Marrakesh.

Marrakesh – what a word! What a strange word! They have
never been there, can't think of anyone who has grown or lived
or died there. Marrakesh. A foreign land, with who knows what
currency or religion or wandering savages! Marrakesh, goodness,
what a word!

'It's her,' Roger says, in a voice more tin than silver. 'No
doubt.'

He points to the back of the card – a white wall vined with

writing: *As eternal as the snows on the highest peaks, as impressive as the Atlas Mountains, as entrenched in history as the palm trees are rooted in the earth, Marrakesh stands as the finishing touch to a picture of timeless beauty. The mightiest kings fought for it; dynasties inherited it; craftsmen, architects, painters and sculptors in all ages were inspired by it. Marrakesh, the imperial city which, at the dawn of its history, gave Morocco its name.* A cheery postscript frills an empty stamp box: *Every imaginable commodity abounds – palaces, hotels, restaurants, golf courses, even a casino!*

No matter how hard her parents Bea and Roger or her husband Peter Michael search, there is nothing more. No tears, no traps, no clues. There is nothing of her there to cling to. Nothing of her eyes (which are green), nothing of her voice (which is firm though not loud), nothing even of her gentle tapered hands that give the children chocolates in lavender foil wrappers and birthday presents twice a year. There is only silence, and then some crying, and no one knows the time.

Roger reknots his chequered tie and vows to fly out there, and Bea wonders what passes for police in Maahrra-Kaahsh. Peter Michael stands with two fingers absently polishing the piano and for the thousandth time thinks over the four years he meant to love her. Aunt Cath waits patiently for the postcard to return from its rounds. Then she clears her throat and says, 'It is getting on lunchtime. The little ones will be terribly hungry . . .'

So they gather round the old oak table and say a few easeful prayers. Then sandwiches are served, tuna salad on enriched white bread buttered right to the edges, and everyone admires the lazy Susan laden with cold cuts and relishes and hard-boiled eggs. There is plenty of everything left over. Roger unravels a celery spear. Peter Michael sheds a hair into his milk and swears. Bea hasn't an appetite.

They want to talk about her, but it takes some doing.

Grandpa Evans recounts how as a girl she loved mystery stories, anything with a puzzle, sometimes reading from them at table, last page first, spoiling it for everyone else.

Roger remembers that she always loved horses –

'Ponies,' corrects Bea.

– but wasn't able to have a real one, on account of allergies, so he'd made a swing from a log, attached to a chain with bolts at both ends, glued on swatches of broom for a mane and tail, bottle-glass for eyes, a bicycle seat for a saddle –

'He even made legs for it,' adds Bea. 'Out of that old canary kitchen chair. Canary-yellow legs, on a horse. Can you imagine?'

– and after all his hard work, she had preferred to gallop about on an old driftwood cane.

'Making those awful noises,' Bea says. 'Neigh.' She makes a pursy mouth, pushes out a harsh, high noise. 'Like that, sort of,' she says, and looks to Roger.

'Horse noises,' Roger clarifies. He shakes his head. 'After all that work.' He means to say something else, but a quietness comes upon him.

They want to talk about her, in a way they are not used to.

'It's just a notion,' Aunt Patti says. 'We all get them. Some more than most,' she chuckles, as one who in her day was known to entertain alarming notions.

One of the modern nieces has heard that Morocco is very much a hot-spot. Cousin David snorts, and says if that's the case, he hopes she's had her shots.

They want to talk about her, but they aren't sure how.

'It's the sun, isn't it?' Uncle Bernie says. 'She wants to be where the sun is. What do you call them? Snowbirds. I would bet on it,' he adds. 'I am that sure.'

Then Grandpa Evans offers a packet of chewing gum to the boy or girl who finds his glasses, and Bea points out that at least the children needn't suffer, and somehow discovers her appetite.

Aunt Cath excuses herself, hinting at indigestion, and goes upstairs, and locks the door, and slides down the wall in the drifting murk of noise and laughter, and weeps the colour from her cheeks and the burnish from her hair, and is brave, all things considered.

At summer's end another postcard arrives. Aunt Cath brings it in, on a tray, almost as an afterthought, with Sunday dinner.

'I thought you might all take a peek,' she says, then quickly sets down the potatoes that threaten to sear her bare palms. 'These will need to cool,' she says. 'That is the trouble with doing them scalloped.'

The card looks homemade. Two images are set on a rectangle of stiff cardboard the colour of sand. In the first, three men each sit astride a sleek tall horse, holding rifles. The men wear white loose clothes and fabric wrapped about their heads, the horses a rich brocade that scarves their necks and masks their eyes. The second picture is a building with thin stone pillars green and grooved as sucked peppermints, and a curved slate roof. Above this picture appears a legend; numbers penned neatly in the margins correspond to text on the verso. One, *The Badhi Palace.* Two, *Dar Si Said.*

The sun bathes Marrakesh in light. Its rays show up the pink marble of the fountains, spread across the tiled courtyards, are reflected, and then bring warmth to the turquoise, greens and whites of the mosaic, finally to be lost amid the stucco of the Dar Si Said, now a museum housing the finest masterpieces of Moroccan art. This same sun illuminates the remains of the Badhi Palace, where a shimmering mirage reveals the wonder of former glories to the dazzled visitor: the gold, the marble and the onyx traded for their weight in sugar by the most celebrated Saadian ruler, Ahmed el Mansour (1578–1603). Again, there is a postscript: (*The perfect proportions of the Ménara pavilion may be contemplated at leisure, mirrored in the quiet, still waters that stand before it.*)

Cousin David wants to know *what* goddamned pavilion? – excuse his French – and mutters a little more, in French.

Just as before, there is no return address, no stamp.

'Collector's privilege,' Aunt Cath says, and blushes at their fond bland looks. 'Though, you know, they're *funny* stamps—'

Then there is a telephone call for Peter Michael, a baby starts to storm. Slowly, randomly, like dried leaves dropping, they all fall their own ways home.

How can they explain her? Driving to and from hockey practice, in the bar of the Curling Club, over the phone, they try. Grandpa Evans catalogues her every childhood lie, confirming his conviction that character is formed early. A few of her friends, some baffled, some hurt, send cards or weepy letters. Jen from work calls with respect to forwarding mail and Em from next door wonders about pricing that antique harpsichord, just in case. How can they explain her? It isn't easy.

Aunt Patti thinks it might be genetic, a brain malfunction perhaps, that makes a person act badly. Cousin David figures a heart that will wander will just damned well wander, and there's no telling why. One of the modern nieces blames the town's lack of options and amenities, though certainly the new arena has turned out pretty well, and now there's that Thai restaurant run by real Thais. Bea takes to saying that she blames herself. Everyone else says it is just *ridiculous* for Bea to be so hard on herself like that – she ought to get out now and again, get her mind off things, have a little fun.

There is no single answer that satisfies everyone, though most agree that the symptoms have been there from the start, in that dark streak she kept carefully hidden but is now plain to see: her generosity that (upon reflection) seems more like bribery; her penchant for time alone, with (it is apparent now) its buried sting of deliberate snub; her shyness (with hindsight) revealed as self-absorption. It is acknowledged that she has made a life of being irresponsible, uncaring, cold. Great-Great-Aunt Dorothy dies (of heartbreak?) believing just this. At her funeral, no one mentions postcards from the East.

By now a sense of resignation has replaced the hope that she will return. Aunt Cath still sets a place for her on Sundays, but no longer fills the glass. Peter Michael is mostly seen alone now, or in the brisk thrall of Mona, his executive assistant, who has always managed his jam-packed schedule and now the rest of his life as well.

At Christmas, Mona forgets to tag the presents she alone has selected and wrapped, and poor Peter Michael has no idea which package is for whom. He stands there by the coughing fire in a jumble of wrapping and Scotch tape and toy reindeer, squinting and sizing-up and allocating. Seven gifts are opened in her name. She sends nothing.

In March a letter arrives from Marrakesh, addressed to ten-year-old Warren Steven, once her favourite nephew. Warren feels funny reading it out loud, so Uncle Dillon, a lawyer from Sydney with two German cars, does the honours.

He slits the envelope very slowly, as though a serpent were snuggled within. Inside is a charcoal sketch dispersed by time and travel to a discreet damp smudge. Aunt Patti thinks it a good likeness of Warren, but with the Smithson, not the Evans nose. Cousin David pronounces it disgusting and awfully unkind. Four-year-old Kenny brings the picture to his face, fascinated by the dark powder settled there. Wetting his finger, he draws circles in his ash-marbled flesh before the mirror. The other children lick their fingers and surround the drawing with new interest.

Inside the envelope she has petalfolded a second, smaller sheet of pink paper, lacking salutations, address, even watermark.

Sunrise over Marrakesh. The dawn adds a note of accentuated contrast to the imperious splendour of the Saadian tombs. Below, a multicoloured crowd invades the winding streets of the medina. Groups of men jostle towards the Ben Youssef mosque, nestling against the Medersa, the vast and superb Koranic school founded by the Mérinide sultan Abou el Hassan (1331–1349) and one of Marrakesh's most remarkable monuments. Your carriage awaits for the Palmerie.

Again, her parents can find no messages. No teary afterword, no solemn pleas of regret. No swift signature, no embedded kiss. Has she forgotten her upbringing? Her conscience? Is there a law against conscience in Marrakesh?

Bea reads it a second and a third time, one black-liquorice fingernail propping up the words.

'I don't know,' she says. 'What am I to do with this?'

One of the modern nieces, who has taken a psychology course at university, thinks it isn't quite normal to send letters like this. It implies alienation.

'Well, alienation is what you get,' remarks Cousin David, 'when you up and bugger off.'

At this time two stories are told. Roger explains how he went to the police station and called in some chips with one or two officers he'd vaccinated for mumps and polio and rubella twenty years before, and expedited a missing-persons. Under 'physical description', he wrote 'big-boned'. Then he thought for a bit, and crossed it out, and started over. After he had started over some six or seven times, he gave up. 'I was worried,' says Roger, 'that people might see "big-boned", and get the impression she was fat.'

Bea recounts a dream in which her daughter lies in a basin of soft ice, wearing a childhood sweater embroidered with a clock. In her dream Bea watches, powerless to do more than stare at this sweater, gone so long without mending, but its clock still ticking away on the body setting like candied lemon into the jammy ice. Bea hopes this dream isn't prophetic, and one of the modern nieces notes that prophecy and symbol are, rather unfortunately, often confused.

Bea falls quiet. 'Actually, I didn't have that dream,' she says. 'Why did I say I did?'

And perhaps it is at that point that they no longer want to talk about her.

'It is odd, about the stamps . . .' Aunt Cath begins, but no one pays attention.

So Aunt Cath stands near the window, listens to the sea roaring along the docks below, imagines the sands whirling and rising free below the foam, settling calmly to the bottom, now lazily changing shape . . .

Finally it is suppertime, and as plates and cutlery clatter across the table, Aunt Cath thinks to herself, *If only*.

Then she says, to no one in particular, 'Will that be enough pumpkin squash? I can never remember who eats it . . .'

After supper she quietly slips the letter and drawing into her pocket and out of their minds. It will not be spoken of. Instead, plans are made for the summer. The family will gather at Cedars Island, Aunt Cath's inheritance. They will lumberjack in the tilting mossy birches, and pick berries till their hands are stained, and set traps for crayfish, and leave chubs on the wharf in the hopes of pelicans. They will bring the children. They will not think of Marrakesh. They will play sand games and refresh themselves at twilight. The horse flies will stay away. The mosquitoes will drown in the silver evening rains. Peter Michael will throw the football, straight and on target, every time. Bea will make wild-blueberry bounce. Roger will barbecue his famous double-garlic steaks. They will all pitch in where needed. They will have a wonderful time.

Aunt Cath hugs the door of her bedroom, wrapped in an old emerald night-gown. Some minutes ago, she climbed from bed to ease her bladder, but now finds herself unable to walk any further.

I will move soon enough it is only a cramp I will just wait a while, she tells herself, but she is anxious all the same. *I have carried them for so long. Too long. I can hardly imagine a life apart.* Once again, she imagines fused ocean and desert, bright sea and spun sand.

Still she cannot move. A shudder traces rapidly up her right side, a mean streak of pain. She feels, then doesn't feel, her right leg seize up, then her thigh, hip, stomach, chest, arm, hand, head. Faces stretch past, out of focus, mouths open. Hands grip her skin, sowing rough red bubbles. She sees all sorts of shadows: torsos, windmills, cats she has known. The room widens, narrows, widens again. She is spinning, somehow, against her wishes, forsaken by gravity and her own leaky will; through the swim of noise and angles, a voice, brisk as thistles: 'Cath? Cath, you sleepyhead! Do you have five dollars for pizza?'

She crumbles, mouth twisted, silent, shaking, knowing.

It has been three months since Aunt Cath's stroke, and they are cautious that Thanksgiving. Even the children nudge each other into calmer states. Aunt Cath sits at the table's head. Her right arm and leg ripple occasionally, nerves sending dead letters. Behind her voice her larynx skips and rasps and her words come slowly, molasses dredged through a cocktail straw. A pretty gilt napkin tucked under her chin catches the saliva that descends in rungs from her seized, split lips.

'Bless you,' they say, and look away. The children are instructed not to hug too hard, and when she automatically rises to serve them, Uncle Bernie proffers a restraining arm.

'Don't overdo it. Just carry one plate at a time, Cath. One thing at a time.'

No one speaks of Marrakesh. She has forgotten them and so must be forgotten. Her place is long since filled. Other chairs lie empty. Death has claimed Dorothy, Miami Beach has claimed Aunt Patti, and Peter Michael is essentially elsewhere – board meetings, business guilds, Venezuela in a week, and what if Mona is pregnant . . .

Roger and Bea sit at the far end, arms linked in a modest show of force. They arrived in silence and will leave in silence – if they can get the car started.

'Oh, but we'll have to get a new one,' Bea says. 'Just ask Rog. Goodness, the windows were stuck shut tonight, not a crack of fresh air – that old beater!'

Roger nods vaguely, offers his arm. This is the way they travel now, in a car without windows, in short cul de sacs. But when they go out, they link arms.

Aunt Cath sees it all, is overcome suddenly by the stiffness that lingers in her right side from eyebrow to ankle, thinks of the stamps, and promises herself, *Soon, very soon.*

She goes upstairs, then, pleading fatigue, and they watch her gravely, with the expectant boldness of young grackles at feeding time. She refuses the listless arms they offer her. Alone, her door shut and bolted, Cath can hear the stereo as it cycles through the stations, the low bass shudder of pop music. Feet shuffle, scrape, change direction, trying out steps. Relieved of the burden of respect, the family grows fluid once more.

Cath tunes her hearing to a pitch above the noise, sits carefully on her settee, tumbles out the postcards, chooses one, reads it with a growing hunger: *Time has passed you by. In the copper souk, perhaps, where the metal is worked by craftsmen following age-old traditions, their faces set in profound concentration. Or perhaps it was in the Langhzal Souk, home of the wool merchants. Or in el Btana, with its sheepskins. Or in the hubbub of the Zarbia Souk, where carpets and caftans are sold to the highest bidder.*

You are in another world. Where the smells of saffron, cumin, black pepper, ginger, verbena, cloves and orange flower enchant the nostrils. Among sacks of almonds, ground nuts and chick peas piled high like mountains, baskets of dates, casks of olives, and, on the apothecaries' shelves, pots of henna, flasks of rose extract, jasmine, mint, kohl, pieces of amber and musk. For all the beauty gathered here, for the sheer joy of the senses, you cannot miss the souks of Marrakesh—

Cath breaks off. There is too much to read, if she starts now. She will be here all day. She will always be here.

*

The old house is freshly cleaned, and quiet. Aunt Cath's three leather cases are packed and stand side by side, an ordered procession waiting for a signal that she herself will give, any time now. She will show them the card and the limpid blue wildflowers wired all the way from Marrakesh, their wavy roots tipped with sand, as though just moments ago plucked from the sea with an upward thrust and a tourniquet applied to clot the wound. They will live for a week or more, and everyone will say how appropriate they were, how exotic but how familiar.

Aunt Cath has worked it out with all the patience of a lifetime of service. She sees that the path most attractive to her is, for once, the path she will choose.

Dragging her suitcases out of sight, checking the oil and windshield fluid in the car, Aunt Cath readies herself. She lets the curtains down in all of the bedrooms, taking care to leave two fingers of light. Her mail will be forwarded to a post-office box near enough to drive to. There are too few jewels left to sell.

She lifts the telephone, picks out the rounds of numbers.

It is a low day, charcoal-grey, the sun seeping out beneath an overhang of clouds. The family gathers once more in Aunt Cath's living room. The children are peevish, the adults hushed and tense. Everyone waits without complaint.

Watching Aunt Cath, they feel her sadness. That Christmas Uncle Bernie will break down, shockingly, while carving white meat, and recall that he saw then in Aunt Cath what he had seen in *her*, just before *she* left; *seen it, known it* . . .

But then, they suspect nothing. All they see is sadness. Though it is strange that when Aunt Cath speaks, she does not cry.

'I have a letter, from a friend of hers, in Marrakesh. She died there, last week, at peace and happy. It was cancer, you see, but she— She did not wish it made public.'

Cancer. That's it, that's why, they think. That's the answer. Now they understand. Who wouldn't have done as she had done? Moved away in her pain like an injured wolf from its pack, wanting to spare them her weird disintegration, the slow, certain loaming of her tissues and marrow.

Cancer – it is the key they need. They explain her to each other in the light of this revelation. They recall how kind and unstinting she had always been. How generous, giving what she could while she still had time. How tactful, keeping it to herself, never losing her dignity. How quietly courageous, to the very end refusing to be a burden. Cancer – how terrible! – and yet it relieves them, it fills in gaps.

'Upon her wishes she was cremated. Her ashes will go to Cedars Island. She was loved, well loved. She was well loved, and though we all will miss her, we will remember that she was loved.'

There is no more. There could not have been.

Many conversations follow the hush, but none will be remembered.

Catherine is nearly sixty when she arrives in the place she knows as Marrakesh, well into the evening, in the longest light of spring. She pulls into the driveway, drops her good hand over and grinds the stiff gear into park. Stepping out of her car, she walks up the path to the house, white frame with a hoopy skirting bending like a bustle across the cliff's lip, its windows storm-shuttered against the near sea.

The sound of the wind in the foliage, chirping birds, the heady odours of jasmine and honeysuckle and the persistent perfume of the famous Marrakesh roses, saffron, poppies, antimony for black, the trees weighed down in their abundance.

In the garden she finds flagstones painted with images of the desert: a sun red-gold as a baking apple over plumes of blown white sand; wiry cacti; fragile dusty cities. To her left, a skeletal greenhouse. To her right, a fluted hand-stitched canopy. It's a roof, she thinks. A roof, for the souks of Marrakesh.

Carts overflowing with oranges and roasted grains, storytellers, musicians, public scribes with their black umbrellas, fortune-tellers, potion vendors and healers all contribute to the unreal spectacle.

Under the canopy, racks of driftwood, scaled and woolly with seaweed and dried sponge, are piled high with trinkets collected from the beaches, nubbed wrinkled starfish, sand-dollars, wave-sculpted aluminium cans; sea-glass by the barrel, speckled and smooth; old coins mixed and matched to fill hope chests for those on a budget. So many treasures, so many left to build.

East of Marrakesh, water, water, everywhere!

Cath can't stop smiling – it must be the air, the strong sea air. She walks into the house, parts heavy bead curtains, steps between terracotta pots. She touches everything: oiled wooden walls, the kites that hang from the wicker furniture, the slender pewter table dressed with a furious patch of hand-blown glass, bright and creamy as fresh marzipan, turned in the shape of a hummingbird. On this table Cath tumbles out the letters written from Marrakesh, posted from Scrimms, Nova Scotia, a mere hundred miles from the family seat, where she is now, where she will remain.

Then she tilts her good ear towards the back of the house, says gently, 'Laura – don't be afraid. I've come to help you finish it. I belong here too.'

The halting reply, the rummaging for words, the simple response: 'Hello Catherine. Welcome to Marrakesh.'

In the morning, they sit in the garden, listening for the propeller cries of the fishing boats, and suddenly Cath is crying, barely believing. 'O Laura Laura Laura – I am finally out of reach . . .'

She has never returned, Aunt Cath, and her house was eventually sold, her share kept in trust for the children. They speak of her often, and with love. She was well loved here, and she will be missed, but they will always remember that she was loved. They wish her luck and wisdom in the wilds of Marrakesh. But they will not try to follow; they have things to do and mouths to feed and new lives to moisten, and they like it here, where they are, where they were born.

Handsome Freaks and Other Flowers

Everyone has a vision. For Professor Trevor Kyle, it is *A Complete Illustrated History of Northern Ontario*. Working with diaries, oral histories, ordnance maps, early town records, Professor Kyle transcribes the evolution and liquidation of Ontario's north: the spectral burial mounds of the Laurel; the cliff paintings of the Blackduck on Blindfold Lake; the arrival of white voyageurs, surveyors, navvies; the relentless repossession of the better lands from the Saulteaux, Assiniboine, Cree and Ojibwa; the deliberate isolation of the French on the barren north-eastern shores. The miraculous gleaming stretches of railroad, the steady gutting of forests. Kyle assembles a book that is part documentary, part manifesto. It is his life's work. It has a single printing.

In his chapter entitled 'Northern Diversions', Kyle devotes

several pages to Killgarnie's Circus Colossus. Incorporated in 1880, Killgarnie's carved a spectacle out of the Canadian Shield. Its big top alone covered four acres; the rest of its tents spread some three acres more, shunning host towns' hot tar bellies for scrub land near the fairgrounds, where the water was. Killgarnie's was the first three-ring in the country, and the only one to feature a steam calliope, Arabian horses, full menagerie, no-net high-wire act, four-horse chariot race, clown brass band. Its sideshows boasted bare-knuckle boxing, midget wrestling, Black Museum, camera obscura, dozens of sure-thing games of chance. Most infamous was The Curiosity Room, stinking of pipe-smoke and spirit gum, loaded by low oaths: 'Freaks. Goddamn freaks.'

Still, they couldn't take their eyes away. Shut up into the mines and mills all day, they might have been used to dense things.

Under the heading 'Tragic Shadows', Kyle meticulously reproduces five photographs from Killgarnie's own archives – dark, streaky portraits of the denizens of The Curiosity Room, caught on stage, mid-step, as though painfully extruded through a cracked, imperfect dye. The Mustachioed Madam, a freshly oiled soup-strainer adorning her top lip, her jaw sporting dapper muttonchops, what looks to be combed muskrat sewn into the bodice of her dress. Simon the Swallower, king of the geeks, his neck coiled in upon itself like hemp and distended, the base of a milk bottle jutting from his mouth like a pharmacy stopper. The Scallop (a Maritime favourite), soft body pillaring into a face waxy and ornate as candle windings. The Eel, skinny and pliant, eczema-scaled, sucker-mouthed. The Maple Lady, displaying her three extra spoking appendages, an unruly tree of hands between wither and bloom.

'For many,' Kyle writes, 'their night at the circus ended here, with a pleasant shudder. A shudder, and a prayer: O Lord, to be born like that – how much happier to be whole!'

About the freaks themselves – their lives, their fates – Kyle does not elaborate. He notes that, in the 1940s, an American outfit registered The Curiosity Room as a trademark. Killgarnie's freak show came to be called The Last Caravan. It was the last open door.

Trillium was not born strong. She was born surprised. They extracted her from the shreds of Zena's uterus with tongs that barely cradled her head and shadowed her open blue eyes. But she did not flinch or cry or wet herself. She was surprised, that was all.

Zena thought she was dreaming when she saw the smooth dovetail of the infant trunk, the crinkled oversew of skin spanning the tiny thighs, the perfectly sealed joints of the knees. She thought, *I am drugged I am dreaming,* and this thought overtook the dream, and displaced it.

Dr Mickle checked in. 'And how are we, Mrs Macleod? Feeling fine?'

Zena tried to look fine. Fine like a trooper. Fine like right as rain.

Dr Mickle stayed, toeing awkwardly up and down. He cleared his throat. Tugged his beard. Swiped at his glasses, his head side-to-siding like a metronome's needle.

'You're no doubt aware . . . don't extend past her knees . . . not fundamentally *serious* . . . mind at ease . . . purely mechanical . . . Mrs Macleod, if you'll just . . .'

Things became dulled. Part of Zena dulled also. Part of her

stayed sharp. *How clever of him to notice,* cackled the sharp Zena. *Whoops, no legs! A button missing from a shirt. Long waist tapering into a dolphin's snub – how lovely! Why, on the right wheelbarrow, she'll be the belle of the ball!*

The dull Zena set up sensescreens. Both Zenas wept, stared, slept.

Back at home, in the armchair, or squatting over the toilet, trying to clear her leaking bowels, Zena recalled the months of pregnancy, moment by moment, stumble by stumble, searching for that subtle pivot where the ordinary became the damaged. Was it the time she had awoken early, jaundiced with bile, turned over her ankle on her way to the bathroom, tumbled down three stairs? Had she dissolved the nascent limbs on New Year's Eve when, wanting for once to let her hair down, she accepted that second, prodigal glass of champagne?

Zena resisted certain judgements: that it was a natural conception; that she had carried responsibly; that the doctors made no mistakes or substitutions. She wanted the blame to be fixed, not floating. They decided not to have another child, but to do their best by this one. Doug got himself fixed. Zena was tired all the time.

Trillium was an easy baby. She slept through the night and nursed enthusiastically, open-eyed, watching, rolling if she had to in order to face the light. Placed near the swell of a sunbeam, Trillium oriented herself to it, bumping along the bed, stretching rapturously into the warmth.

'Look at that! She's just like a sunflower. Or a seal. A seal on a rock,' said Zena, and so she was, and a sleek one too. In the wide bright crib, body softened by her flannel sleeper, Trillium was complete.

'But then,' Jean reminded her, 'you take a step back.'

Of their relations, Doug's Aunt Jean was the only one they saw regularly. Once a month she made the trip from Rainy River, visited her friends in town, gifted Zena with a fruit cobbler or a half-pound sack of wild rice she packed herself. Politely disappointed but doing her part, casting homilies before her like barley-seed to fowl. *Things must take their course. Sunshine follows rain. Bricks alone don't make a home.* Trillium was hard on Jean, so far removed from the perfect Pampers baby she had anticipated, written triumphant letters about, bought tiny, glamorous outfits for. Trillium was hard on all of them, without being hard at all.

'It's a trial for Zena, poor dear. She sleeps. As for Douglas – you know how he gets, all thin-lipped and quiet – he never lets on. Still waters run deep. Poor Douglas!'

Poor Douglas never complained. Doug was an improver, ill at ease in a slap-dash world. He worked overtime, read book after book, trawled for advice the way others did trophy fish. He worked at everything, at staying fit, at eating right, at sex. A few months after the birth, he brought home a self-help package called LoveMaker, half-price from a friend in direct-mail. He told her that so proudly, as if waiting for her to chuck him on the shoulder and whisper, *Oh boy Dougie you are one well-connected fella you are one smooth operator!* Zena was just fine with their love life, but Doug wasn't, apparently, and he had enough zeal for both of them.

Together they completed Love Charts and Intimacy Indexes, and for weeks afterwards Doug was adamant about consulting these before he greased or nibbled or stroked or held her, until Zena felt less like a lover and more like a recalcitrant skin rash. Finally, as he busily lit joss sticks around the Nuptial Throne, she dropped her acolyte's mask and said, 'Doug? Put those away.

Please, put them away. I want you to lie there. Just lie there. Close your eyes. Don't move . . .'

She had never been so wet, so fast, so limber. She wound herself about him like lichen into sandstone and he thanked her with a climbing series of cries. Afterwards, she gathered and garbaged the glass-stoppered jars, the racy software, the three-colour glossy brochures. He watched her with his heavy raven's eyes, but never said a word.

Trillium grew. Zena planted seeds in the back garden. Trillium, smarter and chattier every day, sat perched on her weatherproof cushion with a miniature set of gardening tools to dig with, chubby arms churning, scooping soil with abandon, pausing for the occasional dazed worm, grubby as string on a roast. She had just read *Winnie the Pooh*, and saw bears everywhere.

'What are we planting, Zena? Are we planting honey?'

Zena scanned the seed packet, tried to make some sense of the blurry six-point text. Her glasses were lost, as usual, hanging from something or buried beneath something. She hazarded a guess.

'We're planting flowers. Hanscombe's Free Something. It's a kind of flower. It's blue. It's supposed to be blue. But we won't know, will we? Until spring.'

Trillium loved the name, rolling it around in her mouth, singing it: 'Handsome freaks, handsome freaks, handsome freaks we are planting you . . .'

Zena could have corrected her, but why interfere? Left to their errors children learned – wasn't that what Doug called 'priority parenting'?

Trillium grew. For years the horse waited patiently, stabled in the vestibule under a dropsheet, where the three of them had painted it, and each other too, ending up in a wild thumping battle with Trillium on top, laughing.

'King of the Hill!' she yelled.

Doug spent ages refurbishing it, adding features: reins and spurs and racing colours. He planed its wooden legs and levelled its coiled-spring feet until it was perfectly balanced. Gently, he set Trillium atop it, side-saddle. As soon as he let go of her, she started to slide.

He caught her. 'What do you think, Trill? Should we give it another whirl?'

Trillium nodded, felt herself righted, then lifted. She watched the veins in Doug's arms, the thin swift tunnels in his flesh. She was riding it – the wonder! – springing and leaping, rattling and creaking, her hands well wrapped in its broom-top mane, holding fast, holding . . .

She awoke with a sore, lightless feeling. She had fallen very hard. Knocked herself out. Now her eyelids were heavy drapes and Doug was the measured sun.

'All you all right, Trill? Can you feel this?' Doug pinched her shoulders, her forearms. 'You took quite a fall there, hon. But you had him.' He waved a flared wood swatch. 'Look – you rode the tail right off that goddamn horse!'

They laughed, and he let her swear twice: *Shit! Damn!* The swearing was their secret. Zena would be furious if she heard the way he spoke to Trillium, the way she answered back. But if you were stuck living in a glass house, Doug said, you might as well learn about rocks.

She explained to Doug that it wasn't the hurt but the bounce that had set her crying. He figured that. Crying would clear that bounce away. Crying would feel good, he promised, holding her hard, fluffing her hair, scalp to ends, the way she liked. She cried a little more.

Trillium grew. In the town she became a kind of emblem. Neighbours dropped in to see her. She was invited to all the birthday parties. It was educational for the other children to have such an example before them. Sympathy, diplomacy, a keen appreciation of one's luck in life, might all be learned through association with Trillium. Everyone said what a sunny little girl, and wasn't it peculiar where the twist lay, in a human life!

Trillium went to the parties and set an example and looked straight ahead, never down. She was not a cripple; she was disabled. She was not a mixed blessing; she was a treasure. She was not playing catch-up. She was not a sad sack.

For a spring treat they went to the circus. Zena was uncomfortable with the live animal acts. Doug was anxious in crowds. Trillium loved the excitement, the eyes staring elsewhere for a change. Zena glanced at her watch, at Doug, at the sticky littered ground. At a man in a gorilla suit shooting a stream of apple juice from a bottle strapped to his groin. She shut her eyes, thought of her dining room, newly stripped. Three good coats of paint, she reckoned. Three coats, then see.

Zena couldn't understand what about this meagre entertainment so appealed to Trillium. There was an ageing strongman, whose foam barbells flexed visibly when he hoisted them, grunting mightily, above his pulsing accordion neck. A team of pimply tightrope walkers, who managed tentative cartwheels and celebrated unduly, exchanging countless high fives. Two clowns whose comic repertoire ranged from farting to falling over and back again. A dim, stooped old bear, prodded by a trainer on to a trampoline, where he settled into a swingy sleep. Amore (The Billy Goat of Love) who 'kissed' children, except that he was biting them, except that he had no teeth. Three clever dogs who dribbled beach balls and barked lugubriously to 'Stand By Your Man'. The ringmaster punctuated his patter with coughs, measured death rattles marking time until the audience departed, when he could drain into the duff old tenting and add his skin to its stains.

Trillium was mesmerized, eyes huge, unblinking. Doug tied and retied his shoelaces. Zena tapped him on the shoulder, and without looking up he said, 'I know. But she loves it.'

Trillium turned to Zena, hugged her, wordless in her pleasure, fierce in her thanks. Doug dropped an arm to nudge a popcorn nugget into Zena's unprotected ear.

Laughter and antic blows. Nasty harpy clowning. Candy corn and grief.

This was the state of Killgarnie's Circus Colossus, that once houseproud institution born and raised in Ontario's deep woods, famous enough to draw crowds in the American border towns, boasting at its peak a cast of over eighty, and on its payroll nearly thirty more – carpenters and tailors and cooks and whores.

This was the state of things.

Trillium turns twelve the year the pictures begin to disappear. It is early January, bitterly cold under a webbed grey sky. She wears her new Clone Technologies *Sprinters* hydraulic legs: heavy, with thigh-sockets and muscle detailing and a polyester wrapping tinted to mimic flesh. Pressure-sensitive flex controls are attached to her shoulders. To operate them she must swing her arms, left-right, left-right, balancing this motion against the brief lag before the legs engage, willing her body in-line, her legs at their joints hissing and whistling like long pierced balloons.

She is alone in the house, a bungalow with low ceilings and small, regular rooms done in tongue-and-groove pine pretending to be cedar. Beeswax candles. An intermittent theme of sunflowers. A spread of six-odd books makes up the stagnant coffee-table library. On the opposite wall a mirror hangs; below it she notices the twin punctures, not yet puttied over, where it has been raised. Without her stilts she would not be tall enough for this mirror. Odd. She turns to study the familiar photographs of herself and Doug and Zena at a meadow picnic, frolicking on rafts in a shallow inland pool. But they are no longer where she remembers them. Everywhere on these walls, it seems, changes are underway.

Pivoting slowly on one stilt, she spies a book she must have passed a hundred times, *A Complete Illustrated History of Northern Ontario*. She moves out of range of the mirror, begins to read.

The junior high in Absinthe dates from 1942. The stairs are steep and the halls are narrow, and it takes a two-handed push to split the heavy front doors. The thrifty, wartime classrooms have fixed seats and desks, no space for a wheelchair. Clearly this will be difficult for Trillium. As Zena sees it, there are two options: either Trillium will make the daily commute to a newer school in nearby Mowcher; or she will work through a series of self-study modules at home. At home, she can set her own pace, her own standards. There will be few distractions.

Then a letter comes concerning Trillium, signed by Meredith Coulthart, on behalf of Health and Welfare Canada. Ms Coulthart is writing to advise that a new special-needs school is slated to open near Thunder Bay. The school is wheelchair accessible, and offers full board, custom beds for custom bodies, in-house nursing, a library, an adapted pool and fitness centre. Teaching centres on the standard curriculum, including family-planning and career counselling. Zena thinks this all sounds pretty good. She thinks if she were Trillium this school would be like paradise.

Doug reads the letter only once. He grins, a short tight compression, and says, 'When will we get to see her? Or is that the point?'

Zena goes over it again. It seems so clear. She asks Doug, please, for his firm opinion. He says leave it up to Trillium – he'll be happy if she is. Zena hates the thought of her daughter alone in Thunder Bay. But these are formative years, and Trillium, with all her warmth and intensity, needs other people, other voices to counter those so strong in her head. Maybe she'll feel less excluded. Maybe she'll grow immune to difference. Others must have.

But there are delays in construction, strict bylaws not to be skirted, and another letter comes. The school is a bust. Ms Coulthart is doing what she can. She is extremely hopeful for next year, when the new budgets will come through. Companies are being approached, sponsors. She will be in touch.

Trillium reads the letter. Then she wheels herself outside, thinking to drain something. The back meadow lies like canvas against the cloud-jacketed sun. To the left, near the culvert, a white bird balances on one leg, eyes steady, muscles sprung. The grass blows high and graceful. Each noise has its echo. From the road, the staccato grate of dry leaves on concrete. From the house, the screen door slapping against its fixings, Doug's falsetto cooking croon.

Tomorrow after school she and Doug and Zena will visit the junior high and practise. First, the front steps. Then they will have a go at the doors. Maybe the kids will still be there, watching her as she left-rights up the stairs, forming behind her in a wary, embarrassed line, unable to pass, liable to be knocked for ten-pins should she slip her grip and fall. Sometimes, she is afraid. If this fear had a shape, it would look like stairs.

Trillium rests on the convex of her lower body, the part she calls her root. Down there it is an odd mix of firm and very soft. She knows she must take care of her root, the most important part of her because the most dangerously bruised. She has seen trees bend and clatter from their sockets, the dark tangle erupt from the earth, a meeting of the mighty and the hidden. She suspects that beneath her root there is also a tangle, but there is no way to know this, because to see her own root she must already have fallen. She knows that her root must never be seen, however sweet the joy of falling, of falling low and loud and hard, of having in her such a place to fall from.

Doug signs up for a photography course in Dryden. He tells Zena that he needs a hobby, something fun and bright. He's always been a slave to the image, he adds; he's always been a visual person. Zena can't seem to recall that side of him. Perhaps he has always been that way, and she just never noticed. Perhaps it has surged in him, lately, while she was somewhere else.

'*Bonne idée,*' Zena tells him. 'Get you out of the house.'

Doug nods dreamily. 'I'll need something with adjustable aperture. Obviously, it has to be fine-calibration capable.'

As always, Zena thinks, he's got the lingo down pat.

Doug drives out to Dryden twice a week. He buys himself a camera so heavy and expensive it requires a separate rider on their insurance. It has a terrific adjustable aperture. Capable of very fine calibration. The man in the camera shop has never known one to beat it.

A month or so into his course, Doug fashions a darkroom out of a prefab garden hutch shaped like a miniature barn, complete with red vinyl siding and white trim like trouser piping.

'Pretty impressive,' Zena tells him, staring at the artist's rendition on the flat-pack box. 'With a quack-quack here, and a quack-quack there, you'll be Old MacDonald.'

Once operational, the hut is just three strides across, slightly longer than it is wide. Bolted to the walls are troughs for emulsions. There's a table raftered with racks and rollers, several pairs of latex gloves like something a surgeon forgot.

Zena requests a tour. The smell bothers her, sweet and artificial, like grape jellybeans. Over one vent hangs a frill of baby-blue fabric that might have made a saucy nightie in 1959. To Zena this gives the place the air of some squatter's hovel.

She has a few suggestions. 'It doesn't have to be such a blot. You could at least hang some proper drapes. And maybe some window-boxes.'

'It's functional.'

'No, it's the Brothers Grimm.'

'Objection noted, and dismissed,' Doug says. 'I'm not renovating.'

Soon he is up there nearly every day, sometimes staying into the night. Gradually, the shed grows to resemble him, taking on his shape and manner, so that by looking out, Zena can gather his mood. Now it looks taller and spiffier (she sneak-planted pansies beside the door), and this means Doug is happy there. Happy only there, Zena thinks – not without relief.

There are other things on her mind. Trillium is doing school by correspondence, with Doug's exacting help, and is lonelier than ever. She spends hours at the library, and once Zena catches her leaving Whitechapel Manor, a local nursing home. Zena has her reservations about Trillium spending time in institutions, especially ones where people go to die. Taking stock, Zena appreciates how different all of their lives are becoming, and how minimal the overlap. Sharing the same source but diverging, like the strands in a long, undone braid.

Even Jean is distant. 'I've had headaches four nights running,' Zena says nonchalantly, easing her cart round a corner. 'You don't suppose I'm coming down with something?'

'Mmm. Did you notice that the mayonnaise coupon is good only for the family-size jar? At least, that's their story at the checkout. I consider that out-and-out misleading.'

'You're not listening to me,' Zena accuses.

'That is because you slur your words.'

'I'm slurring my words because I'm ill. It may well be a virus. I definitely feel faint . . .'

'Viruses prey on the weak of constitution,' Jean observes stoutly.

Zena sighs, heads for the cereal aisle. There, the boxes make bold promises: *Part of a complete breakfast . . . fortified with folic acid . . .* Everything is recently improved. Health, happiness, inner peace – all distilled to a simple selection, a brand choice.

Trillium first hears about Colonel Bob Whiting from the head librarian with the Chinese printed dresses whose name she can never recall.

'Oh, he's something all right,' the librarian tells her. 'Not many left like him. He'll talk the wings off a magpie, given half a chance.'

From this description Trillium pictures Colonel Bob as a wild, bluff man, big as a barn, laughing. Instead, he is thin and quick and dark, with an overhang of quiet gloom that makes her sleepy. He wears a cloth cap sunk over pale, bran-coloured hair, and a high turtleneck. When she introduces herself, he nods thoughtfully.

'Fine handle,' he says. His own name turns out to be showbiz. He isn't really a colonel. He worked in a touring troupe, riding stunt saddle, shooting targets blindfolded, upside down. His skill and courage packed houses, raised the roof.

'Time of my life, the circus. Best folks I knew, watch your back in a house of mirrors. What was theirs was yours. Tough as horsehair, warm as muskets. Time of my goddamn life.'

Trillium begins to visit regularly. She stays all afternoon, and he plays music for her on a record player he has to sign out, songs with names like 'Holly's Gone Like Hollyhocks', that mean nothing to Trillium.

One day he does not put on any music. Instead, he hands her a photograph: a man standing in a clearing before a huge, moon-marbled wheel of tent. The man is nearly naked, though his flesh supports a mass of fantastic growths, some almost fungal, some clustered, tufted with coarse hair. On his head one spectacular nodule buttresses a crudely formed globe, attached to a sign – *The Human Map* – close-printed in letters inexpertly looped and joined.

Trillium stares at the photo, not fully understanding. Then she looks up. Colonel Bob has removed his shirt. He stands before her, a mobile relief map: swollen fleshy drumlins, scenic scar canyons, bold juts of bone without function.

'They took off the bigger ones. The ones on my head,' he tells her. 'Would've killed me otherwise.' He points to the picture. 'I rode with a helmet. Covered me from the shoulders up. Never took it off when I was on stage. They'd never have let a freak ride. But I had to ride.'

The shift nurse walks in, fixes Trillium with a gooseberry look, asks Bob to get decent, please. He leaves with the nurse. He does not replace his shirt.

Trillium visits Colonel Bob once more. She brings a bushel of fresh apricots which he divides equally with her. On leaving she is told he isn't well and can no longer receive visitors. She is not informed when he dies. She is not invited to the funeral.

Days later she finds in the meadow a granite bulkhead two-feet high. She writes on it in black permanent marker: *Colonel Bob Whiting.* There is more, but it barely shows against the dark impacted stone.

For Christmas Trillium goes to a Care Club Fun Camp near Georgian Bay. On the day she leaves Doug brings out a black-and-white photograph in a wan birch frame he made himself: Trillium, resting in a basin of tall grass, back against an ironwood tree, in three-quarter profile. She is truncated at the waist. Doug calls this cropping.

'I've sprayed it with a fixative,' he says. 'So it shouldn't run. If it does, you let me know, and I'll take the bottle back for a refund. It's guaranteed.'

Trillium glows. She can't stop looking at it.

'Isn't she beautiful?' she asks Zena. 'Come on, don't you think?'

Zena hands over her own presents for Trillium: a leather journal, complete with pencil, embossed tastefully with botanicals, hand-sewn to withstand hard wear. A portable CD player, in a fetching shade of lilac, glossy and sleek as a Smartie. Trillium is pleased, but only pleased; she holds Doug's picture more closely still. Zena tries not to be jealous.

'Hey, good gifts! I guess you're pretty lucky, huh?' she says.

Doug heads for the garage to warm up the old car. Zena wants to cry. She wants Trillium to be five years old again, when her changes were surprising, but always in view. She thinks: I want you to go but I don't. It's not even three weeks but I almost can't bear it. You have become the hinge we open and shut on. You're what's left.

She says, 'I hope you intend on taking that damn duffel coat that cost so much. Dress for the weather – make sure you've got layers on. Take care of yourself. Don't stay up and get all weak and get a flu. And call us when you get there!'

Doug returns wearing his driving mittens and the tall puffy hat that makes him look like a moose in civilian clothing. He whisks Trillium up, she dips and nuzzles; they leave, heads together, her body swaying gently with his stride. The door takes a long time to close.

Later, watching TV, picking moistly at a clementine orange, Zena realizes what bothers her about the photo, feels her insides chill and spool. *Isn't she beautiful?* Trillium asked. And it's true, she was. Except that in Doug's photograph she looked like some-one else's child, a brainy smiley television child, a child to be envied, for being so decisively whole.

It is the kind of picture Doug can take because that is how he sees her. But not me, Zena thinks. Not me. Somehow, against her best wishes, she has traded by increments her pain for some-thing more tacit. Stealthily, she has given up hope of thrilling, inappropriate change. She could not have taken that picture. She no longer has the faith.

The 'camp' turns out to be several buildings clad in grey

concrete, linked by a network of breezeways humid with durable plants. The air is antiseptic, a familiar hospital undercurrent of bleach and handwash and alcohol swabs. Windows are sparse, square, glazed and well draped; walls are bare except where garnished with mercy-art – bad paintings with good intentions. Negotiable surfaces are skinned in a rubber laminate meant to numb sound and sensation.

Trillium's room has a half-height dresser and a low pallet bed and a painting of a boat she hangs her coat on. She uses the room only for sleeping or resting between activities. Days are filled with arts and crafts and story-time and pacy co-ed wheelchair sports. At night there are movies and karaoke and dancing and skits. Everything social takes place in the dark.

All told, there are maybe eighty campers. Some Trillium knows. Others are unfamiliar, with unfamiliar disabilities. Acronyms abound: CF, MS, CP, SB, DS. Medication is universal; each day stutters along to the sounds of pills in plastic thimbles, water filling plastic cups.

Trillium gets to know most of the others on her floor. Susan, a Down's, who gives her friends drawings of blue stick-people with swollen sun-like heads. Mary, a thirty-something with multiple sclerosis on leave from the Royal Bank. Sam, brain-damaged, deaf, paraplegic, whose language consists of a few finger-signs: *hungry*, *sleepy*, *poo*.

At the end of the floor is Robert. Nearly forty, he is fat and soft and white as a grub. Trillium learns that Robert was once unusually high-functioning. He spoke and read very well. He even read a little French. Then his father died, and Robert grew depressed. His mother, alone and unsupported and on a tight budget, was ill-equipped to care for him. Unable to meet his stringent needs, his check-ups and workshops and activities;

overpowered by his rages, sudden and soaking as monsoons, she bought him an adjustable chair and a colour television, and placated him with cola and potato chips. For six years Robert watched so much television and consumed so much cola and potato chips that when they finally took him into care he was a parrot who weighed over three hundred pounds. He knew the theme songs to *Happy Days* and *The Love Boat* and not much else. He had long ago forgotten his French.

Robert spends his days wandering the halls, pausing every few feet, leaning down heavily to observe, one slab finger pressed to the side of his nose. He is fascinated by books. In the library Trillium watches him pick up book after book, studying each one with wonder, with immense sadness, tipping and shaking them, as though hoping its meanings will spill to the ground where he can reach them.

'He can't read,' Robert's associate explains. 'But he remembers that he could do, once. And he doesn't understand what's happened.'

That strikes Trillium as the hardest thing of all. To have loved something and lost its memory – that is the hardest thing of all. She tries several times to talk to Robert. He just stares at her and makes whooshing sounds. For a long time, she doesn't understand. Then one day she goes to him with a book in her hand, the one from the crafts room. A children's book: *Are You My Mother?* She reads to him, quietly at first, then with drama, and he tilts his bulk this way and that, swaying to her voice like some gigantic, broken wind chime. As she finishes the story he takes her hands in his, plump and pale as unbaked bagels, and she feels his tears. When his associate arrives to collect him, Robert turns to her, quick-bending his massive head, and whenever he sees Trillium afterwards, he performs that same queer bow.

As the week wears on, Trillium begins to feel at home. She adapts her sleeping habits, her diet, her distinctions. Smart/dumb is refined to low-functioning/high-functioning; disabled/able-bodied becomes para/quad. For the first time she can remember, Trillium is a spectator, just one in a juggle of awkward bodies, in this land without stairs.

The darkroom sees lots of action while Trillium is away. Doug ping-pongs between there and the house, barely touching down. Zena tries to divert him.

'Doug? Sandy's on the phone. Do you want to meet for dinner tonight, seven-thirty? Doug! Oh, better forget it, Sand. Just . . . Another time.'

Two in the afternoon on a school day, and Doug is playing hooky. At the darkroom she knocks, counts three, slips in, still manages to startle him, like some unwelcome spirit.

'So what are you up to?'

He straightens. Doffs the gloves that make his hands the drab paddles of an amphibian. Shakes out his ragged, discoloured sleeves.

'Nothing. Just working something out.'

'Let's see.'

He turns to look at her, measuring, she thinks uncomfortably, filtering, separating. Then he reaches for a tarpaulin to hood the drying rack.

'It's nothing. Pictures. You know. Same old, same old.'

Zena asks whether 'same old' includes cropping. Doug says no, that's yesterday's news. He has moved on to composites. He must spot her uncertainty, then, her clot of unease, because he takes her hand. She sees how exhausted he is, how grey and drained.

He says, 'Do you think they're meant to be real? Because I used a camera?'

Zena says no, of course not, she isn't a total idiot.

Doug talks right over her. 'I want her to be her best. Not someone's passing glance – but the way I see her. The way she is.'

And Zena thinks of the portrait of Trillium, perched stylishly against the ironwood tree with all the soft-focus glamour of a forties film star, her face and form a blended roundness, her sunglazed hair upswept. Beautiful Trillium. But her hair is not the colour of Trillium's hair, and her body melts into the background; by such subtle amputations is integrity restored.

Trillium walks in the middle. There are more than thirty campers shambling and wheeling their way to a taffy pull. The day is unseasonably warm, the streets are snowbare. Care Club has provided ponchos, *Support Our Fun Camps* printed in a bold yellow, a colour scheme indexed to hoops of sun, to children's smiles. Around them, people stop and stare. Some approach, jingling change. Some avert their eyes to other views, cross the street, studying their watches. The associates walk on the outside, joking and flirting, making a virtue of their normalcy.

They are turning west when the woman passes, trying to shield her young daughter, dressed in a skirt that shows her hipbones and high heels that make her walk falling forward. Her face is rigid with powder, her lipstick the colour of creek mud. Trillium is amazed by her. She has never seen anyone so stark, so cruel-looking before. She stares.

The woman pulls her wobbling daughter closer. 'How can they let *that* on the streets?' she sneers, pointing at Trillium. 'Good God – *how?*'

Trillium sets her head like Doug has taught her, rearing up like a horse, walking tall. But then a twist of something sniggers up inside her, and disrupts her delicate balance. Her stilts give way slowly, she falls, a heavy domino, and then they all fall, until Sam's wheelchair catches Robert in the chest, and he hangs there like a fat perch, surprised to be in a gull's beak, flopping and screaming. The sidewalk seethes. People run over to gawk, to help, tucking gingerly into the ruck of bodies, plucking at limbs and implements in a game of pick-up sticks. The donation buckets overflow.

'We never made it to the taffy pull,' Janet Jingo, the head counsellor, explains later. 'Pretty good day though. Raised over three hundred bucks.'

Spring comes to Absinthe. Zena enrols in a real-estate certificate course at the Landmark technical college. She is the oldest in a class of fifteen, all women.

'They smoke in the bathrooms,' she tells Doug. 'DuMaurier milds. Very grade eight. The ladies' loo smells like a Lucky Strike bingo. Every time I pee I worry about lung cancer.'

Zena sits at the front of the class. She takes notes, and volunteers first for role-playing. She plays a man whose last house was a money-pit. She plays a middle-income single mother concerned about security. She comes to feel that these characters are more real than she is, she and everyone else she knows. More real and more comprehensible.

'It makes me feel useful,' she says, when asked what she's been up to. But mostly she looks forward to the dextrous separation that the course affords her. The twice-weekly journey into new surroundings. Speaking and being listened to. Doing her hair differently. Having her coffee alone.

*

Trillium doesn't wear her stilts so often. They leave bruises on her neck and shoulders. Anyway, she isn't out and about so much these days. She gets HomeTeaching, a programme part-funded by an Ontario government that doesn't know it's there so can't cut it. Meredith Coulthart gets in touch. The new school is a go. Trillium is invited to begin in September. Orientation will be arranged.

Alone, Trillium considers her options, in the meadow, in the easy afternoon light. Fuzzy caterpillar sacs and drifts of pollen spoon along the stems of grass. Slivers of soil appear like scalp when the breeze brushes southwards. A large bumblebee rests phlegmatically in the ruins of some ancient web, twisting dutifully, then folding its wings with clownish resignation. A patch of wildflowers makes a blazing ramshackle lighthouse in the coarse green sea.

Sitting there, she remembers planting flowers with Zena, years ago, behind the house. They were blue and ugly and awkward, heavy on their stalks like old women's handbags. Zena could not bear to display or even water them. Trillium thinks that some flowers can't rely on their beauty or a memorable scent. No one will choose them, bundled with baby's breath, or press their bodies between the pages of favourite books. Such flowers have to learn diffidence, the artless art of saving strength.

Everyone works feverishly the month Trillium is due to leave. Zena nets a honey of a client, a Winnipeg doctor and his family who might be stencils, all four smoky-blond, well mannered. Word is, the doctor's loaded. The office buzzes with estimates of commissions.

Doug is at school by seven-thirty. He prepares his lessons there. The rest of his time he fusses in the darkroom. Preparing his new masterpiece. Variations on the theme of coherence. Zena just nods. *Uh huh.*

At least once a week, Doug phones in sick. Zena and Trillium hold all calls. He has an ulcer that may be operated on any day now – this is his cover story. The consequence of workplace stress and a monstrous and sustained assault by stomach acids. Should anyone call, he is in bed.

'But how can you miss so much work?' Zena wonders. 'How will those kiddies learn? Who'll light their little bulbs?'

'Oh, they'll manage,' Doug says. 'They're up to speed. Ulcers are practically endemic, you know. The board will bring in substitutes. To a man they have battled their own ulcers. They know what it's like.'

But Zena worries. Who knows what those countless hours in the dark, all the while inhaling chemicals, can do to a man's mind?

On weekends, Zena ignores him. She putters in the meadow while Trillium explores, spinning through shoals of grass and daisies like a small, sure tornado. Zena finds it amazing that Trillium can move like that, without vertigo or fatigue. She would love to have that gift, of never getting dizzy.

The second Thursday in August is selected as Doug's big night. He sends out more than sixty invitations, designed by himself, rigid rough-textured cards, wine-red, edged in powdery gold. The text arches across the centre of the page in a precipitously curving script: *Doug, Zena & Trillium Macleod welcome you to a photography showing & sale. All photographs signed & numbered. All proceeds to Trillium Macleod's university fund.*

Doug's work in the darkroom is finished. He lumbers about, a bemused bull elephant, desperate for something to do. He launches himself into domestic labour. Zena offers to deliver the invites, pick up the mixers and a new tablecloth, but Doug says no, he'll handle the works. He becomes the scourge of Safeway, shopping with a calculator and a retail-price index, devising an advanced filing system for coupons. He vacuums in a sombre, methodical way Zena finds terrible to watch. He dons an apron and shower cap to dust in the ceiling corners. He tulips his feet in grocery bags to buff the floors with an old rotary polisher Zena didn't know they owned. He rubs the windows squeaky-clean. He wet-sands the tubs and sinks.

Jean drives in a day early to help, and inspect. 'This old house is shiny as a new penny,' she squeals, while Doug, stationed on a stepladder, rotates the light fixtures into alignment.

'What is this, *feng shui* on the cheap?' Zena wants to know.

But Jean is admiring. 'Can you believe this man? He has done ten years' work in a week! He has gone *all out*!'

Thursday night. Doug wears maestro-black, Zena a silk print dress, Trillium a tunic over a long peasant skirt. The table is covered in a festive yellow cloth, islanded with fruit pastries Zena baked from a talked-about recipe book, and plump red-tinted discs called 'salmon fritters' that Doug bought from Triple Ted Gourmet. They would have hired Triple Ted himself, but he charges a lot, and is known for tucking into his own food when he ought to be serving, and although this is amusing at other people's parties, it is expensive at your own.

Doug has arranged the exhibit in the living room. Twenty-two prints, eight-by-eleven, mounted on high-quality backing. Each is captioned and signed with an uncharacteristic flourish, *Doug Macleod*. He blocks off the room with a baby-gate. This over Zena's protests.

'Of course you don't sneak in early. You're the general public.'

'I also happen to be the landlord,' Zena points out.

Doug just scoffs. 'Lousy capitalist. What do you know about Art?'

Zena sighs, struts off, deliberately treading on his knurled, socked toes.

Eight o'clock. From the stereo, Dave Brubeck in a rare solo recording. From the front hall, bell after bell. In the kitchen, Laurie Fox, point-woman for the Tri-Municipal Arts Report. Heard twice-weekly, on CJRJ.

'Is it okay if I call you a "visual artist"? I dunno, to me, that sounds much better than, you know, "shutterbug". But I don't want to *misrepresent* you . . .'

Laurie has been to Ryerson's School of Broadcasting. A young gun. Doug smiles. Visual artist, yes, it's okay. Everything is okay. He chats obediently into her microphone. Figure-eights through the room, dispensing drinks, hors d'oeuvres, chit-chat.

Everyone invited shows. Donnie Thimble, owner of Lakeland Lumber. Brad and Lissa Makepeace, both paediatricians. The Lockes, who manage the Yacht Club. Various of Doug's colleagues, solicitous about the ulcer. Larry Travic, Zena's boss, and his too-young girlfriend, slim and scandalous in a catsuit and gold belly-chain, sunglasses slotted into her bouquet of blonde hair. The Lunds, who run the Rx drugstore. The Johnstone sisters. They eat off napkins, sip premium lager, sponsor toasts to Trillium, to life in the city, to evergreen luck.

Jean is in charge of collecting plates and glasses. Doug keeps them full. Zena welcomes guests, cocking her great grinning head, listening too closely and laughing too hard, then doing it all over again with someone else. Trillium is gracious, excited, kissing her friends on both cheeks, promising that *of course* she'll be back for the summer, and Christmas too. Miles from the nearest door-frame, she gropes a passing tray for kiwi slice, loses her balance, wobbles like a flan. Zena experiences a small, remote panic. Then she thinks, *Let her go, she's got to learn sometime*, and Trillium doesn't fall.

Two hours into the party, Doug climbs on to a chair, clears his throat, smiles encompassingly, lauds friends and family and the kindness of everyone present, explains the ground rules.

'I want you to feel comfortable. Wander around at your leisure, and if anything grabs you, then grab me. Prices are set, but feel free to make me an offer. Take your time. Enjoy.'

To kind applause, he draws the baby-gate. Lights in the room rise blue like water. Bodies fill spaces.

Stuck firmly at the back of the crowd, Zena sees the pictures randomly, between heads, through a shrubbery of arms. She glimpses lakes and sunsets, all in black and white. Then an old house, its eaves lined with ravens in full song, poised for flight, their bodies strong and thick and merciless. Finally she is in the room and in front of a child, no older than seven, squeezed into a tan canvas swing. The child's left leg is extended, ending in a buckled shoe, her right leg is tucked modestly beneath her. There is no mistaking the face; the tongue between the teeth and the large, surprised eyes. The child is Trillium.

Zena is lost in the details, the expressions, the lines of light and the pitchy seams that conceal the cut-and-paste, the sutures, in these surgical renderings of their living daughter. She smiles a sorry to Bill Locke on her right, stands where he's been standing, looks where he's been looking. A child running, beach towel flowing behind her, a peregrine's wide wings, long hair sculpted by her speed; she has high, spare shoulders and a kitten's long curious neck. Trillium's neck.

Each is more dramatic, more captivating than the last: Trilliums playing in the lilypads and random sandbars of Malcolm's Marsh. Trilliums asleep among edgy knitted ferns. A Trillium on a motorcycle, wearing a winter scarf. Everywhere Zena looks she sees Trilliums, long-stemmed, blooming, spectacularly mobile . . .

Zena is jousted about the waist, pivots to see Trillium stumble past, bouldering through chatting, sipping guests, piledriving poor Larry Travic, snaring an ankle in a telephone cord. The hydraulics shift of their own volition, driving her forward, an automaton, tearing the phone from its umbilical in the wall. Zena follows, coiling the cord, apologizing. Her eyes do not meet Trillium's but their shame crackles between them like a severed electrical cable, flopping and hissing and dangerous to touch.

Jean appears on the staircase, sudden and sour, a wraith with indigestion.

'This is a fine performance!' she hisses. 'Really, you are acting like a child!'

With someone else's snarl Zena grips Jean's shoulders, propels her through the hall and out into the night, slams the door on her faint pummelling, her strident frightened cries.

'Douglas! Douglas!' whinnies Jean.

'Shut up shut up!' shouts Zena. Her hands are lumps, she can't get the door unlocked. She finds a window, wrenches it open.

'Douglas! Douglas!'

Jean manages to catch the key Zena throws her.

Doug starts cleaning as soon as the last guest has left, putting everything back just as it was – six chairs in space for five, the chopped corner of a triangle table out of sight against the wall – replicating exactly their home's unspoken illogic, its lived-in disarray. He removes his pictures from the walls, wraps them in a corrugated brown paper, cords and stacks them like kindling. He sweeps, washes, wipes. Then he extinguishes all but the floodlights, and comes to bed.

In their room, he counts his money. Catching Zena's eye, he says, 'I fought for her. Tonight. Always.'

Zena doesn't remember this.

'While you sat and cried and held your belly, I fought for her, tooth and goddamn nail. But it wasn't ever good enough – right? It wasn't good enough. Anyone could take it away, with a sentence, a sneer.'

Zena wonders at how far off his voice is, how distant and how grating. She sees the curve of solid fat like a halved melon swelling out above his waist, the purple hollows that make cairns of his eyes, the floppy skin of his forearms, stained and shot with sunspots untended. The cropping that she has endowed him with, first from love and later from custom, reverses itself, finally falls away.

'People want pretty pictures. They don't want little girls without legs.'

Zena means to hit him, but can't find her reach. She means to swear ribbons, but her voice is on vacation. So she closes her eyes.

Doug is done talking. His body slumps, his scratchy old clothes folding like laughter lines. Overnight, it seems, he has been used up.

The clock on the night-table flashes twelve o'clock. The power must have gone off. The bed stretches between them like a desert path. Outside, the lights burn for Trillium. Zena supposes she should look for her. Though she can't have gone far. Not in those shoes.

Trillium stays out all night, layered in blankets and a tarpaulin she borrows from Doug's shed. She is thinking of Colonel Bob, of Kyle's *Illustrated History*. She has read the section on Killgarnie's Circus Colossus. Taken notes and names. But it isn't enough. Things are missing. Did The Scallop find her tidal peace? Did Simon swallow his last sword and live to tell about it? Did The Maple Lady cast her pods to unseen places, a farm by a creek that ran deep with gold? Who drowned, who was saved? Who keeps the histories of freaks? Trillium wonders. She will. She will write their stories on the rocks, lever them, one by one, to the centre of the meadow. None will ever be in shadow. None will ever be cut off.

Beside her the legs make hollow, squidging sounds, steeping in the elastic soil. Trillium is immune to the throbbing rain; it does not chill or salve her, suffuse her or make her clean. An hour ago she looked at Doug's scissors and thought of opening her insides up to the rain, letting her shame wash away to leave her pink and gleaming. Now she has changed her mind.

Instead, she will cooperate with the rain, she will become part of erosion. She will sink, inch by inch, to the layers beneath the worms and the roots to where the blind things burrow. They will come to look for her in an hour or two. It will be easy to follow her stilty tracks. They will pull her out with a close sucking sound like lips being smeared. They will pull her from the earth, and they will gasp. For beneath, holding tight to the slippery midnight tendrils of her expanded root, will be the handsome freaks of The Last Caravan: Simon the Swallower,

The Scallop, The Eel, The Maple Lady, The Human Map. People will travel in their thousands to see these huge, high sun-swept wonders, their pilgrimage will score the earth. In silence they will work their cameras, stepping back, back; trying to fit the freaks in their frames. The images will be too large to alter.

The rain is harder now. The soil is creamy at the corners of her mouth. She is patient. She is buried very deep.

All night Zena watches the shape in the fields. Rain bubbles about the window like peroxide at the unseamed pockets of a recent wound. From the kitchen, she hears the whine of the ceiling fan; from the bed, Doug's halfway words. Zena fumbles for Doug's hand, manages only a fingertip, holds it hard. She forces her eyes, swollen with fatigue, once more to the window, finds Trillium, moving against the wind and grass. She holds Trillium tightly in her eyes and Doug in her hand; for a moment, they three are linked, in focus, balanced in the light. Then Zena wonders, picks a nearer point, squints her camera eye . . .

And stands there, waiting for her faith to arrive, and move her, knowing it must not take long.

Terminal Wheel

Ceremony

At the sessions held at the Old Bailey, in the month of July, 1712, Elizabeth Chivers, pleading guilty, was indicted for the wilful murder of her female bastard child, Elizabeth Ward, by drowning it in a pond.

This unnatural woman was a native of Spitalfields, but lived in Stepney at the time of the commission of the murder. The account she gave of herself after she was under sentence of death was as follows: she said that her father lay dying while she was very young, and left her in indigent circumstances, which obliged her to go into service when she was fourteen years of age; that she lived with several reputable families, who deemed her conduct irreprovable; that, approaching the age of thirty years, she lived with one Mr Ward, a lawyer, who prevailed on her to lie with him; in consequence of which she bore the child. On discovering her condition, she removed from Mr Ward's to another family, where she remained near six weeks; thereafter, she took private lodgings, in which she gave birth to a girl who was baptized Elizabeth Ward. The father, true to his promise, provided for the mother and child for about three months, until Mrs Ward, discovering the habitation, exposed her in the neighbourhood, so that she was ashamed to make her appearance. Her milk did not flow, and the child grew light and wasted; still, she would not seek alms or comfort. The child was washed by her tongue, and she fed it from her stomach, as birds do.

Thus degraded by her circumstances, she was tempted to destroy the child, whereupon she took it into the fields and went with it into the deepness of a pond, where it could not swim. Some few people near the spot, happening to see what passed, took her into custody, and carried her to Bow Street, before a magistrate, who committed her to Newgate Prison.

All the time that she remained in this gloomy prison, her mind seemed numb, and she would not confess, even to the clergyman who attended her. This divine noted that her act was the cruellest imaginable, and that she was not driven to it. The father had all the while provided for her, and would have done so still, had she not destroyed the child. She was asked if she had not entertained a mother's love, and she replied 'G—! Yes! And have I not shown it?' and would say no more, except that she had only meant to rinse the child in clear water, but had seen something there, in consequence of which she had formed her unnatural design, though she would not reveal what it was she had seen.

The terrors of conscience that this poor creature silently underwent were clearly of the most shocking kind. What a deplorable state must that wretch be in, to be unable to repent – we know not to what lengths our passions may lead us!

Elizabeth Chivers suffered the dreadful sentence of the law on 1 August, 1712.

Anniversary

She has to wait ten minutes – lucky to wait only that long, really. She tucks her neck, sniffs for perfume. Her skin is hell on perfume, on silver and perfume, tarnishing one and absorbing the other. She counts the bottles, brittle bronze flowers sprouting akimbo from the gravel mouth of the alley. There are eighteen bottles. She counts the heaped plastic cups. There are twenty-two cups. Her birthday. An omen? There is a jag of old counter top, a soggy gleaming condom, its ring jammed into a crack in a wall, wriggling in the low wind. Near the rubbish skip an old man sits, invisible beneath his hood. At his feet two pigeons peck solemnly at a scrape of vomit. She signals the minicab by tossing her head in its belladonna print scarf.

'Ring for a cab, love?'

'Yes, ta.'

He quotes her a flat rate, then asks her destination.

'Terminal,' she tells him. Though she means, *Eventually*.

When she arrives Gerry is out front, lounging against the door like the man in the whisky advert. He straightens her scarf, lifts her suitcases easily, though they are heavy for her. She dragged them three blocks – mad to waste forty pence on a stoplight.

'Door's open,' Gerry says. 'Be right up.'

He smiles at her. His brows are dark, deep, strips of felt on a blackboard brush. In one of the magazines she used to browse through at the newsagent's, such a brow meant strength in a man.

Below his brow he is smiling; the smooth loop his mouth makes, the even corners, might have been drawn with an icing-plunger.

They do not speak on the way up. They walk because the lift is too small for him and her and her luggage. There are four flights of stairs. Fourteen steps each. He has told her they are made of *Italian marble* and that the railing is a *balustrade*. She was amazed at its richness when she first came here, wanted to rub her cheek along the cool *Italian marble*, ragdoll her arms and legs through the spliced wooden *balustrade*.

He pulls the door shut behind him and it tinkles to signal that the lock is engaged. There is a niche by the door made especially for storage; a panel slides across it, maintaining the clean flow of the room. She steps lightly in one place, trying to relieve her sore, flat feet. Everything aches, all of the attachments of her body: her arms, her breasts, her head, her feet. This was not covered in the magazines.

Gerry tucks and retucks his baggy cotton pants, fiddles with his stained, linty jumper. When he sits down he stutters. He tells her she looks rosy. He mentions three things that are a shame: school-leavers, the mood-drug Ecstasy, armed robberies in Cadogan Square. He mixes drinks in a blender. She can smell vanilla and banana and a ribbon of strong spiced rum.

'I shouldn't—'

'It goes in mine.'

He carries the drinks in on a smoked-glass tray. The glasses clatter gently. He waves her to a chair.

'You'll like this. It's mostly milk.'

She bends her neck, sniffs experimentally.

'It's a special kind of milk. It's new – it's filtered in a new, improved way. They strain off all the bacteria. Then they add vitamins and enzymes and butterfat. They say the milk is purer. I don't know. It isn't cheap.'

'It wouldn't be.'

'I drink it like water, now. Like water.'

He drinks with relish, looks at his jumper, riveleted by briskly dribbling milk, wipes himself down with a *serviette*.

'No one ever died of too much . . .' he starts, but doesn't finish.

He looks at her, looks away. Rubs his jaw with a misshapen finger, joints bulging like tennis balls in a stocking. He damaged his hands playing rugby union, jammed all ten knuckles. But he always stayed on the pitch.

She worries that Debs will have her hands full. Elizabeth will be colicky. That cough. Still, she couldn't have brought her.

Gerry is asking about the coach. The departure time.

'Seven-thirty sharp.'

'That's just—'

'Best be off by seven.' She is firm. 'Sharp.'

'Shall I call—'

'No, thank you.'

'– to confirm?'

'No, thank you.'

The apartment smells of washed cotton and lanolin and flowers, nice/musty, like hotel soap forgotten in a suitcase. Gerry tells her that no one has been here. At least, she has not. He says, 'I moved a few things around. Chucked some things out . . .'

She doesn't recognize the living-room curtains, their imposing thickness. She didn't recognize her hands at first, ugly as parsnips, swollen and painful. Why were they swollen? This was never explained.

'. . . here and there . . .' His left hand indicates friendly but deliberate scattering.

In the corner is a coat-stand that she would never use, her one coat. The stand reminds her of a cactus, though its three crooked tines look mirror-smooth. But now, here, in this place, it reminds her of a cactus.

'. . . you know. Got rid of the clutter.'

They met for lunch some months ago, she and Gerry. Not here at the flat, but out of town, in a restaurant where tables were arranged in clusters of three. Each cluster had two waiters. Four clusters, twelve tables, eight waiters. Sixteen hands in sixteen long gloves of white linen, the same putty-white as these curtains she does not recognize. Perhaps they have been chosen by someone else, someone more familiar with gloved hands, fine cutlery, starched puffed napkins.

Then Gerry left her with an envelope. Now he is once again pushing an envelope at her with her name adrift across it in a lilting, machine-made script.

Sixteen letters in her name.

'I'd like you to take it.' He means, *You will take it.*

He slides it into a gap between her fingers. She knows about fingers. On the estate where she grew up, the boys cupped their hands together at the wrist and opened them between the middle and index fingers. The hole was a vagina. They popped a marble out. It was a baby.

She doesn't say anything. Between her fingers scabs have formed, hard pink lattices. Already these frighten Elizabeth.

'Will that tide you over?' He means, *That will tide you over.*

She looks at her watch. 'I've twenty minutes.'

He laughs, shrugs, raises his glass to her.

She offers to rinse the tumblers but he fidgets: *No, no!* He sets them in the sink and squirts some washing-up liquid into each one, lifts the tapered lever that turns the water on. With even a nudge, the water bursts from the tap, steaming, plentiful. Washing up here was a pleasure. He swishes the water in the glasses, pours it out, puts the sudsy tumblers in the rack. They roll about – he has not taken advantage of the built-in rubber spikes meant for tumblers. Seven rubber spikes. Then she sees there are no rubber spikes. It must be a new dish rack.

He lays her few things sensibly on the dining table. A dressing gown, a pant-suit that flattered her hips, some posh knickers that he might have chosen, might have had left over. On each she has carefully sewn her name. Seven times, sewn her own name.

'There. That's all sorted.' He smiles at her, a thin white fluid rims his teeth so that they seem to float in their deep sockets. Then she sees it is his milkshake, not quite dissolved.

With her toe, she turns up a dog-ear in the rug. Stuck to the floor underneath is a page from a forget-me-not pad, in her handwriting. It must have fallen there. She leans in, but it is almost too smudged to read. Three exclamation points. The word *tomato*. Had she really used three exclamation points? How bold. She loves tomatoes, though for herself she buys the greenhouse kind that have never known sun, that taste of flour and grocer's wrap. Gerry buys tomatoes from Israel, still on the vine, ninety-nine pence the pound. Maybe seven to a pound. Dark dark red, and sweet, the seeds inside flat and yellow, they will not grow. She has heard that tomato seeds will not grow, even if well sunned and watered, even if they have everything. Why should this surprise her?

On the paper the letters fade, as though she has forever lost those words, and what was underneath them. Once written.

'I'll just pack these, then.' She rises, unsteady, begins to fold the clothes.

But she can feel him at her side and at her back, helping her to help herself. He has become two men, two waiters, with four quick hands in putty-white gloves, and a beard, a minky beard.

He is breathing very near her, a few millimetres from her. His breath smokes, it is milkshake white, it has been painted by his mouth.

'You know it will lie empty. Empty.' He might mean the flat.

'And these too?' She paints her own breath a different kind of white, warmer, the colour of her own milk, drying, on a hankie, at the tips of her breasts, on sleeping lips.

'What's that?'

She points at the set of towels he bought for the bath, Egyptian cotton drawn into countless fine loops, dyed a jolting curaçao blue.

'And these too?' She means, *I'll take these too.*

He stares at her, he is trembling, the stains on his jumper expand with his breath but do not contract without it.

Gerry is a good way along with the luggage when he remembers to lock up. She is closer to the door.

'Keys,' she offers, opening her hand to catch them.

'I'll manage,' he says, squeezing past.

Waiting for him, she is restless. The marble looks wet and wavy, inviting. The perfume has steamed from her wrists, dissolved by her dry mineral skin. Seven-o-three. Three minutes tardy. Three minutes of fourteen hundred and forty in this day.

Three hundred minutes earlier, she sat narrowed into the corner of a surgery waiting-room, reading a month-old *Now!* She was so bored she didn't suss that the woman was from Ladies' Christian Aid. They talked about high prices and how babies knew to fret before rain. The woman left behind a circular, bordered with coloured blocks and ride-a-horses: *Congratulations on the birth of your baby and welcome to FIRST THINGS, a place to meet and make friends and share the experiences of early motherhood. We will have a visiting speaker or activity each week. Please ask for details of our Cradle Roll and Birthday Club.*

She wanted to ask, What is a cradle roll? But the woman had moved on.

'All set,' Gerry says, descending. As he passes, she breathes herself skinny. He whisks right by her; she is a shadow he does not see.

In the car the seatbelts cradle and lull her, the dashboard lights concentrate her eyes while her mind makes pillows. They spiral through streets like stove coils, sooty and hot, finally spinning on to the high street. They pass a famous church. Gerry slows in order to point out the steeple whose flawed design made the chamber too narrow for its bells.

'"Those who don't learn from the past . . ."' he quotes, shaking his head, as though he imagines that history is always elsewhere.

School Photographer, Safety in the Car, Building Relationships, Make Your Own Jewellery, Safety in the Kitchen, Babysafe First Aid (immunization and injury), Birth Control, Travelling With Baby, Getting in the Swim, Safety in Toys, Toothcare. These were some of the topics covered by Ladies' Christian Aid. *Consumer Rights.* *Safety in the Street. Thanksgiving Service. Recognizing Signs and Symptoms. Dietary Needs. Relationships Now that Baby is Here.* These were some others.

Love comes through prayer, the circular reminded. Love comes.

Seven twenty-two. Her coach is bound for Colwyn and her new flat in Sparrow Lane Estates. Three rooms, each with a single window barred against burglars. There are more burglars there than anywhere, though there must be less to steal. Gas is controlled by a meter, coin-operated. She may paint the walls but must have the colour vetted – it won't do to tart the place up and risk putting off the next tenants. There is a playground with uterine tubes made from PVC and a wire-cage fortress the little boys defend with knives and bends of metal from the torched nicked cars. There is a midnight curfew that she is expected to keep. Midnight – makes it tricky for the working girl. Any noise, they will review the lease. Any goings-on, they will review the lease. Any loud parties, drug use, prank fire alarms, fan heaters – they will review the lease.

Gerry bumps her shoulder with his shoulder.

'All right?'

'Oh, lovely.'

He parks in a flagged zone, doesn't leave his flashers on.

'Sod them,' he says, and looks happy.

At the corner and up a slight rise is the Terminal. It is hub-shaped, roomy, two blocks around. She has never been all the way through. It is painted orange, the colour of barley, further diluted by banks of fluorescent tubes. Nothing is made clearer by that light. Hugging the skirts of the building are boys and girls in their tight tops, arms banded with reflective tape, red blinking bicycle lamps hitched to their shoulder-bags. Prozzies, rent-boys, coozies, jumps, salties, time-shares, drabs, clips. Ten, twenty pence the pound.

'He fuckin' messed with him, he fuckin' battered him!' one of the girls shouts, excited, gesturing with a pure wild joy. Her red-lit arms flash and spangle, her blonde moppet's hair vibrates.

The cars that pull over are mostly late-model.

'I'm always here,' Gerry tells her. She believes him. He will remember himself as meaning it. 'I want you to ring me once you've arrived. Ring me at work. Tell them it's— Tell them it can't wait. And—'

'I mustn't miss it.'

'The calls,' he says. 'I'm so, so sorry. How she got your number, I don't . . .'

His eyes are wet, they are changing colour. He seems to need to hold her. She lets him, briefly, with these fingers she once took in her mouth, jammed brown knuckles, inky tips.

She mustn't dally. It will be a mad rush for the coach. She mustn't be late. Debs will be waiting for her. Debs will give her a right earful if she's late.

'Ring me.'

She smiles, takes a step, arms straining at her cases.

'Please – ring me.'

'I mustn't be late—'

'Please . . .'

She smiles, swivels, walks away. Scraping across the oily pavement, the wheels of her luggage leave lines.

The coach will leave at eight-thirty. Debs treats her to supper at a chippie – a licensed, sit-down place. She feeds Elizabeth, dozy now, irritated by the bottle. Debs orders a glass of white wine, *chardonnay*.

'Was she any trouble?' she asks. Debs assures her not a bit.

The restaurant has warmer candles on every table, chubby glass salt and pepper pots. Gill-nets hang from the ceiling like upside-down tents.

'Ooo – fancy!' says Debs, lippy mouth wide, nodding, jingling her silver earrings, the shape of a bird in a circle, beak touching tail-feathers, back and neck aligned in one smooth draping arch. Debs orders plaice, cuts it into dainty squares, swirls it with brown sauce, matches each piece to a chip.

Debs boasts of the twenty quid she won on the lottery, using her special numbers: seven and four, the ages of her two lads, and her gran's birthday, twenty-eight. She has chosen these numbers in faith. Her win proves that they are lucky, that if played week upon week they will bring a mending fortune to those Debs loves.

In her high chair, Elizabeth waggles a chip she will not eat.

'Well,' Debs says helpfully, 'both my lads loved bottle better than boob. Their dad too, mind,' she adds. Debs is eating chips and she is eating time. She is sprinkling time on her chips, and everyone around them is hungry.

As she watches Debs, she thinks of the old man at the rubbish skip, thinks of pigeons pecking at a chocolate button, jabbing at it with their blunt beaks, jabbing at this thing they couldn't capture and couldn't break. *Jab jab jab.* A penance. The old man watched for a time, then tenderly ducked his hood and vomited a wide, vivid stream. As he settled back his hands intersected, thrilled apart, conjuring.

Debs is going on about her new man, Gar, who just hasn't got it in for the boys the way their dad did.

'He hasn't got it in him, he hasn't,' explains Debs.

'I'm glad.'

'Has he?' Debs inquires hopefully.

'He's not that kind,' she says.

Debs takes her hand; she is crying, suddenly, she is crying on to the last of the chips, and her tears melt their thick brown oils.

She chooses a seat by the toilet, in case she has to change a nappy, in case she sicks up. Debs waves at the window as the coach slowly reverses. Debs is the tallest of those waving; her hair, newly frosted, glistens in the splayed white light. She makes complicated kissing motions. The last one she makes uses all ten fingers, touched to her lips and flicked forward, arms stretched out, palms up, planed by angular raindrops.

The coach lurches. In her arms Elizabeth gurgles jovially.

'Oh, she's lovely,' Debs gushed. 'All dressed up! Got your eyes, she has. You always see the mummy in the child.'

As the city drains away behind, she thinks of Sparrow Lane Estates; of her three rooms and their reinforced windows; of the gas metre that accepts coins down to two pence; of the signs warning that fixtures will be repaired at the tenant's expense; of the young boy in dark baggy pants who leaned against the fence with a tall can of bitter, one thin arm hung across his girl, a lit fag inches from her eyes. She thinks about the curtains in Gerry's apartment, about how they seem to close all the way now, about the new dish rack and the way the bed was made, all nice and smooth and tucked. About the smell of French-milled soap.

At the surgery, the woman from Ladies' Christian Aid reached down and closed her hand, and when she opened it there was Elizabeth's hair, light and fine as dill.

'What a darling little girl,' the woman said. She looked speculative.

We ask you to adhere to our no smoking, no swearing, no alcohol policy within our building. This on the back of the circular. And a prayer, of thanksgiving.

On the coach, a woman in a perky hat, the attendant, comes down the aisle selling refreshments.

'Do they open?' she asks the attendant, pointing to the window.

The attendant looks thoughtful.

'Just a crack. Any refreshments, my love?'

'Have you any juice?'

'I'll check, shall I?'

While she waits she thinks of the kids outside the Terminal, of ventilated soup vans, of downtown priests in their paper collars, of milk around eyeteeth. She thinks of long ago when there were no cities and she was not alive to see them anyway.

'Ribena,' the attendant says. 'Ribena's all we've got, I'm afraid.'

She has a Ribena. When she tries to pay the attendant says, 'She's a lovely little thing,' and touches her hand, just once.

She warms the juice in her mouth, then softens her tongue to the shape of a spout, passes it to Elizabeth, kissing away any spill.

The envelope Gerry left with her is still in her purse. The air through the window is a frigid solid slice. She empties the envelope. There are fifty-one notes. Ten pounds each. Five hundred and ten pounds. They make a rapid slap as they blow hard against the window, then they fly in their fifty-one directions, and there is silence.

By midnight they are in the mountains. The roads coarsen, the coach grinds and jounces along. Elizabeth is wrapped in the

Egyptian cotton towel. By the yellow strip-light, it is the blue of
blown water, the depth of a pond in a park.

You created every part of me; you put me in my mother's womb. I
praise you because you are to be feared; all you do is strange and
wonderful. When my bones were being formed, carefully put together
in my mother's womb, you knew.

Debs is right. Elizabeth has her mummy's eyes. Elizabeth is
nearing thirty weeks old. Her own age in years. An omen.

When I was growing there in secret, you knew. You knew that I
was there – you knew me before I was born.

Elizabeth starts to fuss. To quiet her, she squeezes and rocks.

Above her a vent whirrs, sending ripples over the towel's
looped surface. In the towel Elizabeth is light and springy. She
settles her, fumbles for the formula. Elizabeth isn't greedy, she
mustn't overfeed her. Any overfeeding, they will review the
lease. Any crying, they will review the lease. They will review
the lease.

She thinks about wading in water, wading very deep, Elizabeth
nursing at her breast, her wry closed mouth enforcing a quiet suction. Elizabeth's tiny hands knead, her feet flower. She relaxes
the flat of her hand, soothes her, makes deft strong circles in
Elizabeth's scalp. Elizabeth loves the water, she giggles and
splashes and wobbles her plump hands.

She is swimming now, on her back, legs churning. Still at her
breast, Elizabeth scuds along the surface. She doesn't look at
Elizabeth, not right at her. A wave in the distance crests, cycles
into smaller waves, each reflective, polished. In the flats of the
waves the water is startlingly clear, she sees her eyes there, six
hundred sets of eyes; her eyes are in Elizabeth.

The days allotted to me had all been decided in your book before
any of them began.

She twists quickly through the water. Slowly, she lets go. Elizabeth hangs on gamely, but she has to breathe; her mouth opens, the seal breaks, she slides away and under . . .

She squeezes and rocks, squeezes and rocks. She is thinking of the Terminal. One day, soon, she will walk all the way around it.

In the towel, Elizabeth is heavy.

'She'll grow up gorgeous, won't she?' coos the attendant at her elbow.

She nods.

'Won't she?'

She nods, but isn't sure, *Yes* or *No*.

Northern Line

The trains on the Northern Line are always the dirtiest. She almost doesn't want to sit down. The carriage is wide-bodied, its slatted wooden floor warped and compressed by generations of feet and trolleys, chewing-gum turds and cigarette filters nudging awkwardly through the gaps between boards. She rests her hand on the seat, upholstered in a worn red velveteen, once bright as a bell pepper, now dulled and blackened by years of dense Underground soot. When she was young enough to think bold lipsticks sophisticated instead of tarty, she sampled a red called Diabolique. It rained while she was walking home. Gradually the lipstick sedged into the fine wrinkles around her lips and made a modest clown's mouth, and when she dabbed at it her sleeve-tip was tinged exactly the colour of these seats. She rarely wears lipstick now, in deference to her complexion, which a lot of people seem to think her best feature. She rarely wears it because no one notices anyway, and it's an expensive way to please only yourself.

What will Kev say? How will it be managed? She left the flat nearly four hours ago, with Kev in anguish over a memo from their landlord citing Christmas trees as a fire hazard. She doesn't share Kev's sense of sacrilege. Real trees drop needles that stab between toes. They cost a lot. Their harvesting contributes to ozone depletion. So they won't have one – it's no tragedy.

She suggested a nice, portable tree, wrought in premium plastics to last a lifetime, available in a choice of sixteen classic hues. She is attracted by the notion of a flat-pack tree in a world that is itself collapsible.

Plastic? We may as well decorate some clingfilm! Kev shouted. Then he sat down to draft a stinging note to the landlord. Darkly, he fried bacon.

(Reason Number One: On a deep level, we don't agree.)

During breakfast, Kev said he was sorry, but it was all such a letdown, and they needn't be stuck here anyway, in this fascist outpost with its reek and noise and inconvenience, if only . . .

She knew. If only she had been willing to shop around. Speak up.

She had some things to do, and Kev was off anyway to pick up wine and mulling mix. Going out for anything special? Kev asked, and she whisked him a wicked little smile and said, You'll just have to wait and see, won't you? All sauce and fizz, with that chat-show grin. They blew kisses round a corner, and she wondered if kisses could really negotiate a corner or if they would simply smack into the wall and lie there, stunned.

The train is slowing down. Her fingertips catch in a flap torn by a penknife. Her scalp is hot; the pores prick with a fine sweat beneath her flouncy black hat, a gift from her friend Sally who works at Liberty, and probably got it end-of-line. She'd take the thing off, but she'd look a mess. Not that anyone would notice. But mightn't they? She looks around. The carriage is nearly full. Near her, schoolgirls in olive tunics going home after end-of-term exams, relieved and noisy. Two clubbers with marathon make-up and hair under a restraining order, carry-sacks resting on their laps label-side out. Dull-eyed shop clerks. A sprinkling of foreign students. Three men in rapid conference over a calculator. An old dear wearing Clarks – resoled rather than replaced, she bets.

Lately, Kev's hands on her body veer shy of where she wants them, just far enough off to thin her pleasure, and when she tries to set him right he gets excited because he thinks she is playing at resisting him.

(Reason Number Two: We are divided on sex i.e. he enjoys it, I don't.)

It is the twentieth of December, she thinks, the twentieth of December, three years from the end of the century. She sends this thought out, willing it to reach the minds of the other passengers. She gives it ten seconds, then scans faces. Nothing.

Kev peed this morning with the loo door open, and didn't wash his hands. She was mildly revolted. Then she thought, I am probably over-sensitive, I have a lot of quirks. Kev kissed her and she wished he'd shaved first. He read aloud from *The Times*, a paper she despised on principle, though she hadn't read it for years. He read the commentary for six full minutes, and she wished he'd shut up.

(Reasons Numbers Three Through Five: Our thresholds of neurosis clash. Our standards of hygiene. Our politics clash.)

On the bench nearest the single sliding door that connects

the carriages, a man in a penitent's high hard collar snores off-beat to the clank and wheeze of the wheels outside. Beside him a woman leans just out of the range of his breath, fussing with her luggage so it doesn't press into her legs, as though that slight, nagging pressure has become a horror to her.

(Reason Number Six: Kev has never ached for anything. He's never been absolutely shattered, and knows nothing of Pain.)

Home, she thinks. Twenty minutes, and I'm home. She closes her eyes, picturing her bath, fragrant and foaming and only her— Then straightens in surprise at a rush of air, superheated, followed by a cold blown underdraught and the hydraulic whoosh of the connecting door. Someone pushes in, stands for a moment, body reeling to the turvy sway of the train, moves quickly to the seat across from her.

Without thinking she says to herself, Junkie. Dead to type, he is. Young. Close-cut hair with a brief fringe over a narrow face picked at by persistent acne, fuzzed with the hope of a beard. Nobbly, scabbed elbows. In that tight tee-shirt his ribs poke up like fossils under sand. His jeans are torn, tattooed, names and slogans hatching from beneath wrinkles when he shifts his legs, the cuffs split and frayed above tall, sloppy, big-toed boots with brass buckles plugged by piped yellow laces criss-crossing. His hands are red, the nails nearly ruby bursting from the plinths of his fingers. He wears several rings – cheap metal crosshatched with complex nicks and scratches, as though someone has tried to engrave them.

He reaches down, and she sees a bundle squeezed into the hollow of his bent bow knees. His hands play tom-tom on the seat. Now and then he mutters something. His eyes are white in their sockets, they remind her of eggs in cups. When he blinks, she thinks of a tapping on a shell.

The door he came through must have been stuck open slightly, because now it shuts, hissing, and the boy starts. Fight or flight, she thinks.

The clipped voice of an announcer breaks into her awareness. The train is going to be held up. An incident at the previous station is being looked into. Routine service will resume shortly. The passengers' patience is appreciated. Every effort is being made.

She is used to delays on the Underground. She has been told by a friend who is engaged to a trauma surgeon that people regularly dive under the trains. Bodies burst by heavy wheels, pop-popping on the powered rail. Every few hours. This seems a bit excessive. But she wouldn't be surprised.

Is it possible that someone has jumped on to the track? She imagines Kev, wearing his one good blazer and his rugby-club tie, his broad face set, stepping delicately into the path of a speeding engine. He has discovered something, a pip of dark matter where his ambition was, and he can't go on. She is not asked to identify him because there is so little left to find: some freckles from his shoulder, a necklace of capped white teeth. Everyone consoles her. She begins differently, in a new key. The loo door is dutifully closed by her considerate lover, who reads the *Guardian* and is at once radical and rich.

(Reason Number Seven: I have fantasies about his death, which I enjoy.)

The lights flicker, ebb. Emergency strips glow along the curved roof of the carriage, up and down the pillars by either side of the exit doors – discontinuous ropes of luminescence that do odd things to faces, hone them in a troubling way. She is aware of heads and necks, their corresponding bodies emerging as her eyes adjust. The noise lessens. Voices are clearer.

Well, that's brilliant timing! clubgirl Dark says crossly to clubgirl Blonde, and Blonde swivels something – a watch? – from the
underside of her wrist and says, Oh, it'll only take a minute.
We'll be all right. We've loads of time.

The boy hasn't changed his expression, but his hands are
moving furiously, tom-tom-tom, and every time someone near
him moves, his shoulders jut forward. Jumpy, she thinks, then
realizes how cold he must be.

Some of the schoolgirls begin singing carols in a *Top of the
Pops* harmony, sweet and knowing all at the same time. They
sing 'Silent Night', and a few people applaud. They bow and
confer. They sing 'Away in a Manger'.

She closes her eyes. 'Away in a Manger' is a lovely song, she
thinks, all on its own, even if it had nothing to do with
Christmas, even if Christmas didn't exist. It is one of her
favourites. She has always loved singing in rounds, the lack of
centre, the precise, predatory circling of phrase and chorus,
resolving at last into harmony.

Earlier, in Camden Town, she ducked off the high street into
the warren of stalls that comprise the clothes market, her coat
close-buttoned to keep her cashmere free of the fried-oil smell
from the vending carts. She spotted some nice woollen jumpers
and decided to check one of them – a periwinkle fisherman's
knit – against those she already had in her closet, and perhaps
she'd return, and perhaps she'd buy it. She skirted a busy Thai
noodle shop. On her way out, she had to pass a woman in the
throughway, sitting up against the iron fence, bundled in blankets. The woman was young but had a plush, fine-wrinkled face
like a leather couch and bright speckled hair the colour of
semolina pinned up with a Christmas angel, equally pale and
blonde, silver-trimmed to turn the light.

Singing Santas, the woman cried. Singing Santas, six pound each.

Beside the woman was a mountain of eight-inch-high Santas, pointy-hatted, their cheeks abnormally rosy, lying head to toe, all askew like prisoners shot into a trench. At her feet, one sang 'Away in a Manger' in a nasal, music-hall bray, and every time it came to a long vowel it stuck and skipped, cackling, *Awaaaayyyyyy-haaayyyy-haaayyyy* . . . Like it was belting out a sea-shanty.

A big hard-looking man stopped to listen. Do they sing anything else?

The woman held up a Santa winningly.

He can be programmed, cantee? Twenny different songs, he sings. Sings like a bird. Two cee cell batteries. Twenny different— It's on the inside of his arm, innit? Printed, on the inside of his arm. Six pound each, won't find better.

Done, the big man said, counting out the cash. Ta, love. Happy Christmas.

The woman was cold, she was obviously cold. The Santas were ghastly. I could buy one or two, she thought, standing at a distance, watching. I could send them out as gifts. That'd be a laugh. I'll wait till he's gone. Then I'll tramp over. The big man shrugged forward his broad, shaved head, tucked the Santa foot-first into the collar of his coat, so that it rode him like a child going piggyback. People turned. She watched him go. But she never tramped over. And like a scouring in her head, she heard Kev say, Why don't you just ask? What are you afraid of?

'Away in a Manger' has ended. 'The First Noel' has begun. Some of the others have joined in singing. A tall slim man she hasn't noticed before is smiling self-consciously; his lips are moving with the music and his gloved fingers tap time.

Though she knows all the words, she doesn't sing. She listens to the voices: the strong clear soprano of the schoolgirls; the muzzy baritone of a bundled-up man at the far end of the carriage; the tremolo of the old dear in Clarks. Suddenly she wants to add her sound to their sound, and she hears herself ask the boy, Aren't you cold?

He looks up so fast she is startled, then he sees her, mumbles.

Warm enough. He has a Welsh accent, she thinks. A trilled *r*, and a long, warm *a*.

They're pretty jolly, she says, brightly.

'Tis the fuckin' season.

She is uncertain, then laughs.

Well, I hope we're not going to be long in here . . .

Ah, they'll be buggering about with the switching. It's always the switching. Trains coming straight on, like. They just wait it out. Happens alla fuckin' time.

The impromptu choir dives into a coda. Someone goes very flat. She winces, shakes her head.

Buncha fuckin' crows, that lot.

She laughs. Well, it's better than being outside. London at Christmas . . .

Ah, it's all right, he says.

He is Welsh. A Taffy. Years ago she bisected Wales on her way to the Dublin ferry from Holyhead; the valleys scarred by slag heaps, grassed over now, plummeted across the landscape like child-thrown clay. The towns were mostly small and slapdash and without clean light; poured-concrete houses, stained and streaky with the damp. She bought an Eccles cake at a small bakery. Some men across the road called to her, she went straight for the car and they watched her get in, and one of them showed his teeth and muttered, *Posh cunt*.

The schoolgirls and their allies have launched into a swinging version of 'Jingle Bell Rock'. People are clapping their hands. Even the clubgirls shimmy. Then they do 'Silent Night'. They sing it all the way through, twice, and at the very end there is a moment when all eleven or twelve disparate voices blend to form a final, single tone, declining into a complex lucent silence which enters her, reminding her of pure steam in the way it fills and cleans.

Then the train shudders, breathes deep in its belly, and starts to roll. Seconds later, the lights come on, and there is a good-natured cheer. The doors open, and two big transport policemen walk slowly in, locking the door behind them, moving through the car, scanning passengers. One of the men consults a list. They stop for a moment in front of the young man in the doorway.

Can I help you? he asks, in a dry, possibly American, accent.

Nosirthankyousir, says the one with the list. They walk on.

They are halfway through the carriage by the time she notices the boy again. He is telescoped into his seat, fringe brushed over his eyes, knees vanished into his fingers. It's him, she thinks. Of course it is.

When they finally arrive in the station, the doors stay closed. There is furious pressure on the door-release button, then someone bangs on the glass. A voice comes over the public address: *We regret to inform you that the doors of this train will remain closed pending the clearing of an incident at the previous station. Thank you for your patience. We regret . . .*

In the carriage, a pettish hum. So close to getting out, and now this.

You'd think they'd at least let us off! complains clubgirl Dark. We're *definitely* going to be late . . .

Clubgirl Blonde is soothing. We've loads of time. We'll get there.

Some of the girls try to rouse support for another round of carols, but no one joins them and one by one, like channels changing, their voices disappear.

She twists around in her seat, peeks outside, sees a group of four men pacing slowly down the outside of the train, pressing their eyes to the windows, consulting a clipboard, looking back in. The men are now two carriages back, but anyone standing has seen them. The boy leaps up, paces a fast circle, sits down. It's him all right, she thinks. But what . . .

The engine grinds, halts, grinds, halts. Lights zip-zap on and off, strobing the faces up against the glass, scooping them shallow. The boy is up, down, up, down. Then to the doors, trying to force them open with the blade of his hand, circling, trying again, finally sitting back down, feet poised, talking rapidly to himself.

I'm afraid they're locked, she says. Didn't you hear?

The boy raises his eyes, now grown dark and spent like the dregs of a bottle, to hers. Gestures to her. *Come closer.*

She hesitates, then leans in. Their heads meet lightly, boughs across a river. His breath is indecently hot and laced with menthol. His voice is shaky and urgent. Listening to him is a kind of burden.

My da, he loves apples. Ten a day, easy. Sad bastard. Loves his apples. The front fuckin' hall, the fuckin' stairs, they're covered in peelings. The bastard leaves his peelings all over the floor, all over everything. He's there on the bed, in his room, stinking of apples. Fuckin' mouldy they are, gone off, full ripe stink. He's lying there, covered in peelings, and cores all brown and bad, all fallen apart. I clear the peelings off him with a mop. I use a mop, till it gets dead clogged, and then a spade. I have to dig the bastard out. I'm looking at him, I think, His fuckin' face must've fallen apart! He's stuffed so many fuckin' apples into his face that his face has, I dunno, gone off, just like an apple, and I'm digging and thinking, Oh, Jesus, what if I get to the bottom and . . .

He stops, no longer aware of her it seems. Staring. Talking to himself. The word *Fuck*.

The lights maintain themselves, the engine spins, fresh air fans her.

She sits back hard. Remotely, she hears feet clumping by the window – the men are right outside. Quickly she gets up and moves to the doors beside her, outwings her coat, blocking their view. They can't knock or shout, she guesses, they can't give themselves away. The men peer in, pause, move on. She waits until she can no longer hear them, takes her seat. The boy is talking very fast, and now and then she thinks she recognizes an occasional word – *Paddington* . . . *Arch*. Then she looks at the panel across from her, and realizes he is reciting: Turnham Green, Stamford Brook, Ravenscourt Park, Hammersmith, Barons Court, West Kensington, Earl's Court, Gloucester Road, South Kensington, Sloane Square, Victoria, St James's Park . . .

Which one is it? He speaks so quickly she can barely keep up. Northern, Circle, Jubilee – the stations of the District Line. She keeps her eyes on the map on the panel opposite her. He makes no mistakes.

. . . Westminster, Embankment, Temple, Blackfriars, Mansion House, Cannon Street, Monument, Tower Hill, Aldgate East, Whitechapel, Stepney Green, Mile End, Bow Road, Bromley-by-Bow, West Ham, Plaistow . . .

His eyes are closed, his hands are clenched, he is chanting.

. . . Upton Park, East Ham, Barking, Upney, Becontree, Dagenham Heathway, Dagenham East, Elm Park, Hornchurch, Upminster Bridge, Upminster . . .

He is out of breath. The American steps back from his place near the exit – she isn't sure why – then she sees two men rumbling through the only open door. The boy leans forward, pressing a softness between her feet. Reflexively, she traps, then covers it, leans serenely back.

The first man in stops in front of the boy.

You there. The lad. Hey!

The boy looks up. Yeah? The word leaves him like a necessary breath.

Get up then. Come on!

They crowd him, moving him firmly along. At the door, one of the men asks him, Weren't you wearing a check shirt?

Yeah.

A blue check shirt?

Yeah.

Where is it now, then?

He answers quietly, Got nicked.

What about your jacket, then? All your gear?

Got nicked. It all got nicked, all right!

They wait, search his face.

All right.

They escort him off the train. Within moments, a team of policemen assembles. Once again, he is reciting. She can make out a few words – *Paddington, Marble, Green* – which are soon submerged in the currents of the crowd. From above the familiar address rings out, an audible thread tying one Underground transfer, one journey, one day, to all of the others: *Thank you for your patience. Please stand clear of the doors* . . .

The train pulls away. The American moves opposite her, where the boy sat. She realizes suddenly that he is taking all of this down. But he won't know what to do with it. Like Kev. It will lodge in his head like a peachstone; wrinkled, fluvial. He will try it out as an anecdote, as a parable of this or that barbed quirk of life. He will wring it meaningless. She knows it is important that he does not see what is down there between her feet, that he be left with questions. She leans forward, peers intently down the car. He turns to follow her gaze. She finds the bundle, caches it into her bag. When he looks at her again, he is visibly confused. The train beds itself in the station, she arches an eyebrow at him, walks away.

She pauses outside the station and gulps air, shakes out her legs, beats her arms up and down her shoulders and sides, thwack, thwack, like dusty carpets. Two turns from home, she hears wings and looks up to see a small bird settle on a telephone wire, and beside it, an angel aloft, noosed snugly, bowing and bending, though the night is still. The bird departs the wire, the angel trapezes on its axis and comes slowly upright; its shaken nylon hair the colour of semolina in the streetlight becomes the smeared pixelled halo of a fading firework.

Kev isn't home when she gets there. Her bath is hot, it is punishingly hot. She dumps all of the bath salts and oils she can find into the scalding water, tinting it the colour of wet kelp. The salts make her buoyant; the oils are an aromatic noise. She jellyfishes so that only her buttocks touch the basin. She thinks about the column Kev read out this morning, like a news presenter, in that smirky baritone he adopts when marking irony. The proliferation of minor conflicts across the globe: annexations, separations, revolutions, secessions. What price preservation?

Too high, opined the author – via Kev – better to let go, better to cut ties than arteries. Holding her breath, slowly submarining, she pictures her own body softening and becoming soluble. A slow, eccentric disintegration. The salts strand her skin, the oils infuse her tissues. She melts with ease.

Before she puts on clean clothes, she opens the bundle the boy left with her. There is an old blue checked shirt. An inflatable neck pillow rolled up in a foil insulating blanket. All of it stiff with soot and grime. A cheap toothbrush kit, fifty pence from one of the vending machines in public toilets. A National Express single, Treorchy to London Victoria, dated six days before. In the left shirt pocket, she finds an old, scuffed map of the London Underground, capillaried with pen-lines, hesitant and doubled, paths in a well-worn maze.

She rolls the pillow into the blanket, tips them into the bin along with the toothbrush. She tucks the shirt into the laundry hamper, packs the map safely away.

In the icebox she finds a bag of Cox apples that she bought last week. Everything in their flat goes bad. She picks them out one by one. Near the stalks the flesh is wry and creased, and rot has left a spoor of dark discs along the sides, and a sweet, liquory smell of fermentation. She looks at them for a long time. Then she gets up, goes to the toilet, empties her bowels. When she is done, she scrubs her hands in the sink brimming with water until her palms are prunes and even the beds of her nails are pink and rasped, then she goes back to the kitchen, slices the apples into a bowl of single cream swept with sugar, and eats them, rot and all.

She is lying in bed, looking at the ceiling when Kev gets in. His cheeks are red and shining from the cold.

Comfy enough? he asks her, and she grins, gets up and pads behind him, joins her arms across his waist. She can feel a beating in his abdomen.

She wants to tell him that she is thinking about this flat, their years together. She is thinking that she is going to leave him. She wants to say that this idea has been with her for a while. She has considered it from a number of perspectives; weighed it, and tasted it, and the taste is pleasant. It is not something she can easily explain. It is not that she is particularly unhappy, or even bored.

She wants to tell him something about herself, something unflattering. That some years back, before he knew her, she somehow became the worst kind of liar. She lied about the most minute details of her past and present, sometimes telling different lies about the same thing, and not caring. Everything she said came out as a lie, even if it was inconsequential, even if she had nothing to gain by it. After a while, her own lies didn't satisfy her, and she began to attribute all sorts of lies to others – to her friends, to pop stars, to those in public office. There wasn't a single thread of her unravelling world that she didn't want to tie in a different way, with a lie. At that time, gradually shunted off by old friends bewildered by her conduct, she became lonely, desperate for human connection.

So she made new maps, extended her habitat. She spent days on the Tube, roaming the busier stations, joining crowds, following people who intrigued her, slipping away when she was noticed. For a time this was enough. Then she began to touch them. She became expert in quick, direct, intensely physical contact with strangers. Sometimes they ignored her and sometimes they swore, and sometimes they moved away from her, swiftly, and sometimes they apologized, and sometimes forgave, and then she couldn't contain her hope.

I wept when they said not to worry, she wants to tell him. I *wept!*

This time in her life, as it turned out, was only a segment like other segments, and began somewhere, and ended somewhere else. It ended at King's Cross, when she spotted a hard-looking man in a puffa jacket, followed him to the station and on to the platform. She hadn't a plan, hadn't any idea what she would do next. So she was as surprised as he was when the train sparked and buckled past them, and she rushed him, barrelling into him at speed – *bang! smash!* – fists before her, tight round weapons. She hit him so hard she fell backwards.

The train stung into the silence between them. *Stand clear of the doors!* Without a word, he stumbled into a carriage, a wrinkle into the bustling, moody fold. The train doors shuddered and the warning bells chimed: *Stand clear, stand clear!* The doors closed, she stepped well back, and felt something spend itself, and leave her.

She wants to tell Kev, I was scared, and excited, and that scared me more. And today I found another map I may follow. I feel just the same.

She wants to tell Kev these things, but she doesn't say anything. She will tell him she is leaving only much later, at Easter, in the kitchen, washing Mason jars for extra glasses during their milk-and-eggs party, and his eyes will skew and run.

I don't understand, he will say. Why are you telling me this now? Isn't this something we ought to talk about? I don't . . .

And she will spend much of the rest of the party towelling up the jars he drops.

Again and again he will press her for reasons, and she will think that, finally, the reason you leave someone is the first one that comes to mind.

She will tell him, I can't keep throwing away apples.

But right now, she wants simplicity. So she holds him tightly, and asks, Did you see the angel at the corner?

He smiles. I don't see angels, he says. I'm far too left-brained.

No, I mean the one outside, on the corner, in the telephone wires.

She must look anxious, because he doesn't take off his boots.

Well, come on then, he says. Show me.

He wraps his coat around her. She drags him by his mittened hand and they take the stairs two at a time, whooping. He is puzzled but plays along; he is sweetly puzzled.

Right . . . *there*! she says, with a finger tracing its plumb line in the air.

They look up, setting their hands like soft binoculars before their cool, rain-wetted lashes, and it doesn't take them long to find it again.

Isn't that ridiculous, he says. Isn't that something!

Forensic

We stand in a gallery, admiring a painting, 'Church and Horse', drinking in its distinctive style: the near-pointillist application of paint; the solid, precise geometry of its figures and objects; the seams of colour, cool and detached as smoke rising in winter. In the background is a white frame church, lean, symmetrical, quarantined by a wood-and-wire fence. In the foreground a black horse churns towards a gate, great nostrils wide as a cave in space, tail blown back by the speed of its gallop, backthrust hoof pointing to a tombstone tilting in its socket near the top of a swayback hill.

Staring hard, tingling, I feel it to be the sort of work that cries out for augmentation: who is in the church? What is the horse running from? I am conscious of movement arrested and paradoxically reversed; so that the horse in motion seems to groan into stasis while the church bursts its roots, advancing steadily, close upon me. This image is what occupies my mind now, when you want to know what I am thinking. I tell you I am thinking of a mistake I once made. It was a mistake of addition. Your arm looped in mine winds a fraction tighter.

'Uh huh,' you say. 'And?'

'Hey – concentrate on the painting,' I say. 'Get your eight bucks' worth.'

You are grinning, though your hand still grips.

'You are one sarcastic bastard, you know that?'

An announcement over the public address drowns you out: Will a Mr and Mrs Piché please identify themselves at the information desk? Their child has been found.

We have been standing there a long time. I ask if you are bored.

'No. Are you?'

No, I tell you. I could look at this painting all day. You nod, thoughtful.

'That horse is going to explode any second,' you say. 'Don't you think? Either explode, or be stilled . . .'

The PA again. It seems there has been a mistake – the Piché child has not been found. The message is repeated, in French.

'You're right,' I say. And I don't know which would be worse.

We are holding hands. This is our first vacation in a year. We work hard, play rarely, with restraint and good taste – a model couple of our kind. We work at opposite ends of town but meet once a week for a quick healthy lunch, to keep things interesting, to lower fat intake.

Coming to Ottawa was your idea. There is a festival on, a wake for the corpse of multiculturalism, and it runs until May something. You found it in one of the three newspapers we read on weekends, selected to cover a range of the political spectrum. We divide these rigorously against gender lines: you skiff briskly through the sports pages, murmuring approvingly when a Canadian has done well, I noting the outrageousness of current fashions, draped and shrinkwrapped on to the slinky models with their jumpy bones and jutting, confrontational sexuality, so unlike us, so very different.

All around us things are picking up pace for the end of the century, making new and disquieting nests for themselves, commencing complex negotiations. Change is general over our land. And here we are.

Settled as you and I have become, we rarely speak of the first home we shared, a basement apartment at 223 Rhymney Street, in the Cathays area of Cardiff, a cobbled warren of semi-detached council flats skinned in stucco pastels, mixed raw gravel, without driveways, without gardens, the windows single-glazed so that the weather and street noise are imported intact. At the showing the landlady stressed that it was clean, affordable – just the thing for a . . . young couple. She grimaced as she said this; the words had a Methodist aftertaste.

Cathays then was a student neighbourhood, a welfare neighbourhood, reeking of smoke and lager and food that had sat on the hob too long. Our own flat was small and square and spuriously carpeted, with old wiring and plumbing apparently modelled on chaos theory. Any pressure on the nubbled vinyl wallpaper produced a flickering in the overhead lights, blurring their already timid, tepid illumination; the hot-water tank rumbled and crouped unless the radiators were set to maximum; the radiators leaked every time the hot water came on. The furniture might have been made from asbestos – sitting for longer than a few minutes produced a searing, scratchy heat. The sofa began to puff its stuffing like spores, and we spent an afternoon frantically taping the tears. Our double bed sagged so alarmingly that one of us always slept uphill and nightly wandered, skidding and flopping on to the other, piking back up. With the hip masochism of the urban pioneer, we prized these deficiencies. In chatty, dishonest postcards to friends back home, we boasted that it was cosy. Authentic. *Come visit*, we wrote. *You won't believe it – it's the real deal!*

It's been a warm winter, not as rainy as we feared, but our demure Canadian immune systems are unprepared for the onslaught of new infections. You've come down with glandular fever, a virus which strikes at your spleen and lymph nodes, enlarging them, parsing their membranes, seeding you with fever, fatigue, a throat white with fungus. Like all viruses, it is impervious to treatment, and you suffer, swollen, moaning, tossing and crying out. I rush to the market, to the bank, to the surgery and back home again. I drop off a key with our downstairs neighbour. I move the phone to a pile of books by your bed. I leave the radio on.

You are ill a long time. I use the word *ill* advisedly.

'*Sickness* tends to connote imbalance,' counsels our donnish GP, Dr Greavy, scribbling the names of various organic remedies on her prescription pad. 'Nowadays we substitute *illness*, a term we have found resolutely non-stigmatizing.'

When I beg her for drugs – any drugs – to ease the peggish drumming in your head, loosen the caulking on your lungs, she smiles and says, 'The best care, in her case, is palliative – and *you* are the palliative.'

When I press her for a prognosis, she is evasive. Better to check in regularly. Will there be any permanent damage? Oh, time will tell – I mustn't rush it. Is there anything – anything – I can do? Well, yes and no. I admit to worries about your spleen collapsing. She admits that medical science is still in its infancy, and that she herself is a devoted ayurvedic. Healing the mind comes before healing the body. This is her maxim. Inked into a blanched porcelain tablet the colour of new teeth, it dominates her surgery wall.

During the worst of your illness, when you are furthest from me, angular and scalding on the bed, I talk to you, providing a focus for your awareness. I tell you stories: amusing conversations I overhear at St David's market, trash from the tabloids, true-life tidbits from the butcher and the ex-rugby jock who cuts my hair. I know you will not remember from day to day, and I exploit this, grimly repeating myself. I play music, neither too slow nor too fast, avoiding extremes of style and mood. I do the laundry, coax dirt from the jealous carpets, change your sheets, change your clothes. I try to pep you up. I spout manageable platitudes meant to soothe and restore you.

'You'll be all right,' I tell you, over and over. 'You're getting better. You're looking well, you've got some colour now.' *Don't contradict me, don't fail me by getting worse*, I am also telling you. *Shh, now, we'll be fine.*

One evening the heating is on the blink, and we are wrapped in blankets, winter coats, stout scarves sent from home. In the upstairs flat, things are thrown by a teen mum and dad with matching scalene faces – their features, like their prospects, already eroded we judge. Some days they start drinking before noon, and then she is a slag, and he is a bastard. By now I can recite this banter from memory.

With the kitchen fan on to block them out, I read aloud a

newspaper feature about the brisk trade in human organs: bright hearts, flat kidneys, even corneas have currency it seems. Some are sold on the black market, but many are given away, flesh exchanged for a useful gap. I scale this as a story, as I do with everything these days. And all the while you child-chatter, doze briefly, sometimes cry, lucid for only moments at a time.

Tonight your forehead is rice paper burning, transparent and hot. If this keeps up I will bathe you in oatmeal and lukewarm water using a washcloth that I've wrung out thoroughly – this my father did for me, but I can't whistle Gershwin like he used to. I will pat you dry with a terry-cloth towel and carry you to bed, dodging the cardboard boxes bloated with unread books and the garbage bags we can't put out in advance for fear of rats and threatening notes from the dustman. I will sponge your sweat and sleep away with the backs of my hands and the edges of my mouth that you can't feel for the tingles.

'Are you kissing me, are you?' you ask, and I say that I am, but so gently that I wouldn't be able to tell either, if I were you.

Your eyes are frowned shut, a starburst of small wrinkles. I ask if you can hear me, and you squeeze my hand. *Yes.* The thermometer is safely bedded in its bracket on the wall. I have just taken your temperature, steadying your head between my knees. I am careful with good reason. Last night you bit down hard in the wake of a spasm and we both watched as the mercury emerged silver from the tube and on down your chin, a careful avalanche of spheres. I salved your lips, checked for cuts, mopped up the powdery glass with a moist paper towel, calmed you down.

'Oh God I'm sorry I'm sorry . . .'

'Hey, shh. It isn't your fault. They're cheaply made.'

'No, but . . . Why am I so *cold*? Why can't I keep my *eyes* open?'

I hush you; run my hand through your hair, clogged with sweat; stroke your bumpy scalp and the back of your neck. I rub your wrists where you have clenched your fingernails in the shade of your fever and left white–pink grooves. You shrug impatiently. *Get on with it!*

You want a bedtime story, preferably about my family, because you know so little about them, because I'm such an awful clam. I am telling you about a Christmas present found among the possessions of my great-grandfather, Melville McNeil. He died, aged fifty-three, on a passenger ship bound for Dover, in the mid-thirties. 1934, I think. Sailing from New York to Dover, en route to Scotland to meditate among the family graves. Four days into the trip, a storm came up and somehow the ship lost steering. It swung around and around in the gale and water was taken on and the lifeboats filled early. He likely died on Christmas Day.

I stop to sip at a glass of iced water freshened with lemon, offer you some. We sit quietly for a while, then you want to know if Melville's body was ever recovered, and I say no. Although this is true, it is tiring to remember, hard to see the point. It is the sort of story told at reunions, a family game played for the sake of rectitude that no one remembers the rules of, or really enjoys.

You are shivering again, long roaming shudders that keep you constantly in motion, rapidly exhausting your reserves of energy. I get up and leave the room to run the cold bath. You don't seem to notice.

Straddling the slippery shoulder of the bathtub, keeping you company, I sketch in some background to the story. My great-grandfather Melville was a businessman. He ran a company that turned waste wood into toothpicks – fifteen different kinds – round and flat, waxed and unwaxed, natural and coloured, plain and flavoured. He made a special festive version sporting gaudy dyed-plastic headdresses. He ran off a limited edition, glazed in silver, to commemorate the Jubilee.

When he wasn't dreaming up toothpicks, Melville was by all accounts a jovial man, whose love for the well-turned phrase exceeded his reach. He is renowned for remarking of his wife, Glynda, photographed in the pouchy, woollen bathing costume fashionable at the time, 'Look at her, will you! Near on forty and still such a statutory woman!'

The Christmas gift Melville received but did not open was snugly packed in a trunk of his things that Glynda carted down to the shipping office with instructions for it to be sent off on the next outgoing boat. When news of his death was received, the trunk was brought back home. Among the contents was a bundle of six letters, all written by Glynda before Melville even left, an advance correspondence to be doled out one per week of his intended absence. They were full of soft gossip, descriptions of the children's funny doings, the minutiae of a life ensconced. For each envelope she designed a clever stamp, filigree rectangles inlaid with quaint reminders of the season: snowmen, reindeer, sprockety evergreens fruited with silk-and-glass balls. *As you read this, my love, we are thinking of you.* Just as though, someone said afterwards, Glynda knew he wasn't coming back.

The gift lay in the centre, beautifully wrapped in a heavy gold paper with red stripes, ribboned with real silk. It was of medium size and weight. Continued shaking generated no tell-tale noise. It seemed to have been stripped of its tag or card – no way of knowing the true nature of the package. It might have been sent as an act of love, or perhaps it was a threat – who could say? This introduced certain difficulties: if it was *from* Melville, who was it for? If it was *for* him, who was it from?

After much discussion, a decision was reached. The gift would remain unopened, as a gesture of respect to Melville, the man. And Melville, the gift, was duly born. It appeared at his funeral, draped in black, beside the empty casket; it sat at the head of the table for Glynda's sixtieth birthday; it shone like a charm for baptisms and weddings; and was a squat, square rebuke at meetings of the estate trustees. Melville's gift could silence and unify the family as Melville had never managed to, plunged into the thick of them all, set skilfully as a toothpick in a complicated cake; and inevitably someone said how nice it was that dear Melville could *actually be here* for such-and-such, to savour it, and lend a little dignity, on behalf of the sainted past.

In later years, Ruth, Glynda's eldest daughter, brought the gift out only at Christmas, in memoriam, to bring good luck. Gradually, it lost its mystery for me. I grew older, impatient with tradition, and learned not to care about the contents of things. What was left was the story.

You are dozing now, crossed arms clamping the top sheet to your chin, an unconscious posture of self-protection. I follow your breathing and the passage of water through the pipes and radiators, a steady replenishing. But I do not grow full. Instead, I continue talking. I tell you about my jittery childhood and adolescence, about the night I spent in a Winnipeg Instabank, about my cousin the savant. I find myself choosing my words less carefully, wanting to tell you something while half hoping it will not stay with you. All of a sudden, with a straightforwardness I might never have managed if you were conscious, I tell you about Emma.

It begins in those gloomy days when your fever arrives. You are unhappy in your new department, having little in common with the other graduate students. I work in a virtual sweatshop –

writing for a CD-ROM about the life of Laura Secord, two-hundred-word snatches to be couriered to a company back home, with payment on receipt. I walk a lot, getting lost. I learn to loathe the accent and the fighting in the streets. In Britain the character of a place is found in its accent, and Cardiff's seems to me messy and lurching and alcoholic, steeped in hops and sucker punches, violent and purring, the language of tomcats.

I meet Emma while running your research errands in the pre-clinical library. She is tall and glamorous against the beery freshers crowd, turmeric-coloured hair loose about her face, blown free sometimes from a corner of her mouth. I watch her smile. She has the classic English overbite which seems to me winning, open – later I will think it feral. She looks up at my accent and silently puts books on hold for me. I joke that we have traded glances and I've left mine behind. She doesn't seem to hear. On an impulse, I ask her to join me for a coffee. Coffee is no favourite of hers, she tells me, demagnetizing books with an efficiency I find powerfully erotic. Does she drink tea? She does. Would she like to . . .

Oh, she is expected after work.

I avoid her after that, smarting, telling myself I hadn't been trying, had merely been friendly. I lurk at the back of the stacks, browsing through books I've always meant to read. Poe, mostly – I leaf through lots of Poe. I sit there for long hours, in a vague, unhappy surveillance, tracing patterns in the leguminous carpet. Emma finds me there, taps lightly on my chair. She fancies a cup of tea.

We have a cross-cultural, youth-hostel conversation, dutifully exchanging geographies. I let slip I might have been born in Edinburgh if I hadn't been premature. She relates her trip to America: to San Diego – too fishy – and Florida – too hot.

Canada is something more than an extension of America, she understands. On her way home she flew over Canada and thought it looked bleak. I tell her yes, it does look that way, if you're flying over Gander.

I claim to find Britain bleak. I accuse it of having an ageing, woozy, prizefighter feel, picking itself up without knowing exactly where it is and not so sure it's up for another round. She regards me politely. And what am I doing in Cardiff? I say I am gainfully unemployed. She looks intently past my left shoulder. I keep on talking. About me. About me and you. I say that we won't last much longer. That between us fissures have long been evident, and now they are widening, and this is a trap. I must be very convincing.

Once or twice more we share tea at one of the shops in the city centre. Never quite at ease, we converse brightly, sideways, hiding in the open, mutually purloined. She talks hopefully about returning to school and coolly about her ambitions and I'm not really listening. She talks about her husband of three years who sells computers and has a speech impediment. I mention reading somewhere that speech impediments make you cocky. She watches me without smiling or blinking and says, 'It can only happen once, you know. I took vows, and I meant them.'

And when finally I lift her hand, it is a water cracker, ink-marbled and dry, and the skin is opaque, like it is all over her, I learn. She digs her fingers into mine in a peculiar way. And we smile, simultaneously, looking down.

Soon we are meeting regularly, twice a week. She takes early shifts, and sometimes, reckless beauties that we are, we leave together, she leading, I following, cradling my knapsack like a chalice that wants a wash.

Emma is organized. She has a tooth mug with her name engraved on the side which she freshens with permanent marker once a month. Emma is neat. After we make love she scissors off me, folds a tissue between her legs, inspects it, crimps it like a square of ravioli, making a measured parcel of our wastes. She is specific about where I can and cannot touch her. I regard this as a challenge.

'Does that feel good?' I ask, a little desperately. 'How about that?'

Her prohibitions make me wild to break them, and when I outflank her and manage a few swipes of my tongue inside her, I am exultant. Emma's bones shift when she rolls on to me, off of me. She kisses in straight lines, faintly, without saliva.

By now your illness has peaked, and begun to retreat. You drift at the limits of my life, checking in now and then with the conscious world like a sweet, forgetful guest. The fever passes and you are apathetic; tired all the time, still unable to get dressed and go out by yourself. I try to be solicitous, but watching your cracked mouth open in sleep, your patchy colouring, your slackening skin, I begin to wonder when a nurse's touch turns forensic, when the light behind the compassionate glance threatens to waver or snuff out. I dab a cotton pad along the crease of your hips, trim your bangs, turn a tongue depressor sideways to scrape the dry skin from between your toes, treating each as a disjunct region. Slowly, your body is stripped of its coherence and recast as rituals of care, excised from the part of me that Emma occupies. Slowly, we assume numerical identities, a ladder of integers summed and split, with myself, immodestly, as aleph. For a while, I am able to keep the terms separate. You are my Two, my extra sneakers. Emma is my Three, my attic with a light on. Desires, denials, injuries, foibles are all sorted in accordance with this partitioning formula: Emma sleeps late. You develop allergies to fabric softener. She prefers a man in a shirt and tie to a man in a waistcoat. You would be grateful if I could keep up with your class notes. She wishes I were slightly blonder. You feel fortunate to have me. I never disagree.

I am at Emma's every Tuesday and Thursday. These are her husband's rounds through South Glamorgan, and he returns late.

'I like you,' I say, offhandedly, during one of these sessions, neutrally stroking her side. She stares at the wall.

'You like me because I'm new,' she answers, matter of fact. 'But it won't last. I won't always be new and sweet. You know how fast it goes. Kiss the kitten. Drown the cat.

'No, don't bother,' she says, as I begin to bluster. 'I feel the same way. I like you too. But I also like beginnings. Beginnings are best. I know you now. Your balls hang unevenly, left to right. See? It's happening.'

After that, for a brief period, I try to win her. I reinvent us in a thousand moments when we live our life like a match struck: blazing, rapid, sulphurous; each look a lyrical gunshot, each touch a bomb in the shape of a jewel. I buy her thoughtful, pointed presents that advertise their engines like a schooner's sails. I tell her that I want to be with her out in the open, in daylight, whatever the cost . . .

'Oh,' she says, shaking out her panties. 'I wish you wouldn't.'
'Wouldn't what?'
She looks steadily past me. 'Push things,' she replies.

And finally, a few weeks later, when I ask her why she doesn't return my phone calls, my sly messages that I leave by her desk on bright sticky paper, she busies herself affably, straightening the spines of overdue books, and says, 'I wish you wouldn't.'

When I get to this point in the story, you appear fast asleep. I check the clock, shrug you conscious, fold a crescent of phenobarb beneath your tongue and lightly douse it, tuck you in. All this while I am talking, desperate in my desire to get it all out, the words wet and steamed, an ablution. You are quiet in the centre of the bed, your hands are tightly closed.

'Night night, sweetie.'

You motion night night, groggy, disowned.

Surprisingly, despite herself, Emma calls. Sometimes she calls me in the middle of the night. I keep my voice low, even though you can't hear it, can't even hear the fire alarm that I set off trying to homemake vegetable bouillon. She calls and we trade enigmatic sentences. I say that I am ill, empathetically, and she says she is so far inside her marriage that she can't see out. We talk meaningfully about mundanities and now and then, as an afterthought, she asks me over.

We say little when we are together, pretending to prize the silence that marks our new maturity, the exalted distance we now strive to maintain. We do not need one another – therein lies our need. By now our lovemaking is fully teleological. Nonchalantly, we bring each other off. She takes me in her lac-quered mouth made oval with a brisk professionalism and I slew two workmanlike fingers, my tongue, about her breasts, her clit-oris, refusing to pause until I feel her clench.

We part with rationed kisses, taking care to make no plans – oh, we sensual creatures, brutally spontaneous! I tip my baseball hat, she pats her hair; from our crumpled embrace we slink away, sorry but preening, grown fat and savage on the risks we pretend we have taken.

The last time she calls her voice is a jar of nails, rattling, and I race out in the dark, leaving the blinds up. You are asleep. When I arrive, she is composed and pale and does not let me in.

'What happened?' I ask, across a trellis of light from her doorway.

She is surprised I came. She really wishes I hadn't.

'I wanted to know . . . I thought I had left something with you . . . It was here all along. I wanted to know if . . . I forgot myself,' she says. 'Honestly, it's nothing – you should get back.'

I think about staying, and making a scene. I have a wild idea that a scene is what we need, that it will somehow repair all this quiet damage, even retroactively. I think about forcing my way in. But then I realize I have already done so. And anyway, she has long since tripped the bolts.

On my return, time has performed its forgetful somersault, and Emma lives elsewhere, and you and I live here. Our rooms seem very close and rough and I am suddenly very grateful for you, for the padding. I pour lemonade, take my requests on the stereo. Emma didn't like this band, I tell your shadow, your snorkelling chest-cough, your breath on a glass, she found them *so* derivative, oh, once upon a time.

When you finally recover, you recover very quickly. One day you are sleeping fourteen hours, the next you are up and about. Caught up in the pleasure of it, I grab you by the waist, lifting, tossing you in mid-air around the blocky, orange-upholstered chairs. We whoop and laugh and dance a manic tarantella until want of breath and dizziness send us spinning to the bed.

'It's over!' you shout. 'Yes! I got rid of it; the *fucker*! It's *over*!'

It's like passing the worst kind of swimming test, like remembering where a lost watch is, like stepping inside from embalming cold. After four months you have been released. Indescribable. Later you badly want to make love. Leaning against the dresser, I enter you for the first time in months, slowly, one hand behind your head, cradling it. Your legs are shaking from the strain after only a few seconds and soon I am supporting all of you, spasming in my stomach and my lower back but not caring. At first we are quiet, awkward, straining to feel everything, gingerly taking pleasure.

And then suddenly you are climbing me like someone about to drown, tearing my hands from your breasts and pinning them against the wall, plugging my mouth with a coil of your hair, silencing me. Your mouth opens on my shoulder, I feel the sticky heat of your saliva and I feel you bite down hard, drilling into the muscle, drawing a web of blood.

'*Fuck fuck fuck* . . .' you are saying, over and over, in a sob hard and white as calcium.

I try to speak and only choke on your hair, I can't pull you off me, can't move away; you are spitting at me, *fuck* and *prick* and *cock* and *cunt*; and I can't stop you, can't control you, this loud surprised vulgar talk, words you and I would never use. You whirl and rasp, grate at me with your weak arms and legs spindled and white from inaction; calling me names, urgent names, none of them tender. I am breathing very hard, I begin to hyperventilate . . .

We share a bath that evening. We do not talk about what was said earlier. You vice my head in your knees, scrub shampoo into my scalp with your ten fingers hung portcullis-fashion. I keep my eyes open, even underwater, even through the sting. I do not complain, though the water has long since cooled. Because wrapped together as we are, we can't get out unless both of us get out.

Some months later we break the bank on dinner and drinks to celebrate our *bon voyage* home. The weather is fine, the day's wispy rain diverted by a trim coastal wind. We get dressed up, walk arm in arm to Henry's, the fanciest cocktail bar in town.

Waiting for our Bailey's Comets you ask me out of the blue, 'Whatever happened to whoozit's Christmas present? You told me and it was endless, but you never told me the end.' You speak in a voice just different enough for me to notice, a tonal modulation that changes striking air, like a tiny spray of scent.

'I probably made it up,' I reply. In your eyes I chart my own rapid slur of recognition; I understand what you heard and what you remembered and the choices you must have made, and I know that our arrangement has been secured. And though I sense that in this transaction something crucial has been lost, traded away, I feel I can live with that.

As it happens, I do recall the fate of Melville's gift. It was passed around, trotted out, narrated, until fewer and fewer people remembered its history and purpose. Gradually the family lost its knitted shape and sent threads down to Denver, Belleville, Salmon Arm and other places. Glynda's daughter, Ruth, died peacefully at the Banff Springs Hotel in 1971, the year I was born. She had married well, as they used to say, meaning that he had money but also showed a modicum of love. Her husband managed a brokerage firm in Winnipeg and they lived in a house in an affluent area with a fishpond in the backyard.

Ruth's legacy, divided among her own four children, was heavy on antique furniture and Royal Doulton figurines. My mother, the youngest, had a fool's choice between a Steinway baby-grand and Melville's battered old trunk. Sentiment reared, she hesitated, her older sister claimed the piano.

When I entered second grade, my family moved to a new, roomier house. The men who helped us move were college students working for their tuition and a little left over for beer. One of them was always being ordered about by the others, in a half-exasperated way: 'Hey Sid, grab a hold of this, will you! Sid, Sid! Wait at the truck – the truck!'

The man called Sid had lazy eyes and a cantaloupe head, and we were informed by my mother that he was maybe a bit slow. This did not make him a bad person, she reminded us. Quite the opposite. Sid was a wonderful worker, able to lift almost anything. So it was a pity about the crate being slippery.

I watched the movers, gliding heavily between our house and their huge yellow truck, each keeping to his route, expression fixed, like a figure on a carousel. I saw Sid lean down for our Christmas crate and straighten, over-compensating and losing his footing, teetering down the stairs, falling then rolling, still clinging grimly to the crate.

The foreman rushed over, spoke gently to Sid.

'It's okay,' he said, over and over. 'It's okay, it was an accident.'

Then the foreman conferenced with my mother. Usually, Sid was very dependable. Definitely the firm would be glad to cover damages. Definitely there would be no more trouble.

'Oh, goodness, it's no trouble!' my mother assured him through a mouthful of packing tape. 'Just a lot of junk in that crate. Now, how much longer did you say this would take?'

I am eight years old. Old enough to stay up past supper, old enough to play outside by myself. That evening, I rummage through the debris outside our house, find the crate Sid dropped, and inside it, Melville's gift. Its frail wrapping falls away. I tug at the clotted cardboard lid. Beneath it is another box, wooden, which oysters open with a halting music on copper hinges splayed and cracked, as though sometime torn apart with force. I full-finger into the gap and feel solidity, then a faint crumbling.

Startled, I withdraw, inspect my hands: my fingers glisten blackly with the powdered sheen of coal, and I know someone has been there before me.

For a moment, I see with borrowed eyes. I see Melville, as he was described to me: handsome, bones the size of two-by-fours, his face beneath his beard warm and gold as varnished bread in the windows of Ukrainian bakeries. I have a child's idea of drowning: something jogs an upright boat and it tips, quickly, sprays its passengers hurlyburly into a peaked black sea. Melville's mouth is open. Maybe he is telling one of his six jokes. Maybe he is taking a bite of something. Then he is underwater. His skin shimmers, his beard loosens and spreads. These are things that happen to him. He is too surprised to struggle much.

I see Melville, and I see something else, separately and more dimly: a pair of hands, plump and veined as shallot skins, moving on Melville's gift, unwinding its wrapping, opening the chamfered chest, triggering the switch that sets the music playing, dipping into the box, withdrawing. The hands are poised. They have just moved, they are about to move, though whether to caress or dismember, I cannot say. These three share space in my mind: Melville, the gift, the hands. Between them, there is some cause.

I stare at this box I have opened for a very long time.

Then my mother calls, and I pause, she calls again and I squirrel the box into a tower of raked leaves, mark its place with a limb of pine, return to the new-smelling house. It is my first night there, socked into a sleeping bag on a makeshift Ikea bed. I dream probably, though nothing sticks. I sleep in later than I plan to, race for the front lawn.

But when I return to my hiding place I find that the leaves have gone with the garbage, and Melville's gift too.

Mountain Man

Growing up I thought it odd that the Mountain Man should come only by moonlight. No one would explain it. Mother felt that a mind brought up on scandal and hearsay was a light mind indeed and undernourished – she could only hope my head was good and healthy. Father dismissed the Mountain Man as an old wives' tale, nodding respectfully to my mother, and wondered if we required God's own intervention in order to clean our teeth. We asked at school and were told to stop spreading rumours and attend to the voyages of Jacques Cartier. Our piano teacher, Mrs Hummins, who wore black crepe throughout her marriage and borrowed smut from the library under her real name, offered no views on the Mountain Man. Nor did Simmy Warden, steady as a fuel pump behind the counter of Lucille's Dairy Belle.

The hills around our town were small but rugged, and we were warned to avoid them. Those who didn't paid a price. Annie Tippott's dog was eaten there, its barrel-cage of bone licked dry and spit-polished, leather collar and tag half buried. Tommy Lightfoot got drunk on spirits there and had a vision that left him daft, a vision of a baby made of windfall sticks, with the red-toothed mouth of a lamprey. Unnatural things came from those dim-peaked hills, aproned with scree, spiked with nettles and gorse where birds ate their own nests in winter. Most dangerous to children was the Mountain Man, familiar but faceless, hard to recall, entering the house through keyholes or the gaps between door and sill, disappearing at dawn when the house awoke.

I nourished my mind and brushed my teeth and tried at school and practised the piano, and as Mrs Hummins' pointer-finger rode the cascading quarter-notes of Joplin's 'The Entertainer', I thought about how those notes hid music, just like hills and moonlight hid the Mountain Man.

These foothills we are driving through remind me of that time, that town, those fears. I tell Ken, half joking, 'Step on the pedal, we're in Mountain Man territory!' But my husband is not a believer. Long ago he lost interest in my legends. He wants to know where the turn-off is, whether to take a right or left. Ken mistrusts road signs – anyone can plant them, pegged insecurely to the ground; a steady breeze can dislodge them. This paranoia has roots; Ken is directionally dyslexic. Journey planners, road maps, compasses regularly betray him. More than once I have seen him miss our corner and overshoot our house.

'Right or left?'

'Left. I just told you.'

'Left? Are you sure? Did you check the map?'

'I don't need to check the map. I remember. We pass Duntroon. We turn left.'

'Will you please check the map, please, thank you.'

He is staring into the rear-view mirror, shoulders humped forward, concentrating. The frigid rain is no longer pelting, on my window it spins and slides, the pattern of a hand. I shake the map straight, trace a random course, murmur knowledgeably. I could be in Wawa or Red Deer – I have no idea.

'It's left all right,' I tell him.

We are heading west, climbing through low hills ridged like a spine bent double. The town we are bisecting is a postcard; immaculate, tree-lined residential streets without driveways, quaintly named shops like the Bun in the Oven Breadery, a heritage train depot, a gas station with diner attached, the sign above entreating, TEMPT YOUR TAST BUDS – GRANDMA'S VEGGIE SPECIAL. Grandma digs deep for the health-conscious trucker. Another sign at the town limits: SLOW MEN IN TREES.

We hum by fluorescent mileage posts and garish, footlit billboards in farmers' fields. Car after car passes on the left, where Ken refuses to drive.

'The maniacs come out on Fridays,' he is fond of saying. 'Better safe than sorry.' In practice Ken is sorry that being safe impedes his ability to make good time. He tailgates, following so closely that I shut my eyes and brace for impact. He flashes his brights, staring into the cars he passes, mutely condemning their occupants. He is merciless towards the old, towards those who smoke, pick their nose, steer one-handed. But especially the old.

'I knew it!' he will proclaim triumphantly. 'I *knew* it had to be a wrinkly – look at the size of that boat!' Those that dare to pass

us are maniacs, those we pass soon for the grave. Only we deserve
the road.

I am wearing a pair of calfskin gloves, bought recently. I had
my eye on them for ever, including the shop on my errand run,
loitering by the shelf, slipping them on, glancing casually at the
price tag, putting them away. They fit perfectly, seamed hands
much finer than my own, supple and surprising as a secret I have
from myself. I wear them in the car though it is warm, enjoying
their calm luxury, refusing to take them off. In my lap I cradle a
bottle of red wine, a *baco noir*, funnel-wrapped in something festive. In my lap it is heavy, soft–hard, like nougat. I enjoy its
weight and solidity, its fluted, expensive shape. We cannot afford
it for ourselves. But Anton is worth it.

(At the wine-shop till Ken nudges me.

'Double air miles,' he says, looking pleased. Air miles were
made for people like Ken, patient hoarders, counting seeds not
crops. I wonder if with each purchase he imagines the card
unstacking at the touch of its logo, spilling mile after mile to tile
the linear distance. I wonder where he wants to fly, this man I
would call earthbound, who has flown only once, and then as a
child, on his way to England for a wedding which was cancelled.)

It has been nearly eight months since we last visited Anton.
For Ken this is too long. He wonders if Anton has made arrange-
ments for the winter: snow removal, gas for the stove. He frets
about the insulation, which in gross violation of its ten-year war-
ranty has burst from the walls and matchstick ceiling like the
contents of an over-boiled sausage. He sincerely hopes Anton
has fitted storm windows, paid his property taxes, had his cholesterol checked.

'He's so naive,' Ken laments. 'The day-to-day stuff is beyond
him.'

I have heard this before. Anton is thought by his friends to have the common sense of a baby and a baby's clean, unspotted soul. A baby can't be expected to care for itself. So Anton is cared for. One friend does his accounting, another arranges repairs to the house. Every so often a crisis arises, like the time Anton's leased car was repossessed for arrears. Then the inner circle talks strategy, using exotic, federal-agent phrases like *damage control* and *best case scenario*. Back at HQ, Ken struts about, shrilling and cooing to beat a pigeon, pausing to telephone anxious communiqués, exhaling his martyrdom in neat metered sighs, glad that he and I did not manage children because one is all he can afford.

(Anton, scion of wealthy itinerant Pender Island hippies, is the first and best friend that Ken, prodigal of the Ontario nickel mines, makes while away at university. They share digs, philosophies, clothes, friends, women. Together they chug fifty ounces of beer in fifty minutes. Together they buy a Winnebago, paint it peaflower-yellow and slogan-black, carve Canada along its Rocky Mountain seam, inhaling nature through a ten-inch bong, working odd jobs. Together they find *Nix*, a DIY magazine of fiction and commentary so trenchantly radical it is ignored equally by the Left and Right. These stories are dredged up often when they meet, soaked in nostalgia for their prankish, lusty youth, grateful for the men it has made them.)

We have visited Anton for years. When he was based in Montreal, Ken and I went down by train. We ate at the streetside cafes of Prince Arthur, window-shopped on Laurier, drank in fashionable bars, by day rank and spooky as haunted houses. Later, Ken went alone. He brought bagels, sweet seeded rings oven-seared, wonderful with cream cheese in a stolen afternoon. He brought sores on the shaft of his penis and a clotted effusion around the glands, courtesy of a friend of Anton's who was into sex without strings.

(When he gives me the news I am baking blueberry scones. I drop the blueberries into the heavy Pyrex bowl. Some stick to the sides, and I swipe them down with the spatula. They are sealed, bluebottles in jam. Their bodies leave swilly blue trails. I spit into the batter. I spit, and blend. I spit, and look at Ken. He cowls his head in his big white hands.

'It wasn't *his* fault,' he says.

The sores go away with an ointment that I have to apply because he cannot bear to. Twice daily, after washing. It hurts to pee, he complains. It hurts to get hard. In the night I reach out and barrel his cock in my hand, unravel the gauze dressing, take it in two fingers. It performs a jerky sort of jitterbug as I roll, squirts up into the hair of his belly, pungent and gooey as a tansy bud burst in my hands. I am sleepy. I don't clean it up. Ken never mentions it. That's the end of trips to Montreal.)

Eventually, Anton joined us in Toronto, teaching part-time at one of the community colleges. He published a fourth book of poetry, *The Sound of Sands*. The poems had natty, elegiac names like 'Sensus' and 'Sunday in Amy's House'. Many of them concerned the immaculate, faithless marble of women's bodies, the chill mist that rolled from their breasts. I had trouble picturing myself as cold ornament, my breasts as monuments on moors. But his critic friends adored the book. In their reviews they applauded his heady way with language, his keen sense of eros, his innocent gaze full of wonder. Flush, a celebrity, Anton rented a place in the beaches, designed by an architect who sought to marry light and anger at a time when this sort of thing was greatly admired. At one of Anton's parties there I shyly smoked my first joint. A beard with a man beneath it sketched my face in mango *coulis* and told me I had nostrils worthy of Rodin. Ken shared the tuneful ambit of a throat singer. Anton reclined on a pappasan chair, with a pipe and a glass and a saffron blanket, and hoped we would triumph over Time.

'You've lovely eyes,' he said, languidly tracing my temples as Ken shivered with pride. 'Just like the mouth of a crocus. Shall we paint your crocus eyes?'

(Sometimes Ken's mouth moves with Anton's, a slightly delayed, unconscious lip-sync. I have watched him watching Anton, waiting for his cue. I have seen him walk after Anton, stride for stride fitting into his footprints. I have seen him write with one of Anton's collections open before him, making fair copies of Anton's cocky, wastrel poems, colour-by-number Monets, to lie crumpled and blotted, discarded. I raid the wastebasket and choose one. The sentences rhyme awkwardly, words corseted into place by stiff, graceless punctuation. Ambition figures as celestial litter. Love is a plant, which, roughly handled, retracts its flowers, poisoning itself. We run life's rapids as candles floating, and we wander, and we wane. Embarrassed, I read only a few stanzas, then ball them up and throw them away all over again. Though I fix the spelling of 'Persephony'.)

Now Anton lives in a converted farmhouse he bought for a song. Years ago a group of his friends got together and winter-proofed the rooms at the back. They were going to do the rest of the house but there was a falling-out between the tax lawyer and the radiologist and things were never finished. The kitchen is powered by a dickey generator on loan from a dairy farmer up the road. The living room is being painted by some local high-school girls whose narrow, literary voices Anton coaxes two evenings a week. The dining room is pine shingle, barely furnished. Anton is retired now, the victim of academic politics, tall-poppy syndrome, millennial ennui. He has no income beyond scraps of royalties and whatever his friends donate.

'*He* lives on nearly nothing,' Ken says when the bills come in and I must account for the eleven minutes of calls to Regina or Winnipeg, the current eked out to heat the bedroom after my showers, the tweezerfuls of gas that fire the stove. '*He* goes without.'

And when I reply that *he* seems to do all right, considering, Ken sadly shakes his head, and calls me morally stingy.

(Sometimes Anton sends letters in which I am Lupus Enchantress and he the Moon Lion – roaring, voluptuous creatures smack at the top of each other's food chain. He writes:

I thought of you at noon, and made it dusk; the day was over Then, past me, a breeze I barely noticed.

The letters are full of his half-cribbed verse (he calls it *in the manner of*), his showy, cramping images: my topiary soul only he can trim, my necklacing chamomile hair. Perhaps he takes my lack for longing. Perhaps I am the finest injury he can imagine for Ken.

But whenever we meet he is his old self, never a misplaced touch or stray endearment. It occurs to me that I am meant to be the epistolary entry in his register of seductions. Each year another clever Christmas card, another melodic, plagiarized couplet.

'You can set a calendar by him,' Ken says, rosy with relief.)

Visiting Anton at the farmhouse is a big production, with all the gravitas and attention to detail of a move between royal residences. Ken fills the car with gas, phones for road news, sets the heat and lights to timer, searches for pants to prop up his bottom and a shirt that will hide his oval gut, pneumatic as fireplace bellows. I bring a dress, long enough to cover my slumping thighs and waterlogged ankles, thin and swoopy to lend my body that mysterious, time-safe quality. When we arrive a woman will be there to greet us whom I have never met, and it is understood that I will converse with her, and help out where I can.

'Don't you even know her name?'

'It was Alice who answered when I called a few weeks ago.'

'Alice the dancer, with the warm-up tights?' I'd found her rude, with a trombone voice, slippery and blatting.

'That was East Coast Alice. I think this was West Coast.'

'"Television as visual-arsenic"?'

'Amber. You're thinking of Amber. She's old news.'

'Alice who advocated pigshit as a fuel alternative?'

'You're making that up.'

'Am I? Clearly you've never lived with pigs.'

'Look, it was Alice who answered the phone, I told you.'

'So I know her.'

'Alice was just visiting. She's not actually *living* there.'

'Well, who is?'

'*I* don't know! Whoever it is didn't answer the phone, did she!'

Women pass constantly through Anton's home, like infestations of benign pantry pests. He uses them up quickly. No tears are allowed. No protestations of enduring love or blame. Even so, he is fond of them, these winsome youngsters with slender thighs and pale warm skin, still playing with their hair. Hopeful pilgrims, prostrate with admiration for that poem of his that brought them to the peak of something memorable.

I have met so many of them. They speak to me of Anton and

the mystery he holds for them, potent, erotic, terminal. At Anton's I have encountered a Chantal, a brace of Alices, a Renuka, a Juniper, three varieties of Jennifer, a Dianne who was homesick, a Leigh estranged from her husband of seven months, a Thomas whose parents had wanted a boy, a Sybil with an Angie in tow, a Melinda with bulimia who dreamed of pastries and woke up gagging, a Kari with a single blazing streak of silver and dark volcanic moles above her broad man's lips, a Liz who lasted a year before gargling fabric softener and flying back to her family in Dawson Creek. Once I was near their average age, a welcome companion, and then I was their favourite aunt, wise about love in its fragility and insolence and sheer slurpy joy. Now I am an older woman, to be deferred to but pitied, for the way I have let myself go.

(Never once have I spoken against Anton. I say nothing when Melinda asks me if I think her bottom is really so wide. I say nothing when a Jennifer miscarries, too frightened to look between her legs, striking her stomach and screaming, a smear on my Shetland sweater. I say nothing, just jerry-rig bandages from bedding like some old witchy midwife while Anton tracks about like a bumper-buggy, conveying his immense surprise that such a mess can be made of his hospitality, and Ken phones the ambulance and smokes tersely outside till it comes. On the way home he is tight-lipped, and when, still shaking and smelling richly of her fluids, I drape a tender arm across his shoulder he shrugs it from him and asks why I am followed by drama.

'I didn't knock her up,' I tell him.

Ken snorts, and guns the engine. 'You'll never understand free spirits!'

I used to, I want to tell him. I was generous with praise, hopeful, mining those I met for veins of goodness, happy to ride coat-tails. I was pretty, with hair that grew back after brushing; hips that cracked only in the funny positions I would sometimes adopt for my lovers; a throat with a slope a liquid bead could follow without getting trapped or diverted. So much was simple for me then. So much more could I withstand. My tolerance, I want to tell him. See how you have lowered my tolerance!)

'Right or left?' Ken wants to know. He glances sideways at me, monitoring my wakefulness, ready to make conversation should I doze off. Someone has said that creativity, real creativity, is not at all like grinding sausages. When it comes to chat, Ken is a shameless sausage-grinder. I'm not allowed to sleep while he drives; we must share the boredom, the flat-out, yawning, jaw-straining boredom. So he drives, and I stare, and now and then he grinds me a sausage.

'They've invented a new kind of salmon. It's always hungry. It's engineered that way.'

'I'm engineered that way,' I tell him. 'Maybe I'm part-salmon.' End of sausage.

The distance we have to go stretches before us, patchy as sod. My gloves show lines, smoker's wrinkles; when I spread and fist my hands they look like paws. I am thinking. I am thinking that the Mountain Man is part of my history. As some girls dream of seahorses, I dreamed of him. My mother was right, it was not a healthy fascination.

When I was eleven I took a borrowing card at our local library. I scanned the stacks, thumbed the encyclopaedias, tracking the Mountain Man. I'm not sure what I expected to find: secret stories; hushed, scared text bent into italics; charms and potions and protective medals. What I saw was portraits of long-dead men with moustaches, shotguns spinning on their knees. The lore of tobacco advertising, not the shocking, punitive histories I craved. *Mountain Man – any of the pioneers of the North American Rocky Mountains who went to that region first as trappers, attracted by the beaver in the virgin streams . . . Mingling extensively with the Indians, the Mountain Man adopted many of their manners of life and their beliefs as well as their love of adornment. As permanent settlers arrived, many Mountain Men served as scouts and guides, but their way of life was gradually eliminated by advancing civilization.*

Gradually eliminated? I knew this to be false. The Mountain Man was a regular visitor to some homes. He came for Gussie Perch twice in a single month; she nearly died from it. The Mountain Man left a calling-card, a small-knotted stocking jammed right up inside her, never mind the bruises, red and blue–black – the colours of liquorice, we thought admiringly.

Down the street from our house Winnie Logan ran away to find a larger scene and was followed by the Mountain Man. She returned with a husband, some fellow her father found, with squinty brown eyes and a trapezoid mouth like the flap of an envelope, flicking open, flicking shut. His name was Harry. My mother thought it a good match in the circumstances; my father snorted and said probably Harry was tractable.

When Thora Morgan's new baby burped blood after feeding, it was the Mountain Man, conspiring to mix ground-up glass into her formula, as though he agreed with Danny Morgan that a sixth child wasn't a blessing but an expensive curse. It occurred to me that there were advantages to having a Mountain Man. He could be carried as a kind of armour against blame: bad weather that froze harvests, plagues of weevils that escaped silo fumigations, almost anything. In our town, poor but rich in human error, his hunting grounds were always kept well stocked. In my house we were lucky. We were passed over, at first.

My family ran a general chemist's shop. It had a gable and cow bells on the door and a hand-cut sign fibbing about the date of establishment. It was my mother who made a go of it. She was clever at sums and arranging, knew that prints of tiger lilies next to the bath salts enhanced their appeal, knew that stacked tins of infant formula were useless without the calming influence of rattles and toy swings. She designed legible, authoritative labels for the brown prescription jars, added to each crisply folded white bag a spray of peppermint, and coined a slogan around it: *The South Street Pharmacy and You – 'Mint' for Each Other.* She made herself, as my father punned, indispensable.

But she worried about us, splitting her time between the store and her home. Worried we might grow up wild, a troop of banshees. She wanted a girl to help with the housework. Good, dependable help. Father agreed, got her opinion on the best local girls.

'Sally Richmond—'

'Slow. Fat as a sow, and untidy.'

'Mercy whatshername—'

'Mercy is right. A nonsense girl.'

'Abigail—'

'A minx. Shameless. Born on her back.'

'Well,' my father said, frowning at his list, fractured by strikethroughs. 'That's that.'

So he asked around, made some calls, and soon a sheaf of papers came from an agency who matched interested girls from all over Canada with families who provided food, lodging, and a basic wage. My parents were interviewed by a woman from London. She wore glasses, and a smart pantsuit that struck my father as costing an arm and a leg.

'You don't buy herringbone off the rack,' he muttered.

The woman asked some questions about our home, what we would require in the way of work. My mother did most of the talking while my father stared at the woman, her glasses, her trim tweed curves. The woman made a few graceful spirals in a plain, linen-covered book. Finally she smiled and folded her book and said, 'I am sure she will be very happy here. Of course, should there be . . .'

'The fee is non-refundable,' finished my mother. 'That is perfectly clear.'

At the door the woman adjusted her glasses, gave us a fine sugar look.

'Lovely girls. Lovely manners!' And that was that.

The girl who arrived at our door a month or so later was ripe and round and Catholic. Her name was Marie-Anouk; she came from a Québec town named for a twining of streams. She spoke no English – a detail omitted from the agency forms. She stood on the doorstep with a suitcase and a soft, quilted cylindrical carry-bag, smiling uncertainly. We smiled back. This continued for some time, her smiling, our smiling, both parties gradually realizing that speech was impossible.

At six o' clock my mother got home, found her flimsy schoolgirl French.

'*Bienvenue. S'il vous plait . . .uh, entrez-vous, Marie.*'

Marie-Anouk began to walk, then stopped, dropped her bags, and wept, furiously, while we watched. 'Away from home,' my mother said. 'Natural that she should be nervous. Shoo, now, girls! Take her bags upstairs!'

She swept Marie into her arms, making soothing sounds, dancing her inside the house, past my astonished father.

'What do you say?' he wanted to know. '*Bonjour*, is it not?'

Our home expanded to include Marie-Anouk. She cleaned; swept; dusted; cooked thick-sauced meals; hand-washed our woollens, strong arms red to the elbow, and coupled them to the line with wooden clothes-pins clamped securely between her teeth until needed, folded them in intricate patterns that pushed the wrinkles to the sleeves where they would not offend. She filled her room with posters of Québecois heart-throbs, singing stars we'd never heard of, with names like Gilles and Émile and Robert-with-an-accent, all with dark hair thick as fudge and coffee-ground eyes like her own, framed by long, garden-rake lashes to be envied in a boy. She hid chocolate pastilles in a box on her bookshelf. We conspired to nibble and rewrap them, and if she wondered at the delicate gold-foil discs of steadily smaller circumference day by day, she never said. She made salads with a vinaigrette based on prepared mustard that my mother disdained to make herself but certainly ate enough of. She taught us the kind of French we wanted to learn at that age, how to say *great* and *my very best friend* and *who do you love?* We called her Mary Yuk for short, and found that if we said almost anything, and grinned, she'd grin right and back, and say *Yas, yas,* politely.

We followed her around the house and yard, offering help at the tail-ends of her tasks.

'*Merci* . . .'

'You're welcome . . .'

We trailed around the kitchen as she chopped and rolled and scraped and scrubbed, squabbling over apples sliced for crumble, starting flour-fights as soon as her back was turned, taking our turns with the dishes, which she hated, sudsing and rinsing with a sullen majesty that impressed us as being well worth acquiring. We followed her into the bathroom at night. She was resolutely opposed to our old chain-pull toilet, and seldom flushed it.

Looking into the bowl we stared at her urine, so boldly yellow, a glazy halo around the plump, solid turd. We were amazed by her droppings, heavy and robust and shockingly bright, proof of her vigour, her womanly strength. We devised a contest the aim of which was to generate, by squeezing, heaving and breathing just so, not a sausage-loop in a yolky broth but a real, live Mary Yuk. Points were awarded. Champions triumphed, and were triumphantly dethroned.

'What a find!' Father said, amazed at his foresight in hiring this paragon. He seemed concerned, in his mild way, that Mary Yuk get the right amount of rest and that her appetite was healthy, that nothing trouble the unforced beauty of her dark eyes and soft peat hair, brushed high behind her ears. She expressed an interest in the woods around the town. Sometimes he joined her on walks. My mother had more time to herself, and the shop thrived. My father zapped about like an extroverted bee.

'Well, your da's got his second wind all right,' Simmy Warden chortled to us, winking, and we winked right back, proud of his newfound currency as conversation.

Ken is tapping on my knee. 'Hey. Are you awake? We're nearly there.'

'I am awake. We're nowhere near there. We're here.'

On the hard shoulder in front of us a narrow transport-trailer lies jack-knifed, smoking. Traffic cones divert two lanes into one, and though there are few cars, we are barely moving. Ken thinks transport-trailers should be banned outright, as the last link in the causal chain which includes frozen food, free trade, fatalities.

'No one needs what they deliver,' he says, as a prelude to honking his horn.

I nod, but I am elsewhere. I stand Anton's wine in the arm-rest drink holder, lean back, stroke my hands in their gloves over my sore abdomen, feeling for the firm lump I am hosting, the exact size and shape of a damson plum. During a routine check-up my doctor, a serious young woman I inherited when old Dr Bilky died on his skis, spends several minutes probing my belly with her spaded hand.

'We'll need a good look at this,' she says. 'How's your Thursday?'

At the ultrasound clinic I scan the signs which warn and scold: *Please inform your attendant if you belong to any of the following patient categories: high blood pressure, expecting within fourteen weeks . . . Please inform your attendant should you have objections to a supervised student performing these tests.* A lady volunteer in pale mustard ushers me in, smiles to convey broad-spectrum sympathy. In the long interim, she adds a relish-green cap, then a ketchup scarf. All she needs to complete the costume is the frankfurter and the bun.

The examination room is gloomy, busy with instruments, it reminds me of the engine rooms in *Das Boot*. I sit in a stainless-steel lawnchair. I do not have to take my clothes off.

The technician asks me to rub a mint-green gel over my stomach, hovers a shaver-like instrument over it. Kindly, he tilts the screen so I can see: a dense, dark ellipsis; inside it, something whirls languorously, like planet gas. The technician is slim and round-faced and evenly pimpled, a doughnut with strawberry sprinkles. Now he clicks his mouse aggressively, frowns, adjusts the image on his monitor.

'Bit of debris in there.' He fiddles some more with his mouse, then notices me again, informs me that we are finished and that I am welcome to rinse off the gel in the dentist's sink. I decline.

I am also told I will wait up to three weeks for the result, no telephone calls, please. I leave. The human hot-dog waves me out.
Get 'em while they're hot, I chant to myself, though the joke was
at its sell-by when I made it an hour ago.

And a few weeks later I receive in the post a single card, with
the date, and the result: *Fibroid cyst of no clinical significance*.

At first I am disappointed – even my spurious growths don't
rate a second glance. Then I am relieved. And then, disquieted.
I play a game with myself where I press against objects in passing,
slide a hand over myself, waiting for it to pop aside. I think of its
contents, blended stunted cells, mindlessly reproducing their
odd disoriented structure, a smooth debris. Sometimes I am conscious of it, bumping into my ribcage like a diving bell navigating
a hulk, gliding by the flat of my sternum, spinning along my
liver's sleek flukes in a parody of gravity.

There is something seductive about this hidden presence
within me, bouncing gently (as I imagine it to do when I shift
my centre of balance). Gradually, it takes on a sentient,
observant aspect: monitoring my caloric intake, ensuring the
blood supply for its own growth, delegating the various mission-
critical tasks of my body. *More oxygen to the brain please . . .
White blood cells required in Sector Eighteen*. I find myself inter-
acting oddly with people, at once overtly mysterious and
sweetly condescending, conscious always of this entity I
harbour, the soft semi-parasite, pliant and foetal, syphoning
from my veins, leeching back as chlorophyll to change my
many colours. I begin to route my senses through my stomach,
and hear better, and see better. I decide to grow my hair out,
and my nails. I want everything in me to grow, cell forests in
full flower; when they open me up in a month's time, I will be
tropically lush.

And when, during our skimpy, slipshod lovemaking, Ken passes his damp palm across the dromedary hump in my belly, I think of the technician's instrument, and giggle.

'Warmer,' I tell him. 'Warmer. Warmer. Colder.'

'Just let me know when you're done,' he says tightly, knowing he is being made fun of, not knowing why.

'Right or left?'

'Left, I told you. Not here. The next one.'

Ken slows down at the final turn into the lane, all hanging willows and windblown ash, bare as posts, now, crunchy gravel, an insurrection of dandelions. He pauses a moment here, respecting some personal, silent segue.

(It has happened once or twice in the past that Ken has tried to break from Anton. When Ken and I were married, Anton was not invited. Something had risen between them. Ken has hung up the phone on Anton, he has refused to answer hectoring, hobnailed letters. But even this much means physical exhaustion, night fears, the classic symptoms of withdrawal. They make up like lovers, giggling into the telephone, joining up as one against the rest of us, we cut-price Capulets and Montagues who would stand in their way. Ken always goes back, a tired lover out of options, vowing to get it right, this time.)

'Ready?' I ask. Ken smiles, reaches out and musses my hair with a wayward tenderness that nearly catches me up.

'Ready ho!' he replies, cracks his knuckles, noses the car ahead.

There doesn't seem to be a light on in the house. Ken sneaks around the side to check the kitchen. I hear a sudden shout, a cracking of branches, then Ken and Anton appear, followed by a polished, skirted brunette of perhaps thirty.

'Meet Terra,' Anton says. 'T-e-r-r-a,' he explains. 'As in *Terra firma*.'

Terra strides over to me, jams a stick in the ground, docks her cheek for a kiss. 'Anton's done your charts,' she says archly. 'You've got Leo rising. Drink?'

We move inside, heading for the living room, sparsely set with skimmed-off furniture: some long-stemmed lamps; a low L-shaped couch in blue denim with matching armchair; an orphaned coffee-table dotted with raw-cork coasters; a chair with a strong new-wood smell, a slice of trunk scooped to make a seat in a frame of interlaced poplar saplings, trimmed to size. It seems Terra has a way with wood. We murmur appreciatively while Terra nods sagely, savouring her powers of craft.

The ceiling has a mid-life sag. Ken makes notes: what needs fixing, what is holding up. We accept fresh organic drinks, another thing Terra has a knack for.

'Fruit power,' she says proudly. 'Mother Nature in a glass.'

Mother Nature in my glass is suspiciously frothy, meant to detoxify my system – similar claims are made for shampoos and laxatives. Ken gets the alfalfa–aubergine medley, guaranteed to kick-start his synapses.

'I'm thinking more clearly already,' he says cheerfully.

Terra permits a frosty flush, the pink iced top of a daiquiri.

I climb into the conversation with a weary, practised skill. I smile at an amusing story about Terra's grandmother and a toothache and a sled-dog and a length of waxed string. I express my optimism that things will improve with a change in government.

'One's as bad as the next,' Ken says. 'Just a different hand in the till.'

Anton opens his hands, beautifully. 'What does one do? One continues.'

We all nod seriously at this, as though our oracle has burped, spat, and finally spoken. Then we munch prawn crackers *sans* prawn. 'Why support a corrupt fishery?' Terra demands, with the conviction of one who has spent her life scrutinizing the world's seafood stocks.

(The far wall is steeply decked with books. I side-tilt my head to read the titles. Foucault's *History of Sexuality, Volume I.* Multiple editions of Joyce. Penguin Modern Poets. New Canadian Classics. Shelves of compilations and anthologies. Anton collects anthologies. He is himself an analect, his discrimination assured through authoritative, well-packaged taste. Jane Austen – *unrivalled observer of Regency manners and mores.* Charles Dickens – *caustic commentator, prolific genius, originator of serial publication and the social novel.* These are his sources, his influences, his templates, his creditors. Anton has the writer's gift of being able to make the ordinary strange. But he had to borrow it, and he's still paying it back.)

Terra's hand is out, inviting me to take off my coat, stay a while.

I disengage the snaps, flaps and zips of my woebegone parka, struggle it over to her. Flopped on to the coat rack it slouches conspicuously, the guest in the corner.

'Gloves?'

'Not just yet. Circulation,' I explain. And then I get up. 'Excuse me.'

(One of the side-effects, real or imagined, is the creeping cystic pressure on my bladder. It starts in the very base of my belly, a meandering pressure on a day-trip from somewhere else, expands into a flexing fist inside me, opening and closing with a rhythmic, down-sloping grip. In public, at the cinema or during my rare guilty forays out for lunch with friends of my youth and university (who still address me heartily and determinedly by my then-nickname, 'Sleepy', and recite a lengthening list of deaths, divorces, sad bodily decay, then ask 'what I am up to', as though my life allows me to browse luxuriously a palette of brilliant, primordial possibilities), I exchange a secret smile of female difference and solidarity, take my handbag to the washroom. I hummingbird above the off-white oval seat that some virus-fearing, enterprising Christo has draped with single-ply, and squeeze and squeeze – only to dribble disappointingly. I stand, reallocate my clothing, waiting for the fist to return, as it will several times in a given hour, hoping that on my return my bored companion will not say, as they sometimes say, 'Well, thank goodness! I was beginning to think you'd locked yourself in.')

I find my handbag, smile at Terra. 'I'll just be a moment,' I say. She nods in sympathy. Ken waves, and returns to claiming truth values for fiction.

Once out of the living room I turn right along a short hall, then right again to the stairs, flimsy pine wafers slotted into a painted concrete retaining wall, crumbly where I bump it. Halfway up, a shelf built into the wall holds a sticky bottle of Irish cream, tubs of cocoa and chicory and a taxi-rank of fly-encrusted jars, jams and preserves left by the original owners, preserved by Anton as sacred relics with a ceremonial function. Each harvest he says a prayer of health and thanksgiving, offers a jar of crabapple chutney to the God of Unkempt Fields.

The bathroom is a large square whose four banked walls depict the signs of the zodiac, though space constraints dictate that some of the names be shortened (I sit face to face with that greatest of all archers: 'Sag'). Towels hang neatly over the shower bar: a blue towel, a flowerpot print. Pot-pourri in kindly ceramics. Oils of lavender and bergamot for diffusion. Automatically, I go to wash my hands. Flustered, I towel off the light beading on the leather, allow a compact glance in the mirror. I am surprised to see a faint webwork of scratches, uncertain snail spirals etched by a knife, a file, a hard, cracked fingernail. In places the cuts are deep, flashing the mirror's silver backing.

I am on my way out when I smell the chlorine, duck my head into the laundry room, catch a white undulation in the sink, then, as my eyes adjust, a precision of collar and sleeve. In the bleach solution the cloth is translucent, a spruceworm's slight horns. *Stains dissolving erased,* muses a voice in my belly.

When I return Ken and Anton have embarked on one of their velodrome arguments, in which they circle an absent centre at speed, on parallel tangents, not spiralling but revolving, and Terra weighs in with observations of a perilous neutrality, scornfully ignored.

'Well, that's what you said,' he tells Ken.

'It's not what I *meant*.'

'If you say, you mean, by definition.'

'Why does he have to defend the way he feels?' Terra asks. 'If he feels it, he feels it, and that's that.'

(I have watched Ken endorse the gun lobby, move to abolish euthanasia, advocate means-testing for health care, all in defiance of his privately held beliefs, all to outpoint Anton. He likes to prepare for Anton, reading books and journals and screeds he never has time for, with his remote-control job. He envies Anton his casual access to the Zeitgeist. So he studies; snips and Scotch-tapes this learned paper self, steps into it. But when he moves, he rustles.)

'That strikes me as fishpiss, through and through!' Anton says. Ken argues valiantly (cue panic of rustling), and Terra is a heroic buffer, sustaining most of the direct hits.

'Fishpiss, fishpiss, fishpiss!'

I play with Mother Nature's coaster. Its uniformity is marred by scars on the surface, a golden-ratio tracery. When Melinda lived here she kept soy milk in the cupboards and on the refrigerator were low-fat diets cut out from magazines. Liz painted afternoon water-colours. Thomas rode horses. Each of them must have left traces in this house: hair, jewellery, brushes, lines on the walls. Who has hidden these?

Terra asks about Toronto. She has never been there.

'You were born there,' Anton corrects her.

'Oh, well. Then yes,' Terra says. 'But I mean really.'

'Have you ever been stuck in a traffic jam?' Ken asks her. 'Or on the wrong escalator, and you couldn't get off?'

'Well sure,' she says. 'The traffic jam, anyway.'

'Then you've been to Toronto.' Ken launches into a detailed critique of life in the city, its ailments, its indelicate flotsam of squeegee kids and youth crime and encroaching suburbia, corrupt mayors and high produce prices and small businesses crushed under avalanche taxes. Toronto has failed Ken. He isn't where he wants to be, and he can't seem to get there. Because of the traffic jams, the escalators, the kids in hooded sweatshirts who beg alongside pets, capitalizing on their cuteness, threatening to get something for nothing.

'Well, I better get cracking,' says Terra, draining her glass in a noisy gulp and standing. 'Won't be a sec.'

Automatically, I rise also, shake off the calls to sit down, follow Terra to the kitchen.

'You're tense,' Anton is saying to Ken. 'Look at you – throbbing like jungle drums.'

Then I am behind the swinging door and into the kitchen. An old-fashioned kitchen: double-basin sink, wood-and-formica counters, broad banks of cupboards packed with cloves to ward off mice. Hanging wire baskets tilting with ropes of garlic, dried sage and rosemary, each bunch tied off with a bright check neckerchief.

Terra is not a potterer. She knows exactly where everything is. Her infallibility both chastens and annoys me. Not once does she pause, as I do, trying to locate the cap off a jar, the cupful of breadcrumbs, the soup stock, the separated eggs.

She skins par-boiled potatoes, holding the sharp knife steady as she rotates a potato around it, pausing to dig out the eyes. Her hands do not slip, her jaw and torso remain rigid. The potato in her hand has sprouted a smooth round orb at one of its ends. She peers at it, working out how to cut around it without wasting any flesh.

'Can I help with anything?' I ask dutifully. She shakes her head.

'Thanks. It's under control.'

Every now and then Terra looks quickly at my hands and I realize my gloves are on – my gloves, my beautiful gloves. They look well against the maple draining board.

I'd take them off, I tell her, but for my eczema, worse with the changing weather.

'It's seasonal, unfortunately. Humidity or heat, in any combination.'

I describe my summer hives, clustered cones which colonized

my hands and elbows, weeping custard-yellow tears. Three mornings running, my bedsheets were stiff with pus.

'I went in for tests. The intern doing the biopsy was anti-Novocaine – God knows why, maybe they had an argument. But he was very pro-saline. You know, plain old saltwater.'

'Did it work?'

'No. It hurt terribly. I fainted on the spot, as soon as he nicked off the top. Slice, spurt, I was out like a light.'

Terra is looking a little green.

'Supper's almost ready,' she says. 'You might be more comfortable out with the boys.'

'Oh, I don't know.'

'Well, it's pretty much ready,' she says with relief. 'Basically, I had to heat it up.'

We sit around the table like a string quartet. Before us, serving bowls steam like the insides of animals; beeswax candles cast a hollow light, and smell like vanilla.

'Is it vanilla?' I ask.

'Actually, a blend,' says Terra.

Terra looks at me, I look at Ken, Ken looks at Anton, who is wearing his poet's gaze, wisely considering the rest of us in light of himself. I offer to say grace.

'Dear Lord, forgive us for what we are about to eat,' I say. 'Just kidding,' I add.

We begin. Pared roasted parsnips, oozing a shocking creosote juice. Halved avocados like beetles' backs. Terra ladles out a thick vegan potage with lima beans, pinto beans, carrots, celery, cress and large clumps of bean curd floating in a savoury broth. The curd is sponge in my mouth, meshy, pupal. I barely choke it down. Ken eats with relish, asking for seconds and beaming like an ambitious searchlight. I tell Terra the food is lovely, ask for one or two recipes, contribute a wry anecdote about a sign we passed on the way.

'"The right lane must exist," it read. A doctrine and a dilemma, all rolled into one.'

Anton counters with an artist, first name Torrence, showing at a downtown gallery, who sculpts in pastry, irrigated constantly by a matrix of saucepans at a measured drip-rate – the particular arrangement of pans selected chosen from hundreds of possible combinations, requiring eons of effort and the grease of numerous arts grants –

'Here he speaks as an expert,' Terra interjects.

– the concept being to erode the flour-paste figures incrementally, creating art and its dissolution at every step. Sometimes, in an act of rare commitment, she eats the pastry, even inviting others to sample it.

'Word was it tasted very good, maybe a little long on butter,' says Anton.

This brings the house down. *Oh, Anton, you old roué; how I roué the day we met!*

'True story,' he says, extravagantly crossing his heart.

(Once, Anton asks me whether I have any 'ideas'. Ideas for what? He means his kind, of course, *literary* ideas, prosey thickets prowled by plots and devices, populated by characters, events, symbols, a host of things that mean and mean and mean some more, when looked at in the proper way. Ideas with central heating and a double garage, an income. Ideas with legs. Should I have any, I'll keep them to myself. I know him as a thief, even then. Especially then. A lucky thief. Anton metaphorizes ancient matriarchy as Kotex virtues, *absorbency* and *flow*, and is hailed for his insights into the feminine. Nonsense. He is a workaday phrase-maker, clever as twist-ties, accurate as arrows tipped with bits of Ken.

But by tradition we are meant to treat him as a storm-lantern, light of last resort, blazing and fragile, dependent on our butane and goodwill to make it through his dark nights. 'Do you know a Muse who makes house calls?' I ask him.

He smiles, a good-dog smile. I smile, a get-your-own-goddamn-slippers smile.

'Then no thanks,' I tell him. 'Besides, I hear writing makes you poisonous.')

I become fascinated with my spoon. I bounce it right up to the edge of the table. I think of the sound it will make if I drop it. I want to drop it. In my gloves my wrists bulge above my cuffs. The broad sac of flesh at my thumb tingles with a trapped blood stutter.

I am glad I have worn my gloves to table. I eat very carefully, as society ladies used to, cutlery blazing like Rumpelstiltskin's needles, stabbing and ferrying to the rhythm of my blood. If I did have eczema, it would respectfully remove itself, in deference to these magical gloves.

'We've barely heard from you all night,' Anton says, taking a breath, addressing me. 'Enjoying the old homestead?'

'Just great, thanks, Anton. As always.'

Later, I help Terra wash up.

'Hydrophobic or -philic?' she asks me.

'I'll dry.'

(The dishtowel is an endangered species list in alarmist yellow, fashioned in sections, like a heritage quilt.)

Terra whips her jacket off rather than spoil the silk by rolling up her sleeves. Beneath it she wears a white tee-shirt, tucked into her slippery bell-shaped skirt. She winds a chopstick into her hair to keep it off her face, the dark strands chuffing and sprouting, splayed out like the cap of a strawberry. Reflexively, I touch my own hair, thicker than hers, coarser. I imagine my fingers as tiny, smooth rolling pins, free of my hand, tumbling her hair. I stare at her, at her back, all planes and arches. When she leans over for a spoon that has skipped out of the basin, I watch her vertebrae press into relief like a branch dragged backwards. Her curt, ragged nails; her arms scudded with grey soap suds. Strong triceps and a pouch of muscle near the elbow. What we used to call a workhorse.

I am busy polishing the stoneware, bunching up three fingers to towel out the glasses, swiping the counter with that stylized, self-conscious motion I adopt in other people's homes. The ceiling light fizzes and flickers.

'It's the circuits,' Terra assures me. 'They do that, sometimes. We think it's the circuits. I know squat about electricity, and Anton . . .'

Here she shrugs helplessly, absolving him, a gesture I have seen perfected by Ken.

'Could you grab that and give it a quick scrape? Don't mind the worms.'

I tug at the lid of a heavy rubber bin. There is movement, slithery grace of nightcrawlers, reddish, with textured tails. A musty haze – a mix of wormshit and fermentation – rises to cling-wrap my mouth and nostrils. I'm getting a little spinny.

Terra is talking to me from the sink. 'You've known him a long time.'

'He and Ken go way back. To the womb, to hear them tell it.'

'Anton says Ken is into human salvage. Tony can be very irreverent.'

'You call him Tony?'

She shrugs. 'Sometimes. In bed.'

I have a picture of Terra and Anton in bed. She is on top, he is barely moving. O *Tony*, she breathes, and his mouth opens. It has a queer look about it.

'He has a quality of innocence.'

'He's been around the block a few times.'

'Still. He has a very attractive smell. He smells fresh. People who are, you know, *wounded*, have a certain smell. Not Anton.'

'I've never sniffed him.'

'A healthy smell.'

'I guess he's got his health.'

'He's got a philosophy . . .'

'Never give, never take.'

'That's right!' She is impressed.

'He's been refining it a while,' I tell her.

'It's a way of unshackling intimacy. No give, no take, no questions, no crime. Right?'

'But what about you? Cooking and cleaning. What you do with wood. Those . . . drinks.'

'Oh, you mean, does he *accept*. Of course. Doesn't everyone?'

I am tired of this conversation. I want to watch her again, the oddness of her moving, the tension in her shoulders. I want to watch the worms, watch them trailing bright serum, a tail-weave of colour and spark. I want to drink the wine I brought. I want to talk about me, even briefly.

Terra strikes a pose I have seen in Jennifer and Melinda, her ancestors in this house. That same posture: hands on hips, eyebrow cocked, an attitude at once possessive and unsure. She speaks in a stage-whisper.

'Have you ever been . . . consumed?'

'I had lice as a girl. They tore a fair patch off my scalp. But I wouldn't say consumed.'

She tosses her head back, sighs and shifts her shoulders. 'It's uncanny.'

Consumed. An eating from within, a toothsome hollowing. Annie Tippott's dog, browsed at leisure and left like campfire stones. It was a ring of bone when they found it.

She nods. 'That's it exactly. A ring of bones, all stacked up, like in the horseshoe game. That's how it feels.'

Anton on his back, ring after ring of Terra settling over him. A whispering.

Terra is looking at me with frozen interest, a dog entranced by a snack.

'Hang on,' she says. 'Your soul, it's caged.' She takes her hands and chop-chops her way around me as though pounding loose bricks from a citadel. After two circuits she stops, satisfied. 'Better, better,' she says.

'That soul of mine,' I say ruefully. 'It's a problem.'

She goes to the door, opening it. 'How're you doing?' she hollers.

In reply, slurry laughter and the clink of glasses. 'Well, wouldn't you know it,' she says. 'They're pissed.'

In the living room we gather, crows with ideas. Mother Nature congeals on two of the three side tables. A bottle of whisky is cradled between Anton's knees. Terra perches on the arm of Anton's chair. He fiddles with her palms, the concave of her hip. He offers her whisky. She demurs. He offers it again.

'Be a man,' he entreats her.

'Anton . . .' I begin. Then I am distracted. Somehow – in

the bathroom? at the table? washing up? – the tiny stitched V joining my gloves at the wrists has popped. I pick at it.

'Ken has been telling tales out of class.'

Ken is silent, glaring into his glass, body defensive.

'Nothing very salty. Ken is *so* discreet.'

'It isn't important,' Ken mumbles.

Terra stands up. 'I think I'll put on some music,' she announces.

'Music, music!' sings Anton.

Some music comes on that I am unfamiliar with. Terra stands beside Anton's chair. His left hand is under her skirt. She sways a little.

'A toast,' Anton proposes. Terra shakes her head.

'It doesn't agree with me,' she says. 'It burns.'

'For luck,' Anton says.

'I don't like the taste,' she tells him.

Anton reaches up and douses the floor lamp. Only the light above the mantel is on. Brightly I mention the long journey we've had, compliment the excellence of the meal, signal my sleepy fullness.

Anton nods. 'Neat or on the rocks?' he asks Terra.

'Neither,' she says.

'Just a sip,' Anton says.

'No,' she says. 'I'll sick up.'

'One sip. For Christ's sake, it won't kill you.'

'Think of honey,' Ken suggests. 'Close your eyes, and think of honey in the hive.'

Terra closes her eyes. She leans her head down, then straightens.

'I can't,' she says. 'It makes my throat itch.'

'Plug your nose,' Ken tells her. 'You won't taste it.'

'He's right,' Anton says. 'Plug it. Go on. For luck.'

Terra pinches two fingers at the bridge of her nose, goes for the glass in Anton's hand. He pulls it away, dodging, making her bob for it, like a duck after bread.

'I'm not doing this,' she says. 'I'm just not.'

'Okay, okay,' Anton says. 'Spoilsport.'

She lips the glass, mouth shrivelled with distaste. Anton tilts and half vices her head, until she swallows, coughing.

I look at the coasters before me. Terra's fingers on the dishes, her chipped, bitten nails. I see her fingers on these coasters, digging, divoting.

I see her in Anton's mouth, held glistening between his white teeth, sparrow's-egg speckled and delicate, outlined against his mouth like a portrait in a locket. Anton wears a cakey grin. If he bites down he will surely crush her.

'One more,' Anton says. 'One more.' He pulls her head back for another swig.

Something flutters from her eyes. She is crying. She is crying *No!*

My hands in their gloves pulse, purging sea cucumbers, a stroke offbeat of my heart. I find the slipped laggard thread and pull hard at it. Stitch by stitch I unlink the beautiful leather. The gloves fall from my hands like an ageing pellicle, revealing fingers specular as new antlers, covered with a fuzzy down. The thread is a long lightning and then it is sand in a sink drain and then it is a frazzle, ugly as wire. The red glove-liner protrudes obscenely, a wet tongue. Gloves without shape are nothing.

First Ken then Anton turn to watch me. I want them to watch me. This is for them.

Under the gloves my hands are swollen and damp as steamed puddings.

'Jesus,' Ken says. 'Jesus, those were *brand new!*'
Stain dissolved erased, chuckles a voice in my belly.

Once Terra and Anton have gone to bed, I come downstairs alone. I leave Ken sleeping softly and wander the house, bright with the full moon's sheddings. In the bathroom I notice a pearly crescent in the crack between bathtub and wall – the split moon of a fingernail.

Scored coasters, trapped hairs. Skin shavings. A splice of blood from a nicked thigh. Fingernails. Hairs packed into marmalade, windowpane graffiti, baby's bright-yarned booties unravelled into a pantry cupboard. My gloves. Cruel antiquities, twists in the order of things. They belong to the Chantals, the coastal Alices, Becca, Juniper, three varieties of Jennifer, homesick Dianne, puking Melinda, brave Joanna, horsey Thomas, Sybil with an Angie in tow, literary Kari, Liz from Dawson Creek. Terra. And now me.

In the laundry room, Anton's dress shirts bob softly, minor ice floes, semi-submerged. I drain the sink, pinch my nostrils against the strong chlorine. I drizzle then pour raw bleach, burning into the shirts, mindless loopy trails like men pissing.

We aim to please. You aim too, please. I do aim. I aim to leave stains.

Growing up I thought it odd that the Mountain Man should come only by moonlight. But I learned. I remember a night in the foothills, carbon black, quarter-moon diced by clouds. I woke to whispering, wooden clogs, a scream high and sharp as a back-and-forth bow-saw. I ran downstairs; my feet were cold. I saw Mary Yuk stranded in her doorway, all twisted up like a salt pretzel. She hadn't any clothes on. Her mouth made a queer gargling.

And I knew that it had finally happened. Despite the locks and other safeguards. Despite the wit and strength of my mother and the excellent aim of my father. I blamed myself. I had gone and looked him up, ignoring the warnings of people who knew better. I had summoned the Mountain Man, and sure enough, he had come for me, settled for Mary Yuk, not wanting to climb the stairs. I watched Mary Yuk with a child's fascination for painful things. I imagined candy-coloured bruises, ropy lacerations, a bright-red scavenging flower in her stool.

'The Mountain Man!'

My mother didn't look at me. 'Yes,' she said. 'Now back to bed. Please. Now. Please.'

(My father and my silent mother stand in the kitchen, peeling spuds for mince collops, she at the cutting board, he leaning over a tub of peelings. I have an idea that his eyes are shut. Without looking at her, he airlifts a peeled potato to the cutting board; without looking at him, she taps the straight blade once, twice, draws it over the back of his hand, a zipper of blood; without looking at her, he presses it to his jeans, counts ten, picks up another potato.)

'Right or left?' Ken says. We are travelling east, climbing through this corrugated land, heading home by daylight, passing through towns like postcards, through low, scoliosis hills.

'Right or left? Which is it?'

It sounds like a routine we have worked out between us, a vaudeville sketch perfected. Ken, brows bowed in surprise, above pound-puppy eyes, plays straight-man to my errant comic. I get the good lines, I always have, and that is part of the injustice.

'Right or left?' Ken asks again. The truth is, I don't know.

I stare, waiting for a sausage. In his hopeless, cautious way, he must understand this, because he leans over, ruffles my hair with a wayward tenderness that nearly catches me up.

'Don't worry about it,' he says. 'Have a nap. I'll get us there all right.'

I know that in minutes we will be lost, into these hills.

'I'm betting on left,' Ken says. He steadies himself on the wheel; he takes a big breath; his eyes rove the landscape, looking for a clue.

'I'll get us there,' he says. 'Just watch me.'

Skinrain

Leon is on his way, he is on his way home. He strides briskly, swinging his heavy briefcase, packed with papers: memos, faxes, contracts, gift ideas from Reader's Digest. The day is wet, and every now and then the slosh and skein of car tyres grazes his traffic ear. The crosswalk storm sewer is clogged and overflowing; a sudden surge of water grips and soaks his ankles. Momentarily distracted, he fails to hear the lunatic grunts of a lone car braking, striking solids, reversing, fading out . . .

Leon is on his way, he is on his way home. He strides briskly, swinging his heavy briefcase. As he walks he imagines the inner workings of an artesian stream bordering a cottage he rents for two weeks in the summer.

'Come back renewed!' his boss always says, hearty as a back slap.

The stream is narrow near the cottage, though of course it must be wider at its source, which Leon has never seen. He has a gaudy, potent dream of one day following the stream, over hills smooth as bumps in a blanket, through cool, bird-stirred woods, to its very origins, and there, lowering himself . . .

A stab of light startles him, the rapier glint off a puddle he might have walked right by. A large puddle, gravel-lipped, busy with ripples like sled tracks. He leans in for a closer look, puts down his briefcase. His briefcase— Where has it gone? It was in his hand a moment ago.

In the clear water he can see his face: sweet-potato jawline, wide-browed grey eyes, quizzical smile. He tries on a few expressions, bobs to and fro in a brief St Vitus.

'Accidents happen,' sighs a voice to his left.

Leon looks up. There is no one nearby that he can see. The voice hails him again.

'Accidents happen in a few inches of water. Step this way please. Please.'

Leon takes a step or two and stops, sceptical. Before him the puddle gleams invitingly, seeming to rise from the road, though this is impossible.

He prods it with his boot. 'You rascal,' he says. 'You rascal – I thought it was you.'

'Go *on*,' a different voice urges. '*Do* something!'

Leon checks the street. Bold paint trails; the disappearing halogens of a speeding car. Otherwise, he is alone. He taps gently at the shallow pill of water. It feels dense and pliant. Experimentally he plucks its edge, rolls it away from him, as he was once taught to ladle soup. The surface wobbles like fortified gelatin; bits of twig and crumbly soil stucco the underside. He tucks and rolls, achieving a fine waxpaper finish, he lifts it – it is lighter than he thought. Now he works confidently, ironing out creases, using a bottlecap to cinch the last bit into place. The rubber cap-liner is a token in some forgotten promotion, a simulacrum of a playing card: YOU HAVE GAINED THE JOKER! THE JOKER IS WILD!

When he is finished it is tight and dry, a sea scroll snug in the bell of his umbrella.

'This is a wonder!' he says, and heads home.

Just a block from his house a man takes photographs behind a fancy tripod camera with a bright, showering flash. Leon tilts his head politely, but the man appears not to see him, intent on his spooling and clicking. People want pictures of everything.

The house seems to have warped slightly since he left this morning, raked to one side, like a sailor's cap. His lawn hangnails from its flagstone cuticles, retreating in raggedy strips. The bay windows have the glazed look of heated plastic. A natural effect of the rain, no doubt. Natural as a rainbow.

Leon gives each eyelid a tug to clear his vision, walks through the sliding front doors, glances at the post, tucks the umbrella into the stand, then remembers, totes it upstairs.

Ramona is in the living room, filling out the daily crossword. As always, she uses a pen, to prevent backsliding.

'Welcome home, warrior,' she says. 'Warrior being a seven-letter synonym for soldier. And vice-versa.'

'You look subtly different,' he tells her. She laughs, slides down the bench to greet him, captures his mouth in a long, drinking kiss.

'There,' she breathes, releasing him. Her lips are white–pink, strawberry hearts, pleasantly tart, much warmer than his own.

'Do I feel cold to you?'

She kisses him again. 'Not yet.'

They sit down to eat. The meal, a stew, is hot and finely sea-soned. He takes seconds, touches napkin to teeth to clear the clinging shreds of herbs, pronounces it a perfect supper.

'Delicious!' he raves. 'The flavours really meshed.'

They share a few inches of vintage port in a souvenir tumbler. *Sun y Florid* , it reads. Somewhere, Leon thinks, those faded letters are enjoying themselves, free of all responsibility, handed loss on a platter. There, in the tawny light, she covers him, mapping her body on to his, the rich odour of root vegetables. They improvise a happy mess; they lie in the bed they made. She props her chin on his chest, a tee on a golf green, and stares up at him.

'What will you remember?' she asks.

Hours later, masked by her mild breathing and dream-talk, he steals from the room, finds the puddle, wrapped closely about his umbrella's metal stem, transports it to the study, unrolls it along the floor. It glistens and pulses, heaving tiny, urgent breaths.

Again he sees his face there, widescreen, a smile broad and bright as whales surfacing. 'Goodnight!' he says, and it shivers at him weakly, with a moderate thanks.

Leon is on his way, he is on his way home. Striding briskly, house-keys jagged in his pocket, their pressure on his pelvis reminding him of the closeness of nerve to world. The air on his bare neck is bakery-warm. The sun shone brightly all day, drying yesterday's moisture to dust. On the opposite sidewalk, two men carry an empty cot, tan canvas over an aluminium frame, shedding sizzling drips on to the ground. The canvas is dark with damp.

'Nice afternoon,' says Leon, with an inclusive grin. The men just carry on walking. People are busy. If time is money, conversation costs.

Two turns from home Leon hears a miniature scream from underneath a truck – *help!* spoken without consonants. He has a moment of indecision.

'Oh, hell,' he scolds himself. 'Is this what things have come to? What if it was you?'

Tracing the sound is difficult because of the truck's low bodywork, a vestigial skeleton. Eventually he spots a driver's side glimmer, the light from an eye in the bowl of a spoon, crawls over to examine it. As he works he watches his reflection, all etching and contour – a monochrome tattoo. He looks drawn. His cheeks are orchid curtains parted by a peeping nose. His mouth is slack and rubbery, a collapsed inner tube. There's inkwells where his eyes were, shadows of wounds on his temples . . .

There it is. 'Poor little fellow!' he says, sympathetically. With his thumb and forefinger he finds its raised edge, rim-rolls it like a Persian carpet, taking care to avoid tearing or spills, pops it in his pocket, next to his newspaper.

The crosswalk is alive with plastic yellow tape. A twist jitterbugs up to partner him, does a few mid-air steps, spins him out and back, dips him, favours him with a dry, airless kiss, skips away. Reflexively, he reaches for his briefcase . . . What has he done with his briefcase? He looks up to see it soaring, split like a pistachio nut, casting its contents from sea to sea. His flyaway papers litter the street, a tedious ticker-tape, settling on windscreens, shop windows; one is sucked like a stocking over a pedestrian's nose and mouth.

He barely walks a block before he is home. He doublechecks the address, just in case. Things have worsened since he left it last. The lawn pares back like gruyere before the blade. His verandah tilts precipitously, the gables droop, the bay windows flicker with swamp fire. More unsettling, all of this makes sense to him, it has the clarity of something learned by rote, the clarity of grammar.

He lets himself in, it's as easy as wading. Ramona looks very fresh and healthy. Appealing, like fine produce.

'You've had a scratch!' she says, examining and then gently manipulating his forehead, scraping, scraping. The soft, skinny sound of a sunburn peeling.

'All gone!'

Leon sniffs, sniffles, jackhammer sneezes. 'There's something funny in the air.'

'My new perfume. They've synthesized harmony into a smell like ageing roses.'

'"A rose is a rose,"' he recites, one arm extended in his best Lord Byron.

'And so on. A fellow on the radio had a point: "Science trims our lives with greatness." I was of two minds.'

'Two minds are better than one. And what about yours? Anything doing?'

'Oh, a little bit of this and that.' She stares at him. 'Your clothes – they're a mess!' From one billowing sleeve she conjures a loose cotton gown, pimento-green and collarless, with an alpine neckline. It bowties at the back, just above his buttocks.

'Let me put this on.' He stands patiently while she strips his jacket, tie, Oxford shirt, pants. He raises his arms and leans forward so that she is able to pull it over him.

'Better?' she asks.

'You make me better,' he tells her. 'You always have.'

They go to bed. She is shy with him. He makes a comb of his

knuckles, ripples it through her hair fluently as undertow. When his arms begin to ache he unwinds his tongue, licking and grooming her, tasting the salt at her toes and the stretched bottoms of her breasts, the sun-tang of her freckles, dotted moleskin. Her spine is a mystery to him.

Downstairs he tips a puddle from his raincoat, palms its calm surface. Wavelets appear, small and straight as dropped hairs.

He wanders over to yesterday's puddle, smartly dowelled along the baseboard.

'Sleep tight,' he says.

'And you.'

Startled, he speaks louder than he intended. 'Back there, on the street – it *was* you!'

'It's late. Rest.'

'You spoke to me back there! Spoke to me, like an old friend!'

The puddle sighs, breeze through a culvert.

'Do all of you speak?'

'Those who have voices. And something to say.'

'What do you call yourself? I mean, what do you go by? I'll have to call you something. How about Seth? That's a Biblical name.'

Seth is silent.

'Why did you choose *me*?' Leon asks. 'This city of millions, this crowded glass . . .'

'Things creep up on you,' Seth says, finally. 'Goodnight.'

'Goodnight,' Leon answers. Then, more sprightly, 'Goodnight, all!'

Back in bed, he closes his eyes, only to realize that they're already closed. Things are creeping up on him. As it should be.

*

Leon is on his way, he is on his way home, walking a route so precise he might have drilled it. No matter where he leaves from or where he wants to go, he always ends up in the same place, a two-block quadrangle centring on his house. Within this pattern reside unarticulated truths: life has a modest diameter; all creatures great and small organize themselves around a theme.

Everywhere he looks, he finds puddles: nudged into cracks between paving stones, loitering by kerbs, making muddy mirrors over asphalt potholes and bone-pits dug by dogs. Tooled up with a whisk broom and a spatula he finds and collects them to store in his study, now a controlled climate, maintained with sun-drapes and humidifiers he has recently installed. With this come rules. For example, the study stays locked.

'For your own comfort and safety,' he informs them. 'Please note the exit nearest you,' he continues in his best flight-attendant. There are twenty-odd puddles: round and ragged, bright and dull, shallow and deep, even and lopsided, clear and cloudy, loquacious and silent. Sovereign continents, each with their local weather system: oily calm, foaming surf, line squall. Each supporting a unique, limited ecology: spine grass, monarch snails, acrobatic waterspiders. Surveying his parquet floor, Leon feels like a duke on the Grand Tour.

As more guests arrive, he starts to lose track, decides to have a go at naming them.

'Well, you're Seth, of course. And you look like a Maryanna,' he says, pointing to a curvy jewel beside him. By the time the collection reaches forty, Leon has run out of names. During roll-call he discovers three Williams. He gives up.

'I feel like a teacher taking attendance. All these names, they're wearing me out. Not that I'm not *fond* of you, just that . . .

Just that naming is an act of violence.' A guilty twinge. 'But Seth will always be Seth!'

Leon pàuses, irresistibly drawn to his reflection percolating from puddle to puddle, contiguous screens. Wherever he looks, a receding echo of the man he was moments earlier. This pale nervous creature – it can't be him. He wiggles his nose. The man in the puddle wiggles back; sarcastically, it seems to Leon. He pulls a goon-face, sticks his tongue out, makes mouse-ears with his hands. The man in the puddle does the same, contemptuously.

'It *is* me – but worse!' Leon says, shocked.

There can be no doubt: he is changing. Why is this surprising? Awake at all hours – miles and miles of walking by day, in and out of bed ten, fifteen times nightly. Turbid dreams, stalked by horrors vivid and foetid as algal blooms. Constant noise, a shrill electric chirping like birds plugged into wall sockets. Disorienting sensations, a sudden upstream pumping in his veins.

'You're a wreck,' Ramona says. 'You're overextending yourself.' She peers at his eyes. 'There's a lot of water in them,' she whispers. 'Not quite see-through.'

'Things are clear. They are clearer than ever!'

'Will you go see a doctor? A specialist?'

'I see beautifully. Here, hold up your fingers – go on!'

She flicks her fingers, rapid dulcimer strikes. He can't keep up, let alone count. 'There. Now, will you go see someone – just in case?'

He pauses, ashamed. She never pleads with him.

'Yes.'

'Tomorrow?'

He is moved by her worry. 'Tomorrow. Tomorrow, indeed.'

They kiss, and he tries to ignore the high, percussive humming deep in his chest, waterfalls in his bloodstream.

Leon is on his way to the doctor, feeling out of place, vulgar as champagne served from a boot. The doctor operates out of a van. He appears at the rear doors, devilishly charming in a yellow fire-proof jumpsuit. 'You never know when you've got to dodge a flame,' he says merrily. 'Best to be prepared for everything. And it's very nicely tailored.'

On cue, a nurse pops out, dressed head-to-toe in stiff blue linen. 'A wonderful woman,' says the gallant doctor. 'Ornament to the profession. And a good hand with an intravenous. Good, steady hand. Huh! What did you say the problem was?'

'Water on the eye,' explains Ramona.

'All the world's particles are visible in a few inches of water,' Leon objects. 'This is an example of a miracle-as-fact.'

'Why not close your left eye?' the doctor suggests.

'With that eye I have seen marvels!'

'There's a certain dampness . . .' Ramona begins.

'Medically speaking, a certain *moisture*,' corrects the doctor.

'See?' Ramona says triumphantly to Leon.

'I thought I wasn't able to,' he snaps, sensitive to the salt-water seeping from his eyes, lagoons at the ends of his lashes.

'Close your right eye – in fact, close 'em both!' the doctor shouts recklessly.

Leon does so, sending trickle-trails of water down his face.

'Crocodile tears. We'll have to check the pH on those. Nurse! A swab!'

The doctor runs an exhaustive set of diagnostics, test after test: harsh pinpoint lights, swipes with a scanner, a rubber hammerette sounding Leon's skull, making his brain bounce, a weird zippering across his hairline, scrapy rubber ligature, lightning punctures at both wrists. Voices upon voices. The bleaty swill of measuring machines.

'What we haven't got,' observes the doctor, 'is time.'

Leon works a set of muscle pulleys, forces his eyes to open and his mouth to move.

'I used to run a rat race,' he says. 'Then someone speeded up the rats.'

'Go *on*!' This is Ramona. '*Do* something!'

'Oh hell,' the doctor says, running a trembling hand through his hair. 'Time wins.'

'What will you remember?' asks Ramona, and her face changes. 'Thank you,' she says. 'For all you've done. Thank you so very much.'

'A pleasure,' the doctor replies. From somewhere he produces a square, spongy rag. 'May I recommend, for short-term relief, this chamois. Dab and wring, dab and wring.'

Leon makes his rounds in the study. He tries to have a kind word for everyone. He has to – morale is a social imperative.

'You're looking well; oh, you're looking *very* well!' Some of the puddles stay silent, some respond with shy quivering, doubting chuckles, warm wavy shakes.

A garrulous pool shaped like the Seagram's star has a love for Shakespeare's tragedies, on the page rather than the stage.

'Othello had a genuine head for battle.'

'He blew it though, huh?' Leon only dimly recalls the play, but feels sure the hero was bound to blow it.

'Othello was brave, with the brave man's narrow perception. Honour was his mead. He quaffed it, and craved more. But in this case, the mead was spiked.'

'It's a funny old world,' Leon agrees, and moves on. He is in demand.

A trim lozenge seeks his attention. 'Nothing in nature really equals a good *filo* pastry,' it says, with a bric-a-brac sigh.

Leon has to confess, he lacks a discerning palate.

'Technology is a lantern without a wick!' brays one to his left, quivering importantly.

'Better wickless than witless!' jeers another, from its spot on a sawhorse.

'The opium of the masses is now the iron supplement of the few!' pipes up a third.

'How will increasing power in global capital markets affect the lives of communities?' Seth demands from his station snug to the wall.

Leon is intrigued. 'Will I get my newspaper on time?'

'My point is this: the human world is shrinking, that of currency expanding apace. More dollars, francs, Deutschmarks, won and yen are born each day, a mountain of capital miles wide and high. Before we know it, this capital will develop its own brain, form alliances, use humanity as a testing-ground, an agar gel in which to conduct its experiments.'

Leon considers. 'It's a problem,' he allows.

'A problem? It will end love, as we understand it! Put simply, there will be no love. And why? Because forgery is the chief danger in such a world – and love is easily forged.'

'Well, I won't say I'm for *that*,' Leon agrees.

Upstairs, Ramona is asleep, spreading herself into both sides of the bed, staking claims. Leon lolls beside her, watching the minimalist flutter of her face in dream. His own face is soaked with perspiration – from the humidity, he imagines. There's a spending wetness underneath him. Where is it coming from? He touches a finger to his ankle; it comes back wet. He has soaked the bed through. He is generating effects he cannot predict.

He gets up, scavenges a plastic trash bag from a kitchen cupboard, uses it to upholster the wing chair sown with peanuts and used tissues and blinky small change, settles himself.

Leon is on his back in the bathtub, groggily counting the beats between drips from the drain. He has kept to the house for days, out of loyalty and a fear that the puddles will evaporate, syphon off, sneak away. What can he offer them? Why should they stay?

In fact, though, they thrive here. They spread, lining the floors, flocking the waterpipes, flapjacking over central-heating ducts. They are everywhere, and their properties are changing. No longer is each a discrete environment: they whitecap together, ease to calm together, synchronize the swell and ebb of their inch-high tides. Their former diversity of flora and fauna has been replaced by the unreal, pristine blueness of acid lakes, habitats under erasure. Their borders have been reinscribed, water on water, invisible to his naked human eye.

He has trouble telling one puddle from the next, from himself. What is he to know them by? They lose shape, they stiffen, tambourining like overboiled milk. They fill all available space. He and Ramona have no place left to sit or eat or read; no place left to store trinkets or books. Their tables and chairs are spoken for, their shelving units have been reassigned: puddle bunks and puddle perches, puddle playgrounds and puddle town halls. Something must be done.

'Cabinet reshuffle,' he lies when Ramona asks what he's up to in the study. 'Stay clear. You won't believe the dust in here.'

She barges in anyway. 'Stand aside, Bluebeard!' Then wrinkles her nose. 'Ugh! Something's gone mouldy – are you sure it isn't you?'

Inches from her bare toes he spies a puddle sneaking up on her, a shock of green water in mid-spout, shadowing and framing her foot: the dark and the light and the bone between. He pulls her aside just as it starts its slow-motion lunge. He laughs, to put her off the scent. But she is thoughtful, and later he sees her try the locked door, sponge-mop in hand.

Leon takes to carrying his chamois, deftly wiping back encroaching puddles. But this is not enough. There are other intrusions: test tubes, regular glass stamens bifurcating the walls, incessantly passing fluids. Freehand styluses tracing indecipher-able graphs, quickly retracting. Stainless-steel rolling stock. Hypodermics that tap him like a sugar maple, draining him faint. Something must be done. Something must be done. He descends to the cellar, rummaging for ideas. From the bite-size window he spies the neighbour's laundry, hung inside-out with spring clips.

'I have not been thinking laterally!' he scolds himself. Then he races upstairs, outside, inside, to the study.

It takes him twenty minutes to rig up the line, lift and clip each puddle securely to it. Inevitably one or two of the heavier ones burst their fastenings and slosh to the ground, but in the main they seem pleased with the novelty of the posture and free-dom from crowding, experiencing the world in this new way, from above. Each keeps its shape; soft slabs of glass, swaying rhythmically.

Leon stands among them. 'You're lovely,' he says. 'Really, you are.'

A tear blots on his cheek, and soon they are all weeping, the puddles sweetly beading, Leon streaming and blurring. He approaches a near puddle, round and flanged as an organelle, sees himself there, moves on to the next swimmy mirror, looks again. He is changing, changing. There is a looseness of bone, a buoyancy of plasma beneath his dermis. He touches his cheek, breaking the surface; it travels with his touch, a light, sure chop over open water.

'You'll be lonely,' something says.

And he ratchets his gaze away from the puddles, away from his new stained-glass self, away from the hived reflections of that great bulbous tear.

Leon is on his way, he is on his way home. He reaches for his briefcase. Where is his briefcase? It must be far away now, swooping over London, Delhi, Buenos Aires, snapping and jittering, its lock long blown open, his papers like bandages on the atmosphere.

His house – is this his house? The lawn has moulted to a salt-and-pepper polyurethane. The bay windows are hidden behind drab blue curtains sliding on a track to meet in the middle. Where they clear the ground he spies strange, frenzied movement.

Ramona appears in the curtains' gap, with a gown and cap, and a surprise for him.

'Sit in the chair, mister, and close those saucer-eyes!' she commands.

He obliges, but has trouble finding the chair, and more trouble actually sitting in it. Bumping gamely about the room, it occurs to him that his eyes are shut. Hard to tell.

The next sequence takes place beyond his peripheral vision. Someone veers past, circles him, fits a kiss in a trough in the waves now building along his cheek.

'Jessie! Welcome home!' he manages, before the next breaker hits.

'I'm *glad* to be home!' In fairness, it sounds a bit forced.

'Are you here on vacation?' he asks. 'Is it Christmas?'

She ignores him. 'I came just as soon as I possibly could,' she says, to Ramona. 'I flew. It was eighty dollars more.'

'I'll reimburse you . . .'

'Oh for God's *sake*, Mother!'

Jessie wears a gown and mask. He can just make out her eyes.

'How long has he been here?' she asks. Blue–yellow eyes, round and clear as rock pools.

Leon is euphoric. 'We share things we hardly think about,' he cries. 'Like our eyes – our eyes are the same! Like . . .' Words jump his tongue. 'Like water!' he cries. 'Like water!'

And he thinks, It is in water that I know myself. In water.

In water. Water: a colourless transparent tasteless odourless compound of oxygen and hydrogen in a liquid state convertible by heat into steam and by cold into ice, liquid consisting chiefly of this in seas, lakes, streams, springs, rain, tears, sweat, saliva due to appetite, urine, serum, amniotic fluid, morbid accumulation –

Jessie stands before him, hands on hips.

'Who am I?'

– of fluid, hot and cold, salt and fresh or sweet, smooth or still and rough or troubled, hard and soft, aerated, saline, chalybeate, thermal, blue, heavy holy mineral running table a morbid accumulation of fluid . . .

'Who am I?' she asks again, in scratchy, straw-ticked tones.

'You're a tumbleweed,' he gasps, hoping the words sound as he has thought them.

'All dressed up and no place to go,' Ramona says, with a bitter-lemon laugh.

'A tumbleweed with no place to go . . . is no tumbleweed!' This point must be grasped.

But before he can explain it he is distracted by new voices from the region of his ankle. It takes some time to focus, then he is shocked to see a familiar glint roaming end to end through his clothing, spreading confidently as a slime mould with fruiting bodies, stabilizing, its surface darkened by its depth.

'Home sweet home,' says this new puddle. 'Your travelling days are over.'

'I have a certain nesting instinct,' Leon agrees, unsure at last if he is talking or thinking, or neither, or a bit of both.

'The rainforests are losing species like spectacles,' opines a voice in a different register, and Leon understands that another new puddle has sprouted where his left arm used to be. Within short seconds they have thronged the walls; one sits cocked on Ramona's head, jaunty as a beret. The floors, the ceiling, the eddies of air are covered in puddles, glassy platelets, broad wet platters of skin, hovering, dimpling and grinning. They take on facial features. First they resemble well-known personalities, then they resemble no one at all but themselves. One on the lampshade sports a goatee, another inching across the ceiling has acne scars and eyes asterisked with age. As if on cue, two puddles joined in a double helix disentwine, expand individually, slinking and grinning, showing teeth.

'*Do* something!' That sounds like Ramona, from a long way off.

It must have rained skin last night. It must have rained cats and dogs and skin.

'We contribute to our own demise!' a stem-nosed puddle hectors.

Leon adopts a conciliatory tone, though by now he is worried.

'And this will threaten our survival, is that right?'

'It makes us that much less interesting.'

'*Do* something!'

There is a puddle forming in the gully at the base of his nose, threatening to flood it, only to split in a parody of mitosis, two then four then eight, singing in rapid chorus: 'Accidents sell papers, producing a common fear, based on the impossibility of prediction. Some things cannot be known, and interfered with. It's just too, too bad.'

'Accidents happen in inches. In a few inches of water.'

'You're obstructing my breathing . . .' Leon begins, but he is drowned out.

Ssshhh . . . Ssshhh . . . Ssshhh . . .

'Your troubles are over,' they say together. 'Your troubles are over, tumbleweed.'

Above him appears a sharp but transient light, a firefly spinning on a nickel. *Ramona.* She stands looking down at herself looking down, fills her lungs, and dives into him, plunging, neatly finding her balance in this new domain; skimming over his bones like a leaf in current; descending to the photic zone, lightless save for the infra-red of fumaroles, marine volcanoes; navigating his inside ropes and reefs, trailing chutes of bubbles and hair like a chiffon train. Magnified by water, her hands are broad flippers, intensely present compared with his own, translucent, troglomorphic. Here, among the mineral chimneys and clouds of rust-red shrimp, the key to long life is not to do too much. She shows him her eyes, spreading her hands like the doors of a ship's locker, slow-wound with algae, deep undersea. Her eyes have grown and deepened, great bow-shaped eyes, and he itches to climb up into their richly glistening surface. But she hovers, just out of reach, sculling in place, floating over him.

'What will you remember?' she asks, and a heavy moon of water swells and wanes, passes warm from her eyes to his. 'Close your eyes,' she says. 'You won't see a thing . . .'

Leon is on his way, he is on his way home. He strides briskly, swinging his heavy briefcase. As he walks he imagines the inner workings of an artesian stream bordering a cottage he rents for two weeks in the summer.

'It has been with me all along,' he says, faint with wonder. '*I am its source!*'

The leaf-crammed storm sewer has spilled over, making a rank lake of the crosswalk. A predatory bottlecap clamps like a lamprey on to his man-made sole. He manages to dig it free and stares at the rubber cap-liner: YOU HAVE GAINED THE JOKER! THE JOKER IS WILD! He reaches for his heavy briefcase . . . Where is his briefcase? In his hand when last he looked. Now he pictures it aloft, one of a vast migrating flock, flying in formation.

Outside his house a man takes photographs with a flash-camera set up on a dropsheet. Two uniformed men walk past with a wet, bulging stretcher. All the lights in his house are on. Caution tape tentacles his driveway. A high hum loads his ears. The day is wet. The day is wet.

The day is wet. Patches and pots of water gleam in the streets, in the man's mouth and nose, the wells of his eyes. He is nearly submerged when they find him, and when they haul him out he leaks like a cracked clay jug.

'What happened?' Her hands knit knots she can't untie.

'Accidents happen,' says a tall man next to her. He wears goggles and a protective suit. 'A few inches of rain, and all hell breaks loose.'

'What happened?' she asks again, dully, and the tall man draws her close.

'Come now,' he says, bundling her to the waiting car. 'No time to waste. Mind you don't get your feet wet,' he says, as he leads her over the crosswalk through the twilight thick as brine.

Everything Breathed

I'll tell you something about Merrie

The day Merrie's landlords phone with the news, Alex deliberately empties his head. He tilts it and shakes out each ear. Then he sits down and reads, to fill up his head in a new way. In a freebie envirobabble magazine, he finds an article cataloguing airborne pollutants, thousands of them. According to this article, the world is a giant circular exhaust pipe. No place or person exists outside the loop. Everything breathed is shared. This idea at once repels and fascinates Alex. He lets it occupy him.

It occurs to Alex that messy air is a problem he can maybe solve for himself. He finds a do-it-yourself store, flips through the rack of industrial filters. There don't seem to be major differences, so he plumps for something called 'The LungGuard'.

He likes the idea of a sentry at the gate of his mouth. It tickles him.

Back at home, Alex's head fills right up again; a jumbly, partly liquid seeping. It fills to the brim. Thoughts bump up against one another, form towers, cancel out. He thinks about Ellie and why she never cries. He thinks about the two moles on his chest, so raw and bold-black they could be bullet holes. He thinks about Merrie: he hopes she is well and he hopes she stays lost, and this makes him wonder. He thinks about the calls of whales seeking their errant calves, great hoops of sound oceanrolling, loud enough to burst human ears.

He sits and stares at the LungGuard, patiently awaiting its first tour of duty. Maybe he'll give it a whirl. Right now, maybe. The plastic tabs that join strap to mask divot into his jaw. Otherwise it fits just fine. He inhales, exhales, inhales; feels the light suction of each freshly scrubbed breath, and it settles his head pretty well.

After wearing it that whole day, Alex inspects the removable lining, whistles, shows Ellie. 'Will you look at that!' he exclaims. His voice is low and trembles. 'It's caked with grime. All that after less than twenty-four hours.'

Ellie is unpacking groceries, stocking their shelves with the tins he hands up.

He nudges her. 'Surprised?'

She teeters on the stool. 'I don't know, Alex. I really don't.'

And Alex thinks, I could tell her about Merrie right now and it wouldn't make a difference to us. I bet she wouldn't even get off that stool. He scans the list of ingredients on a tin of clingstone peaches: *sliced peeled peaches, water, sugar.* He looks at Ellie's unlined face and his stomach stirs and he wishes people had their limits printed somewhere on their bodies.

'How we doing up there?' he asks her. Ellie is leaning but strangely he doesn't notice, until he moves and she nearly falls backwards.

Alex lets a day or two go by while he decides what to do about Merrie. He phones in sick and loafs hazily around the apartment, frequently dozing off, lulled by the draw and ebb of his breath through the filter. At first he threw away the used linings. Now he keeps them, shoe-horned into natty, red-leatherette photo albums. They are photographs, after all. In a way. On a very tiny level. Alex is pleased that what he breathes is now preserved. Should it turn out that the quick, shady motions of neurons, of thought itself, can be captured and charted, he will be ready, with album after album of miracle fossils, comprising each and every breath.

It jars him to think of Merrie. It is a dagger in his peace. He has phoned Greyhound and VIA Rail – no one has bought a ticket in her name. He has itemized her personal details and description and forwarded them to area newspapers and local TV, where she is already on file. It's pretty clear that he will have to get the police involved.

Calmly, he dials up and files a report. Speaking through the filter makes him conscious of his diction. Merrie up and left last Saturday, her landlords weren't sure where, she hadn't said. No, there wasn't any trouble that he could think of. No, he didn't notice any marks or bruises when he saw her last.

The policewoman asks for Alex's permanent address and whether or not he has a valid passport. Alex wonders what this has to do with anything.

'We'll be in touch,' the policewoman says. She makes it sound ominous.

Alex hangs up but the policewoman's voice is looming in his head. Marks or bruises, she said. He'd better tell Ellie. It's been three days. He'd better tell her something.

So Alex says, 'I'll tell you something about Merrie.'

Ellie is busy sanding down a wooden sphere, maybe three inches across, with a papercut groove along the top. It is one of her mysterious undertakings. Ellie spends hours on her projects. She trawls beaches on their vacations, collecting shells and curls of sea glass she will one day make into lamps. She has drilled and stacked hubcaps for use as umbrella stands, assembled room dividers from linen and PVC tubing. She has fashioned a slinky clinky boa from pop cans hammered flat and stitched with wire toggles.

Alex has a theory about the purpose of the sphere. He thinks that eventually there will be a pair of them affixed to the wall. A small-gauge cable will run groove-to-groove through a loft of air, delineating it, and form their laundry line. This is just a theory.

'I'll tell you something about Merrie that'll blow your—'

Ellie picks up her sphere and her newspaper, takes them to the bedroom, carefully closes the door.

'I'll tell you something,' Alex says to Ellie. They are lying in bed, still dressed, reading, each their own book. 'I'll tell you something about Merrie.'

Ellie shifts until her bottom is pressing into his thigh. 'I like Merrie,' she says. 'Okay?'

'I don't know, I thought you might find it interesting,' Ellie says. She is talking on the phone.

Alex lies rolled in the duvet, waiting for the shower, for the water to heat up. Ellie's water, and before her, someone else's.

Ellie finishes talking, walks into the bedroom, steps out of her bath-towel, shakes out her wet hair. In the flat light, she is dark and slicked, barely dimensional, an otter caught in a pane of glass.

'Morning,' she says, and tousles his hair.

'Uh huh,' Alex says. 'Leave the door open, will you?' he asks.

'I'll tell you something—' he begins. Ellie twirls to face him, grinning hugely, an orange wedge where her teeth were. He is just ready to speak when she hits purée on the blender.

He phones her at work.

'Eleanor Gant, please.'

The woman is conventionally suspicious. 'Who shall I say is calling?'

'Opportunity.'

The woman sighs. 'And would this be personal or banking?'

Alex considers his answer. Things depend on it.

'Personal banking.'

Ellie's working voice is dry, efficient. He tells her he is wearing his red underwear and she giggles. They are having a nice chat.

'Oh yeah, I should mention – Merrie, she's gone.'

Ellie's voice is quiet, dangerous, from the high side of a cliff. 'What's that?'

Alex is shaking, all the different solids in his body wobbling at their own insidious rhythms and speeds. 'Nothing,' he says. 'It isn't the first time,' he says. 'She comes and she goes,' he says.

'Where does she go?' Ellie asks.

'No idea.'

'That's a help,' says Ellie. 'I guess I'm not following you here,' she says, and waits. Alex doesn't say anything.

'This is, you know, a little weird, Alex,' says Ellie. She sounds doubtful.

'I know,' he says. 'It isn't genetic or anything,' he says.

'I don't know that,' Ellie says. 'I don't know anything about that. Just what are we talking about here?' she asks.

'I'm not sure,' he says. 'Merrie taught me everything,' he says, helplessly.

'Look, I'd better go,' she says at length. 'I'm just swamped here. Okay?'

'Okay,' he says. 'Later alligator,' he says, to the dial tone.

After Alex hangs up, he does some hard thinking. It begins with a rhythm: crowbar to wall, wall to dust. He is ten and his house is being dismantled. His father is refurbishing, wheelbarrowing by with waste wood, sheets of gyprock, yards of tectonic tiling. All the paint colours are changing; daffodil flushes to saffron, white cools to cyan. Each act of renovation lingers in Alex's muscles like a sprain. He doesn't want to look, every blink brings an alarming new vista to his attention. Living room gone. Hall and bedrooms gone. In the midst of all this furious activity, Merrie smokes ceaselessly, aggressively, camouflage in a ground war. Alex is aware that she is the origin of these feverish repairs, but isn't sure how. 'I am making space,' Alex's father announces. 'From now on, I plan to keep my eye on things.'

Alex sleeps in and feels a whole lot better. He has a long bath and fingercombs his hair, rubbing in the regrowth lotion with a gentle, circular motion, as the bottle advises. He does not look at his hands, at the sad beached hairs with their translucent bulbous roots. Memories, his barber had the nerve to call them. Memories clogging the bathtub drain.

He rinses off, drives over to the house where Merrie rents the bottom floor. The landlords are a trendy young couple, Toby (a woman) and Leslie (a man).

'Thanks so much for calling,' he tells Leslie seriously. 'I got right on it.'

'Well, I certainly hope she's all *right*,' Toby gushes. 'Oh, we *adore* Merrie. We think she's un*quenchable*!'

Alex nods agreeably. 'Well, she hasn't been murdered or anything.' They seem puzzled. 'I mean, if that's what you were thinking.'

'No-o,' says Toby, eyeing him.

'The truth is,' Alex continues, aware that his hands are drizzling sweat and that he is looking at the ceiling, 'Merrie has . . . lapses. Occasional amnesia.'

Toby makes an O mouth, but she is looking at Leslie, eyebrows raised.

'She always seems to come out all right,' he adds, trying for an upbeat note, and notices Toby staring and Leslie looking into his hands.

When he leaves, Toby is still watching him, and he sees his own negligence in her nutty moted eyes. He wants to tell them how nice it is to finally meet them, but he doesn't want to use the word *finally*.

Alex is still at home, and he is running out of filters. Not for his mouth, but for everywhere else. The LungGuard is not, after all, the alert soldier of its packaging. All day, all night, the world flows by while the sentry sleeps. Alex is becoming keenly aware of all that eludes him, of all he cannot adequately clean and trap. He is jumpy. He washes all of the windows in the apartment and this is some help. He phones Ellie at work several times, to make sure she is there. Sometimes he puts on a false voice, only to hang up, ashamed. It seems to him that this behaviour is connected to Merrie, that it must be so, but he isn't sure how. He thinks of all the other times Merrie has disappeared, but can't recall specifics. He doesn't think he washed the windows then.

He finds himself resenting the envirobabble magazine, even though it's free. It sows anxieties in him. He worries about thinning ozone, genetically altered soy, the plight of the narwhal. About Ellie. It's hard for her, he knows. In her family, emotions are saved not spent. When they visit her family, he is the loudest no matter what the subject or how hard he tries to speak below the current of the room. He has heard the hum of the stove igniting, food digesting, over the voices at her table. Together they have tried to discuss this. Therapeutically. Once she even wept, determinedly, unconvincingly, while he patted her back as though burping a baby.

For the first few months they dated, Alex and Ellie didn't talk about their friends or relatives. This was in the interest of purity. Alex's head was full of links, many of them unpleasant. He felt strongly that Ellie should be free of these.

When they went for dinner on their second date Ellie wore a white silk blouse over wide black pants. A length of silver floss made a bright furrow in her neck. Alex remembered that she didn't eat and smile at the same time. He thought she might not have been wearing a brassiere – they argued about that later.

He asked automatically, 'Is there just the one of you?'

When she grinned, he interrupted himself, and said, 'Forget it – let's not talk about families.'

Ellie speared a clove of roasted garlic and it floated on its tine like the last remaining obstacle. Deftly, she popped it into her mouth.

'Okay,' she said, and their horizon was clear; it was intoxicating.

No news yet from Merrie. Ellie gets in later and later, and Alex is nervous. She is so slender, she can turn sideways and become a narrow spirit, slipping into a private labyrinth where he cannot follow. He tries to keep his eyes on her, but he is only human, he has to blink. He looks forward to the hairpin turn from dusk to dark, when the evening news is on the radio and Ellie is contained. He cooks supper. Ellie lends a hand, washing vegetables, dusting crumbs from the pestle, monitoring a saucepan. Firmly beside her, he understands her boundaries, the fixity of her presence. When she moves, he reaches for the threads of her self that gloss the air behind her, an etched glissandi like a figure-skater spinning, and sometimes even these elude him, and it nearly makes him weep for fear.

In bed he knuckletreads Ellie's back below her neck.

'So what did Merrie teach you?' Ellie wants to know.

Truth be told, Alex can muster up only a memory of sitting at the pantry table, before a lunch Merrie has made – tinned fruit-cocktail slopped over cottage cheese. The syrupy fruit does not so much mix with the cottage cheese as infiltrate it stickily. Merrie smokes out the window so as not to soil his lungs. Thick, grey hide-and-seek smoke. Alex believes that at this time Merrie taught him something – a game, maybe, though for the life of him he can't recall what it was.

'Merrie taught me everything,' he explains to Ellie, for the second time.

But this will not satisfy Ellie. She will want to know more. She will ask again, patiently, When you say Merrie taught you everything, well, what did she teach you? She will want an answer, clean, resilient, that will soak up this mess like a sponge. And all Alex can remember is the game of smoke, and he can barely remember that.

So he tells her, 'She'll be found. She'll be found, and then they'll call me.'

'When she comes back, what does she say?'

'She doesn't come back. They call me. I go. I drive her home.'

'Well, what does she say?'

'She doesn't say. They call me. I go. I drive her home. She doesn't say.'

He kisses Ellie's breasts, her nipples, pink like the inside of her mouth, which he has also kissed. He holds her, too tight. She rolls out from under him, her body pale gauze in the darkness. A pinch of sheet winds between her buttocks, he reaches for it, and then he thinks, But if I unravel it, will she unravel too . . .

And he thinks, Goddamn Merrie! Goddamn her goddamn her goddamn her . . .

Wherever she goes

'If I sit down, it helps.'

Merrie is talking to Mrs Chin, who owns the only stationery store in Apex. She arrived at their house at seven, wondering if she might borrow a *Yellow Pages*, to book in at a reputable motel. She was tired from the bus trip, and limped a little. Mrs Chin asked her inside, to sit down, and then to stay the night – plenty of room. Mr Chin has excused himself, stressing his philosophy of early rising.

The Chin house is neat and well tended, with a gingerbread feel that makes Merrie want to stuff a fowl. Thinking about food makes her hungry and tetchy. Already her hip has begun to generate its familiar fricative twinge.

'Is there anyone we can call?' Mrs Chin wants to know. She tinkles her gold bracelets worriedly.

Merrie says no. Oh, her hip, the grind – she can feel her bone specking away in its shale socket.

'Well, you mustn't be wandering about at this hour,' Mrs Chin says firmly. 'They aim those cars at people, you know, the boys.' She shakes her head.

Mrs Chin is small. Her eyes are wide, warm lozenges, warm black and gold. Her hair is black like vinyl records. A full gorgeous black. Though herself, she wishes she had Merrie's soft wave, her butter-blonde hair.

'It isn't real,' Merrie says.

'Oh!' Mrs Chin says quickly, and pats her own head, and smiles.

The room is smartly furnished. A long striped couch faces two big-bottomed chairs, split by a large television with rounded corners whose screen is very dark. An upright Yamaha piano squats with its rolling walnut cover halfway down.

The piano belongs to Mrs Chin's daughter, Grace, who is in medical school, learning to restore hearts. She will pass her magic hand in its magic glove over the red sucking wrinkle that is a human heart, and lo, it will be well. It will dance a hornpipe, it will high-step round its hat. Grace's equipment fees come to half the tuition – thousands! This is said conspiratorially. Merrie rubs her fingers. *Money!* Mrs Chin nods.

For a few months after she first left for university, Grace wrote long, sorrowful letters about missing home and her friends, her parents, the things in her room. She especially missed the piano.

'Now she doesn't write us so often,' says Mrs Chin. She looks down.

'Can I make you some tea?' asks Merrie, half rising.

'Maybe she has a boyfriend,' Mrs Chin speculates.

'It's no hothouse in here,' Merrie says. Her hands flop from her arms, long and brittle, lilypads at the frozen surface of a lake.

'She plays very well,' says Mrs Chin. 'Grace is the musical one.'

Merrie thinks. 'They say musicians make the best doctors.'

Mrs Chin is surprised. 'Have you heard that?' she says, mulls it over. 'I suppose so,' she says. 'Actually, I wouldn't be surprised.'

They both look at the piano, at the keys, stained teeth in a mouth half bared.

'A heart is a kind of instrument,' Merrie says. 'Strum strum. A pink mandolin.'

'Well, all I can manage is "Ode to Joy",' Mrs Chin says. 'On the piano, that is,' she says, and laughs.

Merrie runs a bath while Mrs Chin exfoliates. Scriff scriff, goes the buff pad over Mrs Chin's planed cheeks, her wide forehead, the fleshy dent above her bobbin mouth. Scriff scriff! The syncopated syllables make Merrie think of hearts, of Grace and her magic hearts. Does Grace have that same gorgeous hair? That black hair showering evenly over her clear, musical heart?

While she waits for the water to cool, Merrie keeps busy. She perches on the edge of the toilet and does exactly ten leg-lifts. She sings a little. She arranges the soap and shampoo so that she will not have to fumble for them. She tests the grab-handles that run the length of the tub. Then she fiddles with Mrs Chin's dainty monk's robe. The sash is disfigured with bunches of knots. Nervous knots, Merrie thinks, worse than useless for holding fast. Finally she slides the robe off her own hutch of a body which she cannot bear to look at except in necessary glances: the grey shuddery flesh at the tops of her legs, the coruscating blue veins on her ankles, the bulging hobbled hip. Only the scar on her stomach looks young.

She thinks, It is because I wear my pants so tight. My pants, they squeeze the song from me. If they weren't so tight, I would leap through that doorway and into space; I would take it in one bound and be just another particle, lost to eyes!

Merrie stays over a week. During that time, she shows Mrs Chin how to bake icebox cookies. She teaches her a variant on twenty-one in which the dealer always wins. She helps her arrange the freezer: packages of peas, fishsticks, chops and turkey cutlets bought in pairs and labelled with the purchase and expiry dates.

Mrs Chin is guiltily grateful. 'Oh, Merrie, you needn't—'

'Idle hands, idle hands!'

Mr Chin works on the accounts and, every now and then, he tilts his fine, elegant head towards Merrie. She tingles, every time.

'Would anyone like a fresh coffee?' Mrs Chin asks, meaning Mr Chin, and he replies, gazing into the corner, 'Isn't it late for coffee?' meaning Mrs Chin, and Merrie marvels at the love that hides behind indirectness.

By now she has the run of the guest room, the largest and best in the house. Mornings, she cooks breakfast: poached creamy eggs, buckwheat pancakes dashed with vanilla and nutmeg, fresh juice. Afternoons, she helps out at the store.

'My Chinese cousin,' Mrs Chin says, whenever a new customer comes in. This is quite the icebreaker.

The store is a wonder of racks and cubbyholes and twirling wire cylinders that hold the exotic papers that Mrs Chin buys from a Japanese woman in the city. Below each item is the price, beautifully printed in a calligraphic hand by Mr Chin. Merrie learns in a few hours where everything is, how much it costs.

'Highlighting marker, fluorescent, dollar sixty-five!' she sings out.

In the evenings, she tries to be the last to leave. The quiet is immense, aerating her bones and joints, a leavening relief.

'We're off to the pictures,' Mrs Chin says hopefully, inviting Mr Chin.

'Inventory!' exclaims Mr Chin, rattling papers forcefully, declining Mrs Chin.

On the way back from the movie Mrs Chin drops her car keys, and has to fish for them in the gravel. Merrie leans down and takes hold of Mrs Chin's scrabbling hand. The hand is a tiny puckering mammal, and it needs her.

They come for Merrie on a working day. Mrs Chin rushes home to see her off.

'Things are coming back,' says Merrie. 'Slowly.'

'You must visit,' says Mrs Chin. 'Please. You are always welcome.'

Merrie smiles. 'Thank you.'

'You must come and meet Grace,' Mrs Chin says. 'You must hear her play.'

'That would be a treat,' Merrie says.

'Do you think she'll write?' Mrs Chin asks. Her hands grip Merrie's painfully. 'I mean, of course she will. Don't you think?'

Merrie looks down at the hands that hold her own hands, thinks of the bathrobe and its mutilated sash. She looks at the gingerbread house on its hardpack icing, and thinks she would like a whisky, would like something. From the squad-car seat she sees Mrs Chin's fluent waving fingers, delicate pistons; she is playing a piano.

She is welcome

Beneath his riding helmet, Alex wears a stretchy latticed hairnet to prevent breakage in the new growth that, as advertised, is melding into a pale down web across his scalp. Over his mouth and nose he has strapped his filter. It adds a humming layer of heat to his breath. When he pedals hard to make a light or climb a skidding hill, the cranial rasp of his own breathing reassures him that he is alive, that he is squarely, determinedly, in the shape of things.

'They've picked her up.'

Alex hears this on his way in. He doffs his helmet, waits for more.

'Whee-aah?' Through the filter his voice is a vowelly thrum.

Ellie walks over, seals a Post-it note over his palm, slots her fingers into his, strokes the tough arc between his forefinger and thumb.

A 519 area code. It's an OPP detachment, somewhere called Apex. Alex unmuzzles regretfully. 'Where the hell is Apex?' he wonders. Ellie shakes her head. She is baffled by the hived small towns of Ontario: fleeting, encapsulated, each with its tackle shop and Legion Hall and array of misleading postcards.

'Constable Someone wanted to talk to you personally.'

'So what'd he say?'

She shrugs. 'He was cagey.'

'Did he say I should phone him back?'

'He just said he called.'

'He called to say that he called?'

Ellie is starting to get that hunted look.

'And that's it?'

She shrugs, eyes darkening, narrowing, flops her tawny hair over her face, culls it with her fingers, shakes away the strays.

Alex finds the phone, taps out the number, waits for a voice, a name.

Sitting in the cold car, willing the engine to turn over, Alex becomes aware of the carbon monoxide coating his throat, of his breath fluttering across the piped white sediments, leaving concentric deposits like the rings in a tree. *Sulphur oxide nitrogen oxide particulate matter (ash coal dust lead cadmium mercury zinc) tobacco smoke polycyclic aromatic compounds radon decay products hydrocarbons moulds fungi bacteria algae pollens spores and their derivatives.* With relief, he replaces his filter. As he wiggles the key in the car ignition, he hears Ellie's singing from the second-floor window, and underneath it the adhesive tear of Post-it notes, clinging, like limpets, like bandages.

Alex has to sign a few papers. Then they sit on their thumbs while a young, good-looking cop fiddles with the electric gate. Merrie waves coyly.

'Quit it,' Alex says.

She kisses her finger and pushes it through the gap in the window.

'I'll zip it right up,' Alex cautions her. 'My finger's on the button.'

The cop shrugs at Alex, raises his eyebrows.

'I'll bet he's got a pointy peter,' Merrie says brightly.

'Jesus,' says Alex, and rolls up the window, ignores her small shriek, accelerates away.

'Slow down, you maniac,' Merrie says, but she is laughing, made wicked by the rush of air, the promise of a new trajectory. 'You *dervish*! Do you want to get us killed?'

An hour into the drive Alex starts looking for a service station.

'Shell!' Merrie cries the name of each glaring, monstrous roadside gas/food/entertainment complex. 'Esso! Sunoco!'

Alex passes them by. Better the independent retailer should get his fifteen bucks. He turns off at a sign bearing a stylized fork and gas-pump. At the end of the short main street is Bill's Total Service.

'Bill's,' says Merrie, respectfully.

It takes Bill a minute or two to realize he has a customer. They sit in the car. Merrie is quiet, crossing and uncrossing her legs. Alex has sworn he won't do this, but he allows himself just a peek in the rear-view – and there is Merrie.

'You looked!' she whoops. 'Got you got you!'

Alex waits for her to quieten down. 'Do you have to pee?'

While she considers this he takes advantage.

'Why do you do it?' he asks her. 'Why?'

She is thoughtful. 'Well, I *do* have to widdle, but I would prefer a cruller.'

'A what?'

'A cruller. A honey cruller – there's a doll!'

Bill is the colour of low country fog. As he lugubriously hoists his arm to the window Alex finds himself counting. 'Fill 'er up!' he says, trying to be friendly. Bill scratches his head, gives him a long foggy look.

'Regular?'

'Yessir!' says Alex, and Bill sighs heavily, moves to the side of the car. Something in the car is ticking, even though the engine is off. The radiator? The cylinders? What in a car ticks? Alex is not mechanically minded, but prides himself on being aware of the details. He gives the clicking some keen thought. Bill's head pops up unexpectedly an inch from the passenger window, startling him.

'Passenger side!' Bill rasps, accusingly.

'What's that?'

'Gas cap passenger side. Not often you see that,' he continues meditatively, 'over here. More likely,' he adds with a searching glance inside the car, 'abroad. What do we have here?' he asks, jerking a thick red finger towards the rear seat.

Alex turns to see Merrie reclining along the back seat, each index finger making slow circles on her temples, eyes rolled back.

'A lady friend.'

Merrie moans softly, the ingénue in a bedroom farce.

Bill tries to squeeze his amazingly fat head into the driver's side window, and Alex moves his own head swiftly to block him.

'She don't look so good.'

Now she wafts a languid hand, floats a brave smile.

Bill straightens inadvertently. 'Ma'am.'

Alex catches Bill's eye, winks once, slowly traces his lips with his tongue.

Bill fills it up.

'I don't know why you had to come rushing,' Merrie says. She has finished her cruller, and is wiping her fingers on the window, making patterns with the residue of oil and sugar. 'Everyone was so nice.'

'Why don't you sit up here with me?'

'My hosts were extremely gracious. They were very cultivated people. No peanut butter on their pantry table. They had a bidet in their bathroom. A bidet! The only other one I've ever seen was the one Marcy Hatch's mother had put in. I can't imagine she knew what to do with it, but she knew it was French. Everyone talked about it. There was an unkind rhyme that went around: "hatch" and "snatch", you know. Unkind. Do you remember her at all? Later she was married and her children were your age. Her daughter was Lori and her son was Stephen.'

'I don't remember.'

'Yes you do. The son was David, and he lost his legs.'

'I thought the son was Stephen.'

She thinks. 'Stephen never lost his legs.'

Alex shakes his head. Her conversation clings, it chaps; he can't navigate it, and drive. He checks the dashboard clock. Eight-ten. He will have to get Merrie home, clean her up, settle her. He'll be lucky to make it home before midnight. Ellie will wait up.

'Will you find CBC please? It's the mystery hour shortly. They've really got the goods this month. Poirot and . . . What's the other one? Miss Marple. They have Poirot and Miss Marple all this month. I've read the books. What's her name? Christie. Her people die horribly.' She says this with relish.

Alex fiddles with the radio. His eyelids spasm briefly. His hands are starting to cramp.

'It's introduced by that man with that voice, you know, all phoney and smooth. I can't stand that man—'

Alex interrupts. 'Did you even tell them? Did you even leave a note?'

Merrie tosses her head, and lets out a soft cry, and Alex remembers the arthritis in her neck. Nothing was taken from her medicine cabinet. She has been more than a week without painkillers or anti-inflammatories.

'All right?' he asks.

She looks away. 'I can manage, thank you,' she says, politely, and he seems to remember, sometime, somewhere, a Merrie who might have carried off that injured dignity, but she is very far away.

'You're welcome,' Alex says. His hands are flat against the wheel, his arms straight out. He steers by shrugging his shoulders.

Merrie laps at a yogurt. Alex brought it, fearing the onset of a storm. When he drives in winter he fills a box with blankets, matches, a family of heating candles in two rows of six, one extra sweater, several bars of chocolate, a bottle of water and a carton of long-life milk. And a wide empty jar to urinate in. Tonight he'd added a yogurt.

'Yum yum,' Merrie says approvingly. She holds the container for Alex to see. 'Extra fruit. Twenty-five percent.'

She slips the shoulder harness, scooches forward, rests her cheek on the back of his seat. Her breath is hot, it smells of plasticine. Alex knows that yogurt is alive with bacteria. Are they on her tongue even now, regenerating themselves, disguised as plasticine?

Merrie is counting trees. She counts the firs and the birches and the maples and the elms and the jack-pines. When there are more firs, they are the winners. When there are more maples, they are the winners. It is a war of multiplication.

'I'll tell you something,' begins Alex. He is driving much too fast. 'What we breathe is killing us.'

'Is that why you wear the snout?'

'It's a *filter*!'

*

The programme has begun. There appear to be three actors playing nine parts. All the character voices are exaggerated, with
plenty of astonished pauses.

Merrie listens, rapt. She repeats key points, she sums up: a
woman's body is found in a library. There is a whole mess of suspects – including a butler (it's true!); including a young man of
family who drives a car Alex once built a model of; including an
old man in a wheelchair whose limbs flop and slither like *stealthy
salamanders* (Merrie's description); including another young
woman, a dancing partner who lives by the skin of her wit – by
God, she's a shiny pebble; including a dancing master, possibly
foreign and therefore suspicious but handsome, yes, with dark
olive skin that absorbs equally the sun and women's greedy stares;
including Marple, serene and cunning, who knows but will not
tell.

'It's the dancing master,' Alex says. 'The Latin. He was married to the girl, there was a baby involved, things were sticky.
The dancing master did her in.'

Merrie ignores him. 'Fink!' she says sharply, to the radio.

His eyes shut, acted on by magnets with a strong attraction.
He jams them wide open, steadily forces the wheel over until he
feels the chunking crunch of the snow-edged shoulder. That's
where you'll go, he tells himself. Another slip like that – *bam-
boom!*

On the radio a roadster explodes in a spray of flame and metal.
They will have to wait for it to cool before they can probe its
wreckage for bodies.

'They'll end there,' says Merrie confidently. 'Ooh –
humdinger!'

'It's the dancing master,' he says. 'Ten to one.'

Merrie sings to herself in a quavery voice. Her hands are

tucked under her. Alex risks a glance, but her face is in shadow.

'We're almost home,' he says.

'I don't care,' she says.

'They've been worried,' he says. 'What's-their-names. About you.'

'I don't care I don't care I don't care!'

'Uh huh. Jesus,' Alex says. 'Enough heat back there?' he asks, once.

Alex wishes he'd stayed on the highway. Watching this road is like staring into a drainpipe; wet dark sides, wet dark surface. Every now and then his headlights pick out a glassy patch of ice and he swerves to avoid it, frequently overcompensating.

'I'll tell you something,' Alex says. 'You can't do this. You can't.'

Merrie says nothing.

'What do you have to go and do this for? You! You have a good life. You have a lot. Look around you.'

'It isn't,' says Merrie. 'It isn't the dancing master.'

'There's an example,' Alex says. 'Now why do you go and say that?'

'Well, excuse me,' says Merrie primly, 'because it's so.'

'Excuse me, but what do you know? They call me and they call me and they call me! What the fuck do *you* know about anything?'

Merrie's crying is soft. In the rear-view mirror Alex can see the top of her head, the crackled white roots in the blonde, the odd round patch of scalp. Outside, a sieved flat snow has begun to spiral from the sky on to his windscreen. A few flakes blow in through the fan slats. Some of the beacons wear snow hats, white, circumambient, inflating flake by flake.

'They can't be for a laundry line,' Alex says. 'They're too small.'

His head billows. He must slow down. Something must slow down.

'You're right about the dancing master,' he says. 'It would be too easy.'

But this is not enough. He downshifts, decelerates, leans across the passenger seat, one hand on the wheel.

'Here,' he says, handing Merrie the emergency box. 'Take this.'

She looks up at him, eyes pooly, unfocused. 'What's this?'

'Open it,' he instructs her, 'just open it.'

Wondering, she opens it, briefly burrows, finds the candles.

'Light them,' Alex says. 'Go ahead – light them all!'

The car is alive with candles. In the side windows their fingertip flames swoop and shimmer.

'And chocolate!' Merrie whoops. 'A feast!'

The car coasts, glides, coupled to the snowgrained road, skims up a hill, then pauses, slips sideways, and chundles on down.

'It's like a rollercoaster!'

'I pack it for emergencies,' Alex says. 'Do you think this qualifies as an emergency?'

On the windows there is a quantity of steam. Things outside are lost. Inside, by the guttering candlelight, Merrie's face is red and young.

'I guess this is living,' Merrie says.

Alex doesn't say. He isn't sure he wants to breathe. He wonders what the candles are releasing into the cramped air of the car. He wonders what this substance would look like, spilled on to the flat tightweave pages of his albums.

The car is slowing down. He thinks that, if there is to be a reckoning, he will pay out loops of a certain line, and Merrie will take it up, and in this transfer something may be saved.

'I'll tell you something . . .' he begins. But the line he pays out is not the line Merrie takes up.

'He was always in my sight,' Merrie says. 'Every day. You remember his routine. He got dressed in his suit and sat in his office. He picked up the phone to make sure it was connected, and he waited. I watched him waiting, I couldn't help it. He watched me right back. By the end, wherever we went, whatever we did, we were seen.'

'Oh . . .' Alex says.

'The door to his office broke, the thingies, the hinges broke, and he didn't fix them.'

'Why didn't he fix them?'

'He just left them. They hung from the door. Silly things.'

'Why didn't he fix them?'

'I knew. We both knew.'

'I didn't know,' says Alex.

'He was curled up just like a jostled woodlouse. His hands were full of pencils. That day Eileen was over. She was talking naughty, we were giggling. I made her lunch. Then she laughed and knocked her juice. Maybe that set him off. When I got there the desk was practically on top of him. He had a bloody nose. He was hollering. All the pencils went *snap, snap, snap*. All the strings in his heart went *snap, snap, snap*. Nonsense. How should I know? Though she would. What's her name? Marple. She would know.'

'I didn't know,' says Alex. 'Why didn't I know those things?'

'Who was going to tell you? He was there and he wasn't there,' she says. 'He with*drew*.'

Through the metal chassis, Alex can feel the wheels shiver, then seize.

'You shouldn't do it,' he says. 'You should stay put. Enjoy yourself. Or go away. Go somewhere far enough away that they won't call me to come and pick you up.'

'You think I should—'

'I just don't want them to call me,' Alex says.

'He went away,' Merrie says, after a pause. 'He with*drew*.'

Alex looks at Merrie. She looks at him.

'I just don't want them to call,' he says.

They have come to rest in the middle of the highway. Without realizing it, Alex has removed his filter. He keyspins off the motor, pops all four windows, wanting to feel the pure iced wind, the cool snapping snow. For a single thrilling moment, he imagines a silent salmon-stream of cars closing in from behind, swerving and dividing and gleaming quickly by. But the road is empty.

Ellie is awake when he gets in, furled up bat-fashion before the television. The television is off.

'She's back.' It is a statement.

'Yes,' Alex says. 'For now,' he says.

'I wasn't sure I'd be here, when you got home.' She scribbles in the air. 'You know. Earlier – the note,' she says. One hand is in her hair, pulling it down. Her shoulders are wire bent beneath the woollen frame of her sweater.

'"In the smoke, there are holes and shapes,"' Alex says, reciting. 'Find a hole. Find a shape. Extra points for a shape,' he says. 'That was the game.'

Ellie just looks at him. 'That was the game. It's nothing,' he says.

She yawns, pops her jaw. 'I'm glad Merrie's okay,' she manages.

'I'll tell you something about Merrie,' Alex says. Find a hole. Find a shape. 'Wherever she goes, she is welcome.'

He undresses, peeling away the sticky shirt; slips his belt, standing on one trouser cuff to lever his foot out of the other. His clothes make random continents on the cool bare floor. Ellie crosses to him, tucks his penis up into his belly, quicksteps on to the roofs of his feet, balancing, rocking him slowly across the cold floor. She is light enough to throw and catch.

From the shower fixture two dim figures bob, and the itchy smell of lacquer spreads his nostrils. The wooden spheres.

'Conditioning,' Ellie whispers.

Ellie rubs against him in the night, and he awakens. In sleep she might be a ghost, so cool and colourless. She might be only halfway there. He thinks that he doesn't believe in visitations, but in disappearances, people blinking out of time. This, at last, is what Merrie has taught him. Lying there, he has an immaculate vision, of Merrie in her ginger dress, her hair glued beneath an ill-fitting toque, trudging through brusque, crusted snow. It is three months from now, and she has disappeared again. The car she drives is found by the side of the road, its hood a broad smudge in the mobile underbrush, dense as smoke, heavy as a hand that cannot be shrugged off.